D1557087

Recipe for Kisses

Caro—
Best roomie ever!

XO—

ALSO BY MICHELLE MAJOR

Still the One

Her Accidental Engagement

A Brevia Beginning

A Kiss on Crimson Ranch

A Second Chance at Crimson Ranch

The Taming of Delany Fortune (The Fortunes of Texas: Cowboy Country)

Kissing Mr. Right

A Very Crimson Christmas

MICHELLE MAJOR
Recipe for Kisses

Montlake
Romance

Published by Montlake Romance, Seattle

www.apub.com

Amazon, the Amazon logo, and Montlake Romance are trademarks of Amazon.com, Inc., or its affiliates.

ISBN-13: 9781503952263
ISBN-10: 1503952266

Cover design by Shasti O'Leary-Soudant / SOS CREATIVE LLC

Printed in the United States of America

To Matt, Jackson, and Jessie—my three favorite people in the world. I love you more than bacon, chocolate, and Rocky Road ice cream.

CHAPTER ONE

Chloe Daniels crumpled the piece of paper in her hand. "How did this happen?"

Her friend and coworker, Karen Henderson, took the letter and placed it on the counter at the back of the toy store Chloe owned in the Highlands neighborhood northwest of downtown Denver. "It won't help to ignore it at this point. How long has it been since you opened the mail?"

"A couple weeks," Chloe admitted, taking a fortifying breath. "Maybe three. I was waiting to get the sales numbers from last month before I opened the bills." She glanced up at Karen, who nodded in understanding. Chloe didn't have to explain to her one full-time employee that she'd waited with the hope that the profits would be enough to cover the rent, utilities, and other bills that were piling up faster than she could pay them.

Since she'd bought The Toy Chest almost four years ago, she'd struggled to keep the shop in the black. The popularity of the neighborhood helped, but Chloe had sunk thousands of dollars into remodeling the store when she'd bought the business to make it fit with the hip, trendy area. Then there were her employees. Although she didn't regret her decision to continually hire new staff and offer benefits and bonuses as she could, her commitment to the women who worked at the shop limited her ability to get ahead.

She focused on the crisp type of the one-page letter and the only three words that really mattered. *Nonrenewal of lease.* There was too much at stake to give in to the familiar fear of failing that had coalesced in her chest since she'd first read those words. "I can't lose this store. It saved me."

"It saved all of us," Karen murmured.

Chloe had met Karen at the first domestic violence support group meeting she'd attended when she moved to Denver. She'd been up to her neck in renovations and had begun to have panic attacks as she dealt with some of the male construction workers on-site every day. Her divorce and the fear her ex-husband instilled in her had still been fresh wounds. She'd gone to the meeting looking for coping strategies to make sure her anxiety didn't jeopardize her new life.

With her grandmotherly personality, Karen had immediately taken Chloe under her wing and offered to be at the shop for support. It was still hard to believe that the sixty-year-old woman, who looked like she was waiting for the second coming of Woodstock, had once been a high-society Park Avenue matron, but Chloe understood too well that domestic abuse wasn't limited to a certain socioeconomic demographic. The two of them had spent long hours in those first few months talking about their situations and how to help other women. Financial constraints were one of the biggest reasons victims of abuse didn't leave, so the plan to hire women referred by the local shelter had been conceived.

"I've got to find a way to convince the new owner to renew the lease."

Absently she picked out one of the small windup toys from the bin next to the cash register. She turned the small gear then sat the orange bird on top of the counter, where it pecked its plastic beak at the paper while walking across it. "I've sunk everything I have into this place. At the rate I'm going, I won't pay off my credit cards until the next decade."

"If only you'd focused more on sales and profit instead of . . ."

Chloe held up a hand. "Don't go there, Karen. The Toy Chest was a new start for me, and part of that is helping other women change their lives." She still had to work out a plan, but Chloe was determined to save her store.

The chimes above the front door jingled as a teenage girl and younger boy walked in. "Welcome to The Toy Chest," Chloe called out automatically. It was morning on a beautiful early June day and only one family, a young couple with two toddler-age children, was browsing in the store. Chloe expected a bigger crowd to come in after lunch, especially since she was hosting a craft class later in the community room at the back of the shop.

"You're not going to help anyone if you go out of business." Karen wrapped her wrinkled fingers around the mug of tea she constantly refilled throughout the day.

"Maybe that's my angle." Chloe caught the plastic bird as it fell off the edge of the counter and dropped it into the bin. "This letter," she said, picking up the piece of paper, "is from a property management company. Who knows if the new owner of the building even understands how important the shop is to the community." She scanned the brief paragraphs in more detail. "If I can figure out who runs BH Holdings, I can appeal to them personally."

Karen set down her mug on the workspace behind the counter. "You assume everyone has your heart, dear."

"Everyone has *some* heart," Chloe argued then shook her head. "Well, not everyone. Not my ex-husband." She folded the letter that threatened everything she'd worked to create these past few years and placed it in the drawer behind the desk. "But I hope whoever holds the fate of The Toy Chest in his or her hands has a bigger heart than this letter suggests."

"We need to think positive," Karen said and gave her a small hug.

Chloe turned her attention to the family who'd approached the register while Karen walked around the counter to check on the other customers. The little girl held two stuffed animals in her arms while the boy, probably a few years older, carried a building set. She talked to the parents for a few minutes and discovered they were visiting Colorado from southern Nebraska, so she recommended several games that would be good for the long car ride home.

Despite what Karen probably thought, Chloe wasn't totally inept as a businessperson, but that hadn't been her biggest priority in running the store. This had been a safe haven for her when she'd needed it most, and Chloe had wanted to make that true for every person who walked through the front door. Now she could add this business to the list of unwise decisions she'd made in life that had come back to bite her in the butt. Maybe it wasn't too late and she could convince the building's new owner to give her another chance.

Just as Chloe started to walk the family over to the display, Karen called to her. "Chloe, I need your help. Right. Now."

The other woman's tone held an unfamiliar note of urgency so she excused herself from the family and hurried around a huge display of plastic farm and jungle animals. Karen held the arm of the boy who'd come into the store a few minutes earlier, while the teen girl pulled the kid's other arm as he squirmed between them. The two kids were clearly related, with the same mahogany-colored hair, although the girl had eyes so dark they were almost black, while the boy's were a clear blue.

Karen was tiny but no pushover and she wagged a finger in the girl's face. "I saw him put the marbles in his pocket. I'm not going to let him steal from this store."

"You can't prove it," the teen said, staring at the boy. "You didn't steal anything, right, Zach?"

The boy shook his head but didn't make eye contact with any of them.

"Karen wouldn't make an accusation lightly," Chloe said as she assessed the children. She glanced over her shoulder, happy to see the family bent in front of the shelf that held the travel toys. She hated public scenes so she needed to deal with this situation before it got out of hand. "If your brother," she said calmly to the girl, "would empty his pockets, I'm sure we can handle this amicably."

The boy eyed her as if the word *amicably* might mean "with a shot of penicillin."

Karen shook her head. "We need to call the police, Chloe. Shoplifting is a serious offense."

Chloe wanted to roll her eyes at her friend. They'd certainly dealt with kids trying to steal toys on more than one occasion. If they could work things out with the parents, the police were never called, but Karen always liked to throw out the threat. She said it was her brand of "scared straight."

"Are you babysitting?" Chloe asked the teen. She looked to be about fourteen or fifteen and the boy closer to eight or nine. "Can you give me your mom or dad's phone number?"

The girl's eyes widened a fraction before narrowing. "There's no one to call," she said with a defiant lift of her chin. "It's just us, and he didn't take any stupid marbles."

"I'm calling the police," Karen said again.

Before Chloe could argue, the girl released the boy's arm. She darted behind him and slammed against the huge Plexiglas display of animals. It was almost five feet high with seven levels of shelves that held hundreds of animals plus prehistoric and mythical creatures. Karen, Chloe, and the boy all jumped back as plastic animals spilled across the store and the display case crashed to the ground, smashing to pieces with a crack.

"Zach, run," the girl yelled over her shoulder.

In shock, Chloe's eyes darted to Karen and the boy. Karen had released his arm in the commotion and he took off for the front door. Karen dashed after him as the teenager climbed slowly to her feet. Chloe's potential customers stood near the far side of the store, four mouths agape.

"You have your hands full," the man said when Chloe made eye contact with him. "We'll stop back after lunch."

"You don't have to go," Chloe said, but they were already hurrying toward the entrance.

She wanted to follow them, but the girl was ducking to the side, clearly ready to make her escape.

"Not so fast," Chloe said and grabbed the back of the teen's soft T-shirt.

"He got away," Karen said as she came back into the store, passing the family on their way out. She stood guard at the front door but kept her hands on her knees as she struggled to catch her breath.

"Call the cops, then," the girl shouted, shrugging out of Chloe's grasp. She crossed her arms over her small chest. "I'll never give up Zach."

"Oh, for heaven's sake." Chloe pressed her fingertips to her temples as she surveyed the damage to her store. She struggled to keep her temper in check. Chloe never raised her voice. Never. "We weren't going to call the police." She pointed at Karen. "You scare kids when you threaten that."

"He stole from the store," the other woman argued. "He should be scared."

"Wait." The girl put her hands on her hips and scowled like only a teenager could. "You mean you weren't going to have him arrested?"

Chloe gave a halfhearted laugh. "For a few marbles? No." She looked again at the mess spread across her shop and thought of the hours of work it would take to sort the figurines, plus the cost of replacing the display cabinet.

"But now?" For the first time there was a hitch in the girl's voice, some of her bravado melting away as she realized exactly what she'd gotten herself into by allowing her brother to run.

"What's your name?" Chloe asked.

The girl's lips thinned and she didn't answer.

Chloe tried a different tack. "What did you mean when you said it's just you and your brother?"

"No," Karen said, stepping forward. "You are not going to take on another lost soul." Karen swept her arms wide. "Look at what she did to the store."

"I know," Chloe said softly. "We can fix the mess." She offered the girl a small smile. "Tell me your name."

The teenager's mouth opened then snapped shut. Her eyes tracked to the now-unguarded front door and she took a quick step in that direction before Chloe reached for her arm.

"Don't touch me," the girl yelled at the same time a deep, masculine voice bellowed, "What the hell is going on in here?"

All three women stopped and looked toward the front of the store. Chloe's breath caught at seeing the man filling the doorway. He was big, broad, and clearly pissed. His dark hair was cropped short with just a bit brushed over his forehead. While his features were striking, they were also hard as a sheer mountain peak. He could have been classically handsome, but there was a darkness about him that made him more intriguing. It was as if she could sense trouble in the thin lines fanning out around his eyes. Chloe had too much trouble in her past. She wasn't looking for any more of it.

He held the girl's younger brother by the scruff of the neck and his gaze landed on the teenager for a moment. Chloe could feel the girl shrink beside her, as if folding in on herself. She was transfixed by the teenager's face and how it went from swagger to absolute terror.

Chloe could relate to terror. Terror used to be her regular companion.

"Is someone going to answer me?" The huge man spoke again. Chloe looked at him, and she had to fight the urge to turn in on herself like she once would have. Because the man silhouetted by the late-morning light looked mad as hell. And most of that anger was directed at Chloe.

♦ ♦ ♦

Ben Haddox was having a crappy morning to top off a crappy week that was the icing on a craptastic month. It was still unbelievable how quickly things had gone to hell in his life. Two months ago he'd been sitting on top of the world. He'd had everything he'd worked for—fame, money, and a hugely successful career. Now he couldn't manage to control any of it, especially not his wayward niece and nephew, who seemed to have descended on this tiny store with their personal brand of destruction.

Zach shifted in his grasp. "You're hurting me," the boy whined, making Ben realize he was holding too tightly to Zach's thin arm.

When Ben released him, the boy took a step toward his sister. "Don't move," Ben said over his shoulder, finding it difficult not to yell the words. Yelling was familiar territory, but it made Zach anxious so Ben tried to dial down his volume.

His gaze landed on Abby and the woman next to her. The stubborn set of his niece's jaw was so much like her father's it made Ben's chest ache. He loved his brother, but the guy had made a mess of his life and these two kids were paying the price. Unfortunately, as Ben surveyed the damage to the toy store, all he could think about was how much this little outing was going to cost him.

The woman moved closer to Abby, drawing his attention. Her body stiffened under his scrutiny and, for a moment, Ben couldn't look away. She was petite, and the shapeless apron with the toy store's logo she wore couldn't quite hide her curves. Her dark hair was pulled back from her face, but a stray curl brushed across her cheek. She had the biggest eyes he'd ever seen, wide and pale hazel. Or was that green?

As he studied her, her full lips pressed together. There was an inherent goodness radiating from her that both intrigued and repelled him. Ben had given up good long ago. He'd gotten where he was in life by fighting his way to the top, being constantly on guard, maneuvering when he could, bulldozing through people when there were no other options. He'd been thrown a few curveballs recently. Or, more accurately, a fastball had slammed into him and knocked him flat on his ass. But he was going to make it past these setbacks like he did everything else, by muscling his way through.

"I'm going to ask nicely one more time," he bellowed at his niece. "What the hell is the problem here?"

"That was your nice voice?"

He glanced at the gray-haired woman standing nearest to him at the store's entrance. She looked like a holdover from the hippie generation with her long braids and the tie-dye T-shirt under her apron.

"As nice as you're going to get when I saw my nephew come tearing out of this place like he's being chased by a pack of wolves."

To her credit, the aging hippie didn't back down. "That boy is a thief."

"I didn't mean to—" Zach started but Ben held up a hand to quiet him. If he'd learned anything as a troublemaking kid, it was the less you said when caught, the better.

"Do you own this place?" he asked the older woman.

"It's mine." He turned as the good girl stepped forward. Her voice was quiet but warm, like a patch of sunshine coming through a window. It made him want to stretch and unwind, like a cat napping in the sun. "I'm Chloe Daniels," she said, "and The Toy Chest belongs to me." The tip of her tongue darted out to trace her top lip. It was a nervous gesture, but his body leapt to attention in response. He was uncharacteristically speechless.

"Your nephew took a handful of marbles without paying for them." It was a statement, not an accusation, and her tone held no anger. Still, Ben's temper flared once more and he cursed under his breath.

"What about all this?" he asked, gesturing to the destruction behind her.

The woman's luminous gaze flicked to Abby. "Your niece was afraid we were going to involve the police and created a rather large distraction so Zach could run out."

"Why?" He said the word through clenched teeth, his gaze locked with Abby's.

"The *cops*, Ben," she said with her usual attitude, but her voice caught on his name. Only for a split second, but it sliced through him all the same. These two kids had been through so much, and despite his intention to make a better life for them, he was already screwing up in a major way.

He rounded on Zach, unable to bear witness to Abby's preternatural world-weariness for one more moment. "Fifteen minutes," he shouted, back to his usual decibel level. "I asked you to stay in the park for fifteen damn minutes."

When the boy started to speak, Ben shook his head. "Empty your pockets," he commanded. "Now."

Eyes on the floor, Zach pulled out the lining of the right pocket on his baggy skateboard shorts.

"The other one," Ben said on a hiss of breath.

Slowly, his nephew reached into the left-side pocket. He extracted his hand again, fist closed.

Ben tapped the toe of his boot on the scuffed hardwood floor. "Show me."

Zach opened his fingers, four colorful marbles resting in the center of his sweaty palm.

It wasn't a surprise. Hell, Ben and his brother, Cory, had pinched more than their share of candy and gum from the local convenience store back when they were hell-raising kids hanging all day on nearby Federal Boulevard with too much time and too little supervision.

Yet Ben wanted more for Zach and Abby. He also expected more from them, although he wasn't sure why. His childhood had been a cakewalk compared to what they'd been through. But he had no intention of letting these kids repeat the mistakes of the adults around them. The precarious lid he held on his temper popped off at the thought that he might not have much say in the matter.

Without thinking, he reached out and knocked Zach's hand, the marbles flying in all directions.

"I'm sorry," the boy shouted. "It was stupid—"

"You're damn right it was stupid."

Zach swiped at wet cheeks with his fingers. "You mean I'm stupid."

Ben's head started to throb. "That's not what I said." He tried to lower the volume level of his voice but couldn't quite manage it. "You're better than me. Better than your dad. You need to start acting like it." He pointed a finger at Abby. "Both of you."

Zach squeezed shut his eyes. "I'm sorry," he whispered.

The realization of what he was doing landed on Ben like a cast-iron skillet to the side of his pounding head. Christ, he sounded like his old man used to, and that wouldn't get any of them on the right track.

"It was a mistake," a gentle voice said from behind him. Ben spun on his heel, lifting his arm to run his fingers through his hair.

Chloe was directly behind him, closer than he expected. As his hand came up she automatically flinched then stumbled a few steps. Ben cursed again as her foot caught on the edge of the fallen display. She tripped over it, falling back onto her elbows and ass. Ben and the older woman stepped forward at the same time. The shop owner shook her head, her whole body rigid with tension.

"Don't," she snapped, keeping her gaze on her knees.

He ignored her, of course, and held out a hand. "I didn't mean to . . . startle you."

She ignored him, scrambling to her feet and crossing her arms over her chest. "Get out," she whispered in a ragged voice that made him feel like a bigger jerk than he already did.

"I was only—"

"Please."

He stopped at the one word, scrubbed his fingers over his jaw. He heard Zach muffle a sob and Abby mumble "asshole."

"This is *my* store," Chloe said, her voice firmer now. "I want all three of you to leave."

"This isn't finished. Abby ruined your display." It took a huge effort, but Ben spoke the words softly.

"Call me Monday and we'll work out payment," she told him, but Ben didn't want to. He wanted to work it out now. This woman meant nothing to him, but he had an almost violent need to know what had happened to her to make her so skittish.

Violent being the operative word. Because he'd seen enough in his life to understand that she'd suffered through some sort of brutality. A rush of protectiveness he hardly recognized roared to life inside him. For Chloe Daniels and for Abby and Zach and all they'd been through to make their reactions to normal circumstances so utterly abnormal.

"Let's go, Ben." Abby was at his side, tugging on his elbow as she grabbed Zach's wrist.

He glanced at the older woman, who glared at him in return. "You heard her," the hippie chick said. "She owns the place and you need to leave."

He opened the door, the cheery sound of the bells above it unsettling in the tense silence. Abby and Zach walked out into the summer sunshine first and Ben followed, but turned back before stepping out completely. "This isn't finished," he said again, staring at Chloe Daniels until she finally looked at him. "You may own the store, but the building belongs to me."

As her lush mouth dropped open, Ben stepped out the door and gave it a hard push to slam shut behind him.

CHAPTER TWO

As exits went, it was brilliant, Chloe had to admit.

It was later Saturday evening by the time she finished sorting the plastic figurines into various bins and baskets she'd dug out of the toy shop's basement storage room.

She'd been so upset by the confrontation with Ben Haddox—mainly at her reaction to him—that she'd considered closing shop for the rest of the day after he'd stormed out. Karen had convinced her not to waste a day's profit and cancel one of their most popular monthly classes over the foul-tempered man and his wayward niece and nephew. But Chloe had thought of little else the rest of the day except the odd trio.

Ben Haddox.

She should have recognized him immediately but had been so distracted by the girl and the mess and her irritating fear at his booming voice, she hadn't processed why he looked so familiar. Ben Haddox was one of the most famous stars of EatTV's programming lineup. He was popular in the way of most celebrities with abrasive personalities. The viewing audience couldn't seem to get enough of the borderline verbal abuse he dished out on his weekly series, *A Beast in Your Kitchen*.

Chloe might be familiar with his shtick but, as cooking shows went, she favored more gentle, down-home, female-hosted programming. Of course she understood Ben's appeal, especially with women. While Chloe wasn't a fan of big, bad, brooding alpha men who practically reeked of testosterone, she knew plenty of women who were. She also understood that thin, bespectacled, soft-spoken men could inflict just as much pain as the obvious bruisers and had been chiding herself most of the afternoon for her overreaction to Ben's outburst.

She'd known almost as soon as she fell that he hadn't been about to hit her and hated how she'd let fear short-circuit her brain in the moment. She'd worked too hard and long on her self-confidence and control to allow one thundering man to wreck everything she'd built.

But Ben Haddox could do more than derail her recovery. He had the power to ruin her life.

Chloe's hope of convincing the building's owner to give her store a chance had walked right out into the fresh Colorado air along with the hulking man. She wasn't going to give up fighting for The Toy Chest yet. She simply needed time to think of another plan.

She gathered her purse, laptop bag, and keys then hit the security code and flipped off the lights for the main room of the store. She didn't like this time of day. The dimming light cast too many shadows as her eyes adjusted to the approaching darkness. As quickly as she could, Chloe shoved the key in the front door to lock the handle then the dead bolt.

"Chloe."

She heard her name spoken just as she felt a presence behind her. Maybe it was her frazzled nerves or another burst of the adrenaline kicked off by Ben's earlier tirade, but whatever the reason, Chloe's reaction was swift and sure.

She yanked the keys from the door and whirled, her finger depressing the button on the can of pepper spray hanging from her key ring before her brain registered where she was aiming.

Ben Haddox let loose the most colorful string of swear words Chloe had ever heard.

"You can't sneak up on me like that," she yelled, but already she was shoving the key back in the lock to open the door.

He didn't answer, probably because he was bent forward, coughing and choking as his face turned an ugly shade of red and he swiped at his eyes.

"Don't touch your face," she said, grabbing his wrists. "It only makes the effects worse if you rub it in."

"You do this a lot?" he asked around coughing fits. His eyes were shut, but she knew he wouldn't be able to see her anyway.

"Never," she admitted as she fumbled with the door.

A group of people came around the corner, their conversation halting as they spied Chloe and Ben.

"All good here," she called. "Just a misunderstanding." She yanked on Ben's arm. It was a little bit like tugging a ton of bricks, but he allowed her to lead him into the store.

"I can't see a damn thing," he growled.

"Temporary blindness," she confirmed as she hit the keypad to disarm the security system and turned on the lights. "Your vision should be better in about fifteen minutes."

He lifted his hands in front of his face then dropped them again. "You're a real expert on the stuff."

"It was part of a self-defense class I took a few years ago."

"I guess it's safer than a concealed carry permit."

She dropped her purse and computer bag. "I don't like guns."

"It was a joke." He coughed again.

"Oh."

He lifted the hem of his T-shirt and wiped his eyes, ignoring her advice. The six-pack muscles of his stomach momentarily transfixed her. Then he let out a strangled groan.

"No more talking," she said, taking his arm again. "We need to rinse out your eyes. There's a sink in my office."

He nodded and grabbed hold of her waist as she maneuvered him through the racks of toys and books toward the back of the shop.

"My eyes won't open."

"It's the capsaicin oil, the active ingredient in the pepper spray." She turned on the water and adjusted the temperature. "It's an inflammatory, so keep your eyes shut while I flush the area around them. I'll need to use soap to remove the oil from your skin."

She positioned him in front of the sink, placing his hands on the edges before bending him forward.

"It feels like someone's holding a lit match to my skin," he whispered.

"I'm sorry," she answered. With a few pumps of the organic soap she kept on the shelf next to the sink, she used a clean towel to rinse his face.

He stilled, his breath eventually slowing as she worked for several minutes. She dabbed at his jaw and neck as the water spilled over his thick brows and straight nose. Her fingers brushed away the hair from his forehead and she was surprised at how soft the strands were to the touch. For several minutes there was nothing but the sound of the water and their breathing. The strange intimacy of the moment washed over Chloe like the water from the faucet. It had been years since she'd been so close to a man other than the customers in her shop. She hadn't been on a date since her divorce, unwilling to allow herself to be vulnerable to someone physically stronger than her.

Although Ben had a good eight inches and at least a hundred pounds on her, in this moment she felt like the one in control. It was only an illusion. The muscles of his arms were thick and corded. Even as impaired as he was, he could overpower her in a few seconds. But she felt oddly safe with him, especially now that he wasn't in the middle of a rant. She had no doubt the temper was coming, and she probably deserved it for spraying him.

But she liked the fantasy of security she had right now. A part of her had forgotten how good a man could smell. Ben's scent was a mix of cedar and spice. Like him, it was wholly male and a little rough around the edges.

He shifted, coughing more quietly, and Chloe started. What was wrong with her? She'd just maced the man who was trying to close down her store and here she was indulging in musings about how good he smelled.

"Can you open your eyes so I can flush them out?"

He blinked then hissed. "Damn, that makes the pain brand-new again."

She grimaced. "Is the water helping at all?"

"A bit," he said through clenched teeth.

"The effects should completely wear off in about an hour." She pressed the rag to the corner of his eye. "At least that's what the self-defense teacher told us."

Ben placed his hand on hers as she smoothed it over his cheek. "I wasn't going to hit you."

She nodded then remembered that his eyes were shut. Somehow, that fact made it less humiliating to talk about with him. "I know. I overreacted, and I didn't mean to spray you."

"Really?" He choked out a laugh. "Because your aim was damn accurate."

"I meant to spray the man behind me," she corrected, "but I didn't realize it was you."

His jaw tightened. "Who hurt you, Chloe?"

Pain ripped through her at the simple question. She yanked her hand away from his. "I think I've washed off all of the spray." She turned off the faucet and pressed a clean towel into his hand. "You can dry your hair, but we should get you a different T-shirt. Yours probably has residual oil on it and if it touches your skin, the burning will start again."

"That assumes the current burning ever stops," he said, straightening. He reached up to drape the dry towel over his head but winced when a corner of it hit his eye.

"Let me," she said, taking it from him. "Does your whole face hurt?" She smoothed his dark hair away from his forehead, careful to avoid touching the area near his eyes.

"Mainly the left side. It was a direct hit."

"Sorry," she said again.

"I'd tell you I've been hit with worse, but my skin is still on fire and the pain from a punch fades a lot quicker."

"But not the bruises," she answered without thinking.

He squinted, trying to open one of his eyes, then cursed again.

"Leave them shut." She liked it better, since he couldn't see the embarrassment reddening her cheeks. She took his hand. "There's a loveseat three steps behind you and a bit to the right. Let's get you settled, and I'll grab one of the store shirts."

His fingers were warm in hers, almost comforting, and again she took too much pleasure in the simple contact. It had been too long since she'd shown physical affection to anyone but her girlfriends and the women who worked in the store. To have her hand engulfed by Ben's elicited a far different response than a simple hug.

One she wouldn't allow herself to examine too closely.

"Stay here," she told him as she pushed him down onto the overstuffed loveseat along the back wall.

"I'm not going anywhere fast."

She hurried to the counter and pulled out the drawer that held The Toy Chest logo T-shirts they sold. Ben was probably an XXL, but XL was the largest size she had on hand. Not a lot of big guys wore shirts with an overflowing toy box emblazoned on the back.

She'd left the door to the back storeroom open, but her step faltered as she returned through it.

Ben was still in the chair, his head tipped back, eyes closed. The shirt he'd been wearing lay at his feet. She might have sworn off men, and maybe burly guys weren't her usual type, but a bare-chested Ben Haddox was something even she could appreciate. He was about as perfect as a man got. His muscles were hard, his skin smooth and golden. He looked almost more like a statue than a real man. She took a small step forward, transfixed by the tattoo covering his right shoulder.

"It's my first kitchen knife," he said into the silence. "I splurged for it after I got my first promotion in Las Vegas."

Chloe stiffened, not realizing she'd moved forward until she was directly in front of him. "Your eyes are closed. How can you tell where I'm looking?"

"Because I feel your stare."

She glanced at her watch. "It's been almost fifteen minutes," she said quickly, unnerved at the accuracy of his comment. "Any progress with opening your eyes?"

His features scrunched, then he shook his head. "Not yet. What's the problem? You disable me then need to hurry me out the door?"

"I want you to be ok."

"Maybe I want the same thing for you," he said softly.

"Then renew my lease."

He tipped his head an inch, as if acknowledging her argument. "I won't talk about business tonight. I'm at too much of a disadvantage."

"I have a feeling you're never at a disadvantage," she answered but didn't force the subject. She felt bad enough about what she'd done to him. He'd been better humored about it than she would have expected under the circumstances. Why push her luck? Instead, she dropped the store shirt into his lap. "Put this on."

"Why? Afraid you're going to jump me if you have to stare too long at my naked self?"

"You're not naked," she said with a huff, "and maybe I'm afraid I'll be tempted to spray you again."

"I could get naked," he said with a half smile.

"You're temporarily blind."

He leaned forward. "My other senses work just fine."

"Getting out the pepper spray," she said in a singsong voice and he laughed before carefully pulling the T-shirt over his head, stretching the collar so it didn't brush his face.

Chloe pressed a hand to her stomach, expecting to feel anxious from his blatant flirtation. Instead some forgotten part of her zinged to life, making her body tingle from head to toe. She used to love to flirt, the banter back and forth and the anticipation of what might come next.

These days she had more important things to occupy her time. But she realized how much she missed the teasing pleasure of mutual attraction.

"Do you want a glass of water?" she asked, seeking a way to keep herself busy.

He shook his head. "Sit down. I promise I'll be out of your way as soon as I can pry open my eyes."

"It's fine." She dropped into the desk chair and spun it to face him. "Actually, it's my fault, but I also don't have plans other than a date with my DVR."

"Did you record me?" he asked, and it was her turn to laugh.

"Ego much?"

He sighed. "I'll take that as a no."

"What about you? Is there someone you want me to call? What about your niece and nephew?"

"They're at home with my dad," he said. "I made dinner before I left so everyone is happy."

That piqued her curiosity. "What does a famous chef make for dinner?"

"Sadly, cheese pizza." He shook his head. "Pizza, chicken nuggets, and plain spaghetti are all I've been able to get Zach to eat since I got to Colorado. I was appointed their guardian, but we're all staying with my dad."

"How long has it been?"

"A little over a month," he said, shifting in the chair. "My brother went to jail and there was no one else to take them."

"How long will you have them?" she asked gently.

Ben shrugged. "He was convicted of armed robbery, so he's got at least five years until he's eligible for parole."

"They'll be almost grown," Chloe said on a gasp.

"Abby's fifteen now so she'll be an adult." He rubbed his hand along his jaw then winced. "She's not even Cory's kid. She and Zach had the same mother. She died last year of a drug overdose so both kids came to live with my brother, Cory."

"So Abby isn't actually related to you?"

He shook his head. "But she's got no one else and she and Zach need each other, especially now. Trust me, I know I'm not a great bet for either of those kids—"

"I wasn't thinking that," she interrupted. "It's really great of you to take them in. Not exactly what I would have expected from Ben the Beast."

"I hate that name."

"It made you famous."

"Isn't that the kicker?" His voice was hollow, giving Chloe the strangest urge to reach out and comfort him. Lost souls. Karen accused Chloe of collecting them, but she reminded herself that this man didn't need her help. He was, in many ways, the enemy. But it didn't feel that way in the quiet of her cozy storeroom.

"I like you better when you're not shouting."

"That's also part of what made me famous." He took a breath and cracked open one eye. "I like you better when you're not shooting pepper spray in my face." He stood, grabbed a clean towel from the shelf, and dampened it under the faucet. He dabbed at his eyes then turned to her, his blue-gray eyes bloodshot but still commanding.

"Better?" she asked, also standing and taking a few steps to the other side of the room. The intimacy that felt safe when he was debilitated with his eyes closed now felt too intense, and she needed to break the connection pulsing between them.

He nodded then glanced down. "Why am I wearing a neon-pink shirt?"

"It's all I had in your size."

He smoothed a hand over the front of the shirt, which clung to his broad chest like it had been accidentally shrunk in the dryer.

"Or close to your size," she amended, swallowing as once again she was reminded of his strength. "We should go now." She walked past him into the main part of the store, flipping off lights as she did.

He followed and she picked up her purse and laptop bag again, reset the security system, and headed out the front door. Although it was fully dark now, Ben almost glowed in the bright shirt, making Chloe smile in spite of herself.

"Where's your car?" he asked after she locked the front door.

"I live close enough to walk."

"I'll walk you home, then."

"You don't . . . I'd rather . . ." She clutched her computer bag to her front. "No," she said finally. "I'm fine on my own." He looked like he wanted to argue so she held up a hand. "It's nice of you to offer, especially after what I did, but this is where we say good-bye, Ben. Thank you for . . . well . . . thank you for being nice about the pepper spray."

He gave a small nod then stepped closer to her. "I'm not nice, Chloe. I get that I scared you, but shit happens and we move on. You said you like me better when I'm not shouting, but loud or quiet, you shouldn't like me at all."

She sucked in a breath as he reached out and traced a finger along her jaw. "I would never lay a hand on you that would cause pain, but I am going to hurt you. I own the building, and this is where I'm opening my restaurant."

A new level of panic spread through her as she absorbed the knowledge that he had a plan for her shop. "Why here?"

"Because I want this space. And I always get what I want."

CHAPTER THREE

"Why that space?"

Monday morning Ben watched his publicist, Michael Ames, root through the refrigerator in his father's ramshackle house near Federal Boulevard on Denver's northwest side, about a mile from the Highlands neighborhood that housed The Toy Chest.

"Because it's the space I want."

Michael set a plate of leftover pizza on the counter and took a bite of one slice.

Ben pointed to the far side of the counter. "There's a microwave in the corner if you'd like to heat it up."

"Did you just suggest I use a microwave?" he asked, swallowing audibly. "What the hell is wrong with you?" He glanced from the pizza to Ben. "By the way, this is phenomenal. What kind of cheese did you use?"

"A mix of smoked mozzarella, Pecorino Romano, and Emmentaler." Ben stepped forward to grab his own slice. He didn't bother heating it either.

"What's wrong with plain old mozzarella?" a booming voice called. "If it's good enough for the Italians, it should work for the rest of us."

Ben looked up as his father walked into the room. "Christ, Dad," he muttered. "Put on some clothes. I'm going to lose my appetite."

"First, remember this isn't your house, so don't tell me what I can and can't wear. And second, give me a break on the fancy cheeses." Harry Haddox wiggled his hips with a smirk then scratched his crotch. He wore nothing but a pair of loose-fitting plaid boxers. In his youth, Ben's dad had been an amateur boxer and his body still held some of its former muscle, but a basketball-sized paunch now drooped over the waistband of his boxer shorts. "I knew you before you were a food snob, Benny-boy. I know your tastes aren't that picky."

"And there's nothing wrong with a microwave oven, Mike," he shouted. "It's called technology, and how else am I supposed to reheat my Folgers?"

The publicist shuddered, whether from Harry's insistence on shortening his name or the thought of someone drinking instant coffee, Ben couldn't tell. "Dad, stop yelling," he hollered. "You're going to wake Abby."

"He already did," the girl said as she stalked into the room. She stopped at the sight of Ben's father leaning down to take a plate from the dishwasher. "Christ, Harry. Put on some clothes. You're going to scar me for life."

"Watch your language," Ben muttered around a bite of pizza, ignoring the fact that he'd said almost the same thing minutes earlier.

Michael quirked a brow. "Are you certain she's not related to you?" He lifted the dish of pizza toward Abby. "Breakfast?"

She rolled her eyes. "I'll have a Pop-Tart."

"There are no Pop-Tarts in this kitchen," Ben said.

She grabbed a box from the pantry like a prize from a penny arcade game. "Harry bought groceries yesterday."

"Shit," Ben muttered.

"No," Michael corrected him. "But mostly chemicals." He finished the pizza then tore a paper towel from the roll, dabbing at the corner of his mouth like he was in a Michelin-rated restaurant. "By the way, Mr. Haddox," he said as Harry leaned in to nab the final slice of pizza, "you have a lovely home."

Abby snorted as Ben coughed to hide his own laugh. His dad's house looked much the same as it did when he was a kid, which was messy, cluttered, and without an ounce of hominess. The linoleum floors of the kitchen had seen better decades, and the appliances were mostly from the Cold War era.

Ben had offered more than once to buy his father a different, bigger, and better house or at least to remodel this one. But Harry was proud and the mortgage was paid, so he saw no need to change a thing. Ben would have preferred to rent a hotel suite or a loft downtown, but the kids had come to stay with his father immediately after Cory had been arrested. He didn't want to uproot them again when they both seemed comfortable in this old house built in the Denver Square style.

"You're slicker than snot on a doorknob, Mike." Harry's booming laugh filled the kitchen. "I like that." He took a bite of pizza then gave Michael a hearty slap on the back. "The Rockies start a three-game home series tonight. Let me know if you want to catch a game while you're in town. I can set you up with tickets, and I'll slip you a free hot dog if I'm working."

"Thanks," Michael said, peering over his shoulder, probably to see if he had grease or tomato sauce staining his tailored suit. "I'm flying out this afternoon, but if our boy is serious about these restaurant plans, I'll be back soon."

"He's serious." Harry's gaze settled on Ben. "My son might have made it big, but he knows family comes first."

Before Ben could reply, Abby nudged his hip. "You're in my way," she said in her typical drill-sergeant tone. He moved and she took a dish from the cabinet behind him. "Has Zach eaten breakfast?"

Guilt stabbed at Ben. Zach had come down at least thirty minutes ago but had gone right to the family room and turned on the TV. Ben hadn't given a thought to making the kid something for breakfast. His first pseudo-parent fail of the morning. Brilliant.

"I'll bring him a Pop-Tart," Abby said, gauging his expression. The girl was spooky with how accurately she could read him.

"I can make omelets," he offered.

"Pop-Tarts are better," she said and plucked up the two that had just popped from the toaster.

"I'll bring OJ," Harry said, grabbing the carton from the fridge and three plastic cups. "That kid's going to need to give up the video games for a few minutes. I want to check out SportsCenter before I take my morning constitutional."

Ben heard Abby groan as they left the room.

"I'll have an omelet," Michael told him, placing the empty pizza plate in the sink.

"Make your own," Ben mumbled, scrubbing a hand over his face.

Michael only laughed. "Back to business, *Benny-boy*. I spent yesterday on the phone with one of Denver's top commercial realtors. If you're determined to open your first restaurant in your long-ago abandoned hometown, he's got way better options for you than converting an old-time toy store into a 'Ben the Beast' signature restaurant."

"Lay off the nickname."

"It's not just a nickname, it's your brand. I still don't understand why you'd want to screw it up by leaving Vegas."

"Thanks to the shooting schedule for the TV show and all the damn promotional appearances you've got me doing, I haven't been in a Vegas kitchen for almost two years."

"But your legend lives on," Michael argued. "There are at least two different investment groups hounding me about their partnering with you."

Ben stalked to the edge of the kitchen. "No partnerships. I told you that." He'd worked round the clock for years to finally gain the title of executive chef. But even when he'd taken over the kitchen at La

Lune, the five-star showpiece in one of the Strip's luxury hotels, he'd had to create dishes that fit with the elite theme of the restaurant. He'd become an expert at sourcing the most exclusive ingredients and using them in innovative ways but had no real style of his own beyond high-dollar excess.

"They'll give you as much control as you want."

"Bullshit." Ben slammed his hand on the counter. "Men in suits are great at making promises before the dotted line is signed. Things go to hell once the contract is locked in."

"*A Beast in Your Kitchen* has been a wild success." Michael actually sounded offended that Ben would suggest otherwise. "It's given you exposure you never would have had, even as a famous executive chef."

"It's also ruined my reputation as someone with real talent. I'm more than a face and a temper." He wasn't sure whether he said the words to convince Michael or himself. As hard as he'd worked to run his own kitchen, Ben knew that even in Las Vegas, people had talked about his histrionics in the kitchen as much as they had the food he served.

He might not have much fondness for his childhood home, but he also wasn't happy living life as the bad boy of the restaurant industry. "I can't even grab a beer without people asking for an autograph or picture. And half the time they want me to bare my teeth like I'm some sort of foodie werewolf."

"You're not getting sympathy from me, Ben. When was the last time you paid for a beer or a meal or spent an evening alone without a gorgeous woman ready for action?" Michael asked, crossing his arms over his chest. "There are perks to the lifestyle. I'm not sure you'd know how to function like a real person anymore. Maybe you are part werewolf."

"Go to hell, Michael."

"A dumpy storefront in an obscure Denver neighborhood might just be my version of hell."

"Do your research. The Highlands is one of the most popular areas in the city. This neighborhood has had a complete overhaul in the past few years." Ben was shouting now, his temper getting the best of him as usual.

"Don't pop a blood vessel." Michael held out his hands, palms forward. "I was joking."

"I don't think you know how to joke." The publicist's sharp focus was one of the things Ben had appreciated at the beginning of their partnership, but now he wanted a break.

"I know how to make you money. Vegas, LA, New York. Why can't you pick one of those? Seriously, Ben, the altitude here is killing me."

"Then leave."

Michael pushed away from the counter, a flash of panic lighting his dark eyes. "You don't mean that."

"I want my reputation back, and I'm staying in Denver. We might not be much, but Dad and I are all those two kids have." Ben felt his gut start to churn as he said the words out loud. "At least for now," he amended, still not willing to fully commit to this new domestication. The ramifications of the promise he'd made to his brother almost paralyzed him with doubt. Altitude notwithstanding, Ben hadn't been able to take a steady breath since he'd arrived in Colorado.

"You can move them," Michael suggested. "Hell, I was an army brat and look how well I turned out."

Ben arched an eyebrow.

"At least say you'll consider a different location. The cash you're going to need to do a build out on a property with no kitchen is mind-boggling."

"It's got to be that location."

Michael ran his hands though his hair, yanking on the dark strands. "Do you know how long that will take, even if we get started immediately?"

"We can't start right away," Ben said. "The current tenant's lease isn't up for another month." At Michael's horrified look, Ben shrugged. "It will give me time to meet with an architect and contractors to come up with a concept."

Michael's arms dropped slack to his sides. "Are you saying you don't have a concept yet? What kind of food is it going to be?"

"I haven't decided," Ben said after a moment. "My usual, I guess."

Michael had been with him long enough not to settle for that kind of answer. "What's the usual?" he asked, tapping the toe of one Italian loafer. "Like you just told me, you haven't worked in a commercial kitchen as an executive chef for over two years. As good as you were at La Lune, that was Maurice St. Clair's legacy and we both know it."

Ben didn't bother to deny it. From the time he'd used his meager savings at age eighteen to move to New York City, his one goal had been to work for the aging French master who ruled the Manhattan culinary scene. St. Clair's reputation was on par with the truly world-class chefs like Joël Robuchon and Marco Pierre White, but Ben had been attracted not only to the other man's creative take on haute cuisine but to his showmanship as well. Maurice had been one of the first true celebrity chefs, and Ben had wanted in on the whole package. He'd done it, too, brazenly waylaying St. Clair in his SoHo restaurant. The older man had been furious and had had Ben thrown out onto the street, only to call him back before Ben had time to brush the dirt off his jeans. It had been trial by fire, but Ben had thrown himself into making it work.

By that time, Cory had started dabbling in drugs and their father was only a year into his sobriety. Ben had needed an outlet for his anger and his energy, and the grueling seventeen-hour days had provided just that.

Maurice had taken Ben with him to Las Vegas when he'd opened La Lune, but a heart attack had forced St. Clair's early retirement. At twenty-six, Ben had been one of the youngest people ever to be made executive chef of a five-star restaurant. Three years later, Michael had visited the restaurant and proposed brokering a deal with the then-fledgling EatTV channel. By then, Ben's temper was legendary throughout Vegas and the restaurant industry as a whole. Michael had pitched *A Beast in Your Kitchen* to capitalize on that and set Ben apart from the regular crop of down-home chefs and overly enthusiastic commentators on the cooking channels.

The show was a runaway success, and Ben had enjoyed the fame and notoriety for a while. Lately he realized that being the loudest person in the room didn't always mean he was listened to the closest. Often it only left him with a sore throat and headache.

"I need a break," he said finally, resisting the urge to shout the words at the top of his lungs. "I want you to clear my schedule for the summer. At least until preseason meetings start for the show."

"Let's get this straight. You don't have a location yet. You have no team or investors working with you, and you haven't even started on the menu." Michael snorted. "Is this a premature midlife crisis?"

"I don't give a shit what you call it." Ben kicked at one of Zach's discarded sneakers lying in the middle of the kitchen. "I'm taking my time with this, Michael. I've earned it."

The publicist bit down on his lip. "You know how fast this industry moves, right? How many hungry guys there are out there, just like you a few years ago, vying to take your spot at the top?"

Anger bubbled in Ben at the veiled threat, but he let it wash over and through him before answering. "Maybe I'm ready to hand it over."

Michael looked around as if someone important might be listening. "Don't say that to anyone but me, Ben. The food industry is a killer. You know that. They'll smell your indecision and start circling like vultures."

"Go back to New York, Michael," Ben said with a sigh.

"You've got an event booked in Vegas at the end of the week." Michael whipped the iPhone from his pocket and punched at the screen. "I can push back a few of your network appearances, but this is an industry showcase. If you cancel at this point, the gossip will be brutal." He glanced up from the phone. "It may even send reporters after you." He swept one arm widely around the kitchen. "We've been able to keep your family business under wraps, but it won't be difficult to figure out once people start looking."

Ben bit back a curse. "Fine. I'll make sure Dad's available for the kids and I'll do the Vegas appearance. I want some time after that, Michael. I don't give a damn about the network or the brand. I've got something more to offer than screaming at people who don't cook the way I want them to."

Michael gave a small laugh. "The line cooks at La Lune might disagree with you on that point. Figure it out, Ben, but don't take too long." He put the phone back in his pocket and headed toward the door. "Your future's not going to wait around forever."

◆ ◆ ◆

Chloe tapped a pen against the mostly blank page of the notebook on the counter.

"Ever think of a career as a graffiti artist?" Tamara Black, who'd worked part-time for Chloe the past six months, peered over her shoulder. "You've got a unique style." Tamara was brash, but her natural enthusiasm won over both Chloe and the store's customers. She'd moved to Denver from Texas because of a breakup that had ended badly. When Chloe had first met her, Tamara had been full of bravado, from her spiked blond hair to the black leather pants she favored. Slowly she was softening, and Chloe had recently helped her enroll in a cosmetology school near downtown.

"I'm afraid of heights," Chloe answered absently then traced another line over the bubble letters she'd written at the top of the page. *Plan for the Future* was what she'd titled the list, but that was as far as she had gotten. Up until she'd made the decision to leave her husband and move to Colorado, Chloe had been content to let her life be directed by the people around her. As a girl it had been her mother's whims. Judy Daniels had moved their tiny family all over Chicago as she switched jobs, boyfriends, and neighborhoods, always looking for her idea of the perfect life. Chloe understood her single mom was under a lot of pressure to make a life for the two of them, and it had been easier to go along with the changes rather than upset Judy's delicate mental and emotional state.

Maybe her mom had wanted the best for them both, but in hindsight, most of her decisions hadn't taken Chloe into account at all. Judy had craved a happiness she'd never found with a string of deadbeat men and dead-end jobs. Her mood swings had morphed into full-blown episodes of depression that had held both of them in their grip for as long as Chloe could remember. For too many years, misery had been her mother's primary companion. Although Chloe had vowed not to follow in her mother's footsteps, she'd ended up living with a different sort of weight on her shoulders.

"I like lists. They make me feel in control."

"You should add 'get money' and 'screw Ben Haddox.'"

Chloe jerked back as a memory of the wildly inappropriate dream she'd had last night rushed into her head. The dream had featured Ben, a blanket spread across a field of wildflowers, and the summer sun beating down on her naked skin. There was sweat and sounds and . . . lord, she could feel her cheeks burning.

"I didn't mean screw in the literal sense," Tamara said with a laugh, watching Chloe. "Although that man is about as hot as they come. Have you watched any of that show of his?"

"I've seen a couple episodes." Chloe moved the notebook into a drawer as a customer approached the register. The truth was she'd binge-watched the first two seasons yesterday, perhaps accounting for the reason she couldn't get Ben Haddox out of her mind. It sure didn't have anything to do with her memories of Saturday night, when he'd seemed vulnerable and almost lost as he talked about his niece and nephew.

No more lost souls.

"He's a total jerk," she said to Tamara after the mother paid for her daughter's art kit and the two left the store. "I don't see why anyone would want to subject themselves to that sort of judgment and ridicule on camera." Chloe didn't bother to mention that once she'd started watching, she hadn't been able to turn off *A Beast in Your Kitchen.*

The premise was simple and not wholly original. The show featured head chefs who had a reputation for being surly and demanding in their kitchens. The staff that worked for them applied to the show and, if chosen, Ben would pay a surprise visit to the restaurant and give the chef a taste of his or her own medicine. After trading insults, and with at least half the show devoted to the featured chefs spouting off about how no one would outcook them in their own kitchens, Ben would challenge each chef to a cook-off to be judged by random customers. The tag line "Can your beast beat ours?" was a dare no one seemed able to resist.

On the episodes she'd watched, Ben had never been bested, either while cooking or throwing down the verbal gauntlet. He seemed able to see exactly where a person's weakness or insecurity lay then needle and push until he drove men and women to the breaking point. The only plus side Chloe noticed was that by getting a taste of their own medicine, most of the chefs featured committed to turning over a new leaf by the end of the episode.

Those silver-lining endings did nothing to ease her nerves at the thought of Ben controlling the future of her business. If he could take down those difficult, hard-hearted chefs, what kind of damage would he do to her if she fought him on the lease?

"He can be scary, too," Chloe added, worrying her bottom lip between her teeth. "At the end of last season, he came close to a physical altercation with one of the featured chefs on the show."

"I thought you only watched a couple of episodes?" Tamara asked with a laugh.

"It was hard to look away," Chloe admitted.

Tamara grinned. "I hear you on that."

"Honestly, I can't believe they let that particular episode air," Chloe said quietly. "Ben was totally in the other guy's face like he was about to lose it. He's intimidating when he doesn't even try to be, but when he's angry, it's kind of terrifying. The other chef started crying, and the producers had to pull Ben away. My heart was beating a mile a minute. If he wanted to, Ben could really hurt someone." How would she stand up to him and come out unscathed?

"I don't know," Tamara said, drawing Chloe back to the present moment. "I can see why someone might be willing to let a man like Ben Haddox do a little dominating."

At Chloe's startled gasp, Tamara quickly held up her hands. "Not me, mind you. You know I learned my lesson and I got a new life now. No one's going to lay a hand on me ever again."

"I never touched any of the participants on the show."

Both women spun around to find Ben standing directly behind them. A glance past his shoulder showed Abby and Zach looking at a display of kites near the front of the store.

Chloe smoothed a hand over her apron. "For a big man, you are remarkably talented at sneaking up on people."

He flashed her a faint smile, but his eyes were serious. "I didn't touch them," he repeated.

His quiet scrutiny was almost more unnerving than his shouting. "You didn't need to," she said with a laugh that sounded more like a nervous croak. "Your verbal evisceration was quite effective."

His thick brows drew down over his eyes, but before he could answer, Tamara stepped forward. "Tamara Black," she said, reaching for his hand then pumping it in hers. "Chloe likes the big words and I don't understand bunches of them, but let me just say I like what you've got going on, Mr. Haddox."

The smile he gave Tamara was genuine, and he nodded toward the bright pink ends of her hair. "Call me Ben, and I like what you've got going on, too."

Tamara giggled like a schoolgirl then pointed at Abby and Zach. "Those your kids?"

"My niece and nephew."

Tamara nodded. "They're cute."

"They're hellions," he muttered.

"Must be how you know they're part of the family." She wagged a finger between Ben and Chloe. "I can tell you two got business, so I'm going to help those kids pick out the most expensive kite we have in stock."

"You go, girl," Ben told her, earning another giggle.

Chloe rolled her eyes. "Have them get two kites." Ben smiled.

"You got it," Tamara said and walked toward the front of the store.

"We don't have business," Chloe said when she was alone with Ben.

"We absolutely have business," Ben answered. "I heard Tamara's comment about not letting anybody hurt her again." He crossed his arms over his broad chest. "Do all of the women you hire have a similar history to yours?"

Chloe found herself busily rearranging a display of yarn-haired fairy dolls. "I haven't . . . they don't . . . my history isn't . . ." She shoved several dolls to the back of a shelf. "Let's talk business."

He only looked at her.

"Please," she said after a moment.

"Chloe."

"Don't do this, Ben." She shook her head hard. "You don't know me. Whatever you think you understand, you don't. You're trying to ruin my life, so I'd prefer to keep my skeletons in the closet." The statement wasn't exactly true. What she would have preferred was to launch herself at him and bury her nose in his neck to see if he still had the same irresistible smell from Saturday night.

"My goal isn't to ruin your life," he said, raking one hand through his hair.

"You're forcing me to close the store that's been my whole life for the past three years."

"This isn't about you. I want the location."

"Where this toy store has been for the past twenty years?" she asked, taking a step around the counter toward him. "There are much better restaurant spaces available in the city, ones you wouldn't need to gut and build out from the studs."

An emotion she didn't recognize flashed in his eyes before he glanced away. "I want this one."

Staring at him for a moment, realization dawned. "This is personal to you."

He shrugged. "I'll share my skeletons when you share yours."

She felt herself swaying toward him, just an inch, but she was actually tempted to share the secrets from her past with this huge, hot-tempered man. How was that possible? Her pulse pummeled in her ears, but it wasn't fear that made it pump so wildly. It was arousal. This strange connection she felt with Ben was dangerous. Chloe had sworn off men since her divorce for good reason, and she still didn't trust herself to make smart decisions when it came to her love life. It was safer to keep it nonexistent. Especially with someone like Ben Haddox.

The bells over the door chimed and she straightened, calling out a welcome to the family who walked in. "What do you want, Ben?"

He watched her for another moment then called over his shoulder to his niece and nephew. As Abby and Zach walked toward them, Tamara went to help the new customers. The two kids came forward like they were being led to the end of a gangplank.

"Let's go," Ben growled. "Stop stalling." Chloe jumped at the edge in his voice and Zach dropped the rubber ball he'd been holding. Abby muttered something under her breath that was definitely R rated.

When they got close enough, Ben pulled his niece and nephew to stand in front of Chloe. "Now," he said.

"I'm sorry," Zach said, looking up at Chloe with blue eyes that matched his uncle's in color but were sweet and sincere as he spoke. "I shouldn't have put the marbles in my pocket." He blinked several times, and Chloe tilted her head as she watched him. Was the boy batting his eyes at her? "I've had a hard time since my daddy went to jail," he said with an exaggerated sniff.

Chloe felt herself starting to melt before Ben yanked on the hood of Zach's cotton jacket. "Too thick, buddy." Abby snickered. "You're up," Ben said to the girl, poking her in the back.

"Sorry," the girl said through clenched teeth. "It was an accident."

Chloe leaned forward. "What was an accident?"

The teenager's mutinous gaze landed on Chloe, anger flashing in her dark eyes. "That I knocked over your stupid plastic animals. You should buy sturdier displays."

Ben groaned. "Abs, has anyone ever told you that less is more?" He reached around and placed a hand over the girl's mouth. He pulled her back against his broad chest and Chloe marveled that Abby, who had been nothing but stiff and surly, actually seemed to melt against him. Chloe recognized a girl desperately in need of attention. She knew first-hand the kind of trouble a teen could find if she went looking for it.

She wasn't sure Ben even noticed Abby's reaction. He simply held the girl like it was totally natural. All at once his hard edges melted away and he became not the badass celebrity chef trying to take away her life but a man struggling to hold his family together. It was the same vulnerability she'd seen Saturday night, and once again, it made her melt in a way she knew she'd regret later.

As if they could sense Chloe's assessment of them, Ben and Abby stepped apart. "So that part's done," Ben said quickly. "How much do I owe you?" He pulled a leather wallet from the back pocket of his jeans and started peeling hundred-dollar bills out of it. "What's it going to take?" he asked, not meeting Chloe's shocked stare. "Will five hundred do it?"

"Do what?" she asked.

"Take care of the damage and whatever else . . ." He broke off as he finally looked up at her. "What did I do now?"

Chloe crossed her arms over her chest and threw back her shoulders. Even if she'd stood on tiptoes, Ben would still tower over her, but right now her anger outpaced her normal anxiety around men. "You want to pay me off?"

He shook his head. "No," he said slowly, as if realizing he'd taken a misstep somewhere in the conversation. "I'm offering to pay for the damage to your store."

"Crappy display," Abby muttered. "Give her twenty bucks for it."

Ben nudged his niece's elbow. "Mouth. Shut."

Chloe looked between Abby and Ben and made her decision in an instant. "I don't want your money," she said, pointing at the girl. "I want her."

CHAPTER FOUR

Ben felt Abby take a small step behind him and his protective instincts kicked in, along with his temper. He shifted so he was looming over the tiny toy store owner. "What the hell?" he yelled. "I thought you weren't calling the cops?"

He heard a gasp behind him and turned to see that Abby had gone pale and twitchy, like she was about to run. He took hold of her wrist, just to be safe, and swung his gaze back to Chloe. She looked nervous at his nearness, but there was something more. It was as if . . .

"Are you holding your breath?"

She started to nod then shook her head. "I'm trying not to smell you."

He bent his head and inhaled the fabric of his shirt. "I don't—"

"You think he's bad now?" Zach asked with a laugh. "You should try sitting next to him after Papa makes tacos." The boy waved a hand in front of his nose. "It's like—"

"Enough." Ben cuffed Zach on the side of the head. "No spilling family secrets." He pointed at Chloe. "I don't smell."

Abby peeked around his shoulder. "He actually showered today," she offered.

"You smell good. It's annoying."

"Would you rather I stink?" Ben asked with a chuckle. He was used to women who were experts at flirting. Yet Chloe's backhanded compliment made his day.

She didn't meet his gaze as she eased back toward the register. "Never mind. I'm not involving the police," she explained. "I want her to work off the money she owes me for the display."

"No. Way." Abby jumped out from behind him. "He offered you more than it was worth. I'm not going to be your slave. That's so unfair."

"Do you have other plans for the summer?" Chloe asked conversationally.

"No . . . I mean, yes," Abby stammered. "I'm going to hang out with my friends and . . ." She looked around wildly before her gaze settled on Zach. "And I've got to take care of my brother."

"I can help," Zach said immediately. "I know a ton about dinosaurs and building stuff. I can be your boy expert."

Ben was floored at the sweetness of the smile Chloe gave his nephew. "I need a boy expert."

"Honey, you need a man, not a boy," Ben said under his breath, earning himself a glare.

"Ben, tell her there's no way you'll let me work here." Abby clutched at her chest, displaying the melodrama teenagers are so good at. "I'm not even sixteen. There are child labor laws."

Chloe laughed at that, a melodic sound that made Ben's breath catch. He wanted to hear more of it. Hell, he wanted to be the one to put a smile on her face.

He was no rocket scientist, but even he understood the hypocrisy of that when he was determined to close down her toy store. "It's not work," Chloe explained in her patient voice. "It's community service, and trust me, it will do you good." She glanced at Ben now and repeated the words in a soft whisper. "Trust me."

Ben, who didn't trust anyone, immediately put his faith in this petite contradiction of a woman. "Fine," he said, ignoring Abby's shriek of protest. "How many hours?"

Something brightened on Chloe's face, as if the fact that he didn't fight her on this one thing really meant something to her. "Forty hours," she said without hesitation. "Ten hours a week for a month. Zach should come with you since his actions started this whole thing."

"Awesome," Zach said, pumping his small fist in the air.

"A month?" Abby's voice was a high-pitched whine. "If I'm stuck here that long, I'll go crazy."

Ben smiled as Chloe rolled her eyes. "You'll live," she said then turned again to Ben. "I also want something from you."

His smile faded. "Me? I don't owe you anything."

"You owe me the chance to fight for my store."

He almost laughed at the absurdity of her pronouncement, but she continued. "I've watched how you operate on that show of yours," she said, stepping forward to poke him in the chest. He knew he should be irritated that she thought he was indebted to her in any way. However, the fact that she felt comfortable enough to touch him, even a silly chest poke, made him happier than he had any right to be.

"You're fair," she added quickly. "As mean as you are to people on *A Beast in Your Kitchen*, it's only to the ones who deserve it. If they turn things around in their restaurant, you help them with publicity and stuff." She nodded, and it seemed like she was trying to convince herself as much as him. The funny thing was, she was right.

Skewed as it might be, Ben had his own code of ethics. Not many people saw through the blustering and verbal barbs he piled on the chefs targeted by his temper, but in his own mind, he tried to honor what he felt was right. Not that he saw himself as a hero, far from it. But he also wasn't the maniacal monster the show's editing portrayed, which was why more often recently the "Beast" moniker given to him at the start of his career had begun to be more of a hindrance to living his life than a help to the success he'd craved for so long.

Chloe's coworker, Tamara, sauntered back to their group. "I've watched how you operate in the tabloids. You're smoother than a baby's powdered bottom."

Zach made a gagging noise.

"I think you'll give me a chance." Chloe smiled at him, not quite as sweet as the smile she'd given Zach but close enough that his heart lurched, the sensation unfamiliar enough to make him press a hand to his chest.

"Tell her she's crazy," Abby told him. "Let's go home. You've already sold me down the river by agreeing to her slave-labor bargain."

Tamara was gazing at Chloe as if her employer had more than one screw loose, but Chloe's gaze never wavered from Ben. It was as if she had faith that he'd do the right thing. He couldn't resist the challenge. "What do you want?"

He saw her chest rise and fall, and her teeth caught on her bottom lip before she answered. He could tell she hadn't planned this, and it made him all the more curious to see what she'd request.

"I owe almost five thousand dollars in back rent," she said, flinching a little when Tamara gave a low whistle.

"You mean—"

"I was going to pay the back rent," Chloe said, looking at each of them. "I meant to but . . ."

"It's ok, sweetie." Tamara placed an arm around Chloe's small shoulder. "Your heart is bigger than your bank account, and that isn't the worst thing in the world." She glared at Ben and he felt his face grow unaccountably warm as Abby and Zach both turned to stare at him.

"What?" he said, lifting his hands, palms up. "This isn't a charity."

When Tamara stepped forward, clearly ready to light him up, Chloe held out a hand. "He's right. But I want a chance to earn back my store. If I can pay you the back rent before the lease ends, will you renew?"

This was the point when Ben should shut her down. Opening his own restaurant had been his dream from the time he'd taken his first job as a teenager in the kitchen at Poppo's Italian Inn near the house where he'd grown up. He'd abandoned that dream when he'd gone to work for Maurice then worked his way up to executive chef at La Lune. The dream had seemed like a far-off plan after his contract with EatTV. Between the show's schedule and promotional appearances, he barely had time to make himself a bowl of cereal, let alone come up with ideas for a menu. But he'd never really given up. Otherwise, why would he have made the promise to Cory and bought this building? Why would he have encouraged the property manager to go easy on Chloe's inability to pay, other than because he wanted her weak and struggling before he took her down?

She didn't look weak now. With her eyes shining and her shoulders straight, she looked fierce and brave and alive. There were a lot of people who thought he was an asshole, but saying no to Chloe now would have been like kicking a kitten. Even Ben wasn't that much of a jerk.

"Back rent, interest on what you owe, and payment for the next two months."

He heard Abby gasp and Chloe made a small noise that sounded like . . . a damn kitten mewling. He opened his mouth, ready to relent, when she nodded and thrust out her hand. "You've got a deal."

"Chloe, you can't be serious." Tamara had her hands on her ample hips now, shaking her head. "There's no way—" The bells above the door interrupted the rest of her tirade.

"That's Mrs. Murphy," Chloe said, waving to the woman who'd just walked in with the hand that wasn't outstretched toward Ben. "I special-ordered a tea set for her granddaughter's birthday." She looked at Tamara. "It's on the shelf behind the register. Will you help her?"

Tamara narrowed her eyes but moved toward the front of the store.

"Your employees are protective of you," Ben observed, still ignoring her outstretched hand.

Chloe didn't bother to deny it. "We take care of each other." She poked him in the stomach with her fingers. "We still need to shake on the deal," she said but poked him again. "Are you making your muscles tight?"

He felt his mouth curve. "Want me to lift up my shirt so you can check for yourself?"

"Going to be sick here," Abby said with an exaggerated moan.

"Wanna see my stomach?" Zach asked and lifted up his shirt, thrusting forward to make a tiny pooch.

"Dude, put that away," Ben said. "We've got to work on your game."

"I like Connect Four," Zach answered. "We can play at home. Dad got me the travel set since we were going to go camping this summer."

"He wasn't going to take you camping," Abby muttered.

For the first time since he'd come to Denver, Ben saw Zach get really mad.

"Yes, he was," the boy yelled, drawing the attention of two women at the front counter. "Maybe he didn't tell you because you weren't invited. Because you aren't really his—"

"Enough," Ben snapped, dropping a hand on the boy's shoulder. He took Chloe's hand in his other one, once again noticing how soft her skin felt. "Deal," he told her, wondering exactly how much additional trouble this was going to cause him.

◆ ◆ ◆

"Ben 'The Beast' Haddox is your landlord?" Samantha Carlton, one of Chloe's two best friends in the world, asked over coffee later that week.

"I don't think he likes the nickname," Chloe said softly.

Sam ignored her. "Since when? Why didn't you tell us?"

"More importantly," added her other best friend, Kendall Clark, "why didn't you tell us the store was in trouble? We want to help if you'll let us."

Chloe sighed and broke off a piece of croissant, focusing her attention on the pastry rather than on the women watching her expectantly. She wanted to talk about the situation with people other than her employees but forgot that her friends might be more concerned with how she was affected. She'd become so used to being on her own, she felt rusty at sharing the details of her life.

Kendall and Sam were the most important people in her life, and guilt tugged at her knowing she'd hurt their feelings with her reticence. The three had met at an evening class at a neighborhood community center several years ago and formed a close, if unlikely, friendship.

Although neither woman had experienced the type of destructive relationship Chloe had with her ex-husband, until a few months ago, bad choices in men had been one of their strongest bonds. But Chloe had always felt like the pathetic stepsister when compared to Sam's beauty and dedication to the inner-city kids she helped and Kendall's drive and determination. In truth, she hadn't told them about the store because she didn't like needing help. Her role was as mother hen or caregiver, and listening to other people's problems seemed much easier than sharing her own.

The result of growing up with a parent who had issues with depression was that Chloe had learned to pretend things were always fine in her world. Judy hadn't been like the other mothers, and she'd quickly learned to hide that aspect of her childhood. She hated the shame of admitting her own problems, even though she'd initially chosen a career in social work so she could help other people deal with theirs.

"It didn't seem like a big deal," she admitted. "Stan still owned the building when I bought the business from him. He wanted the storefront filled with shops that meant something to the community. He'd owned The Toy Chest since it opened, and to him that was more important than how much money we brought in each month. He was happy the store he loved was going to remain in business when he retired.

When he died suddenly almost a year ago, his family put the building on the market."

"Did your rent go up when the new owner bought it?" Sam asked, taking a sip of her chai tea.

"Yes, but the woman at the property management company was understanding when I made irregular payments." Chloe swallowed back the embarrassment clogging her throat. "I should have known something was wrong when the café next to me went out of business so quickly. The owner was old and had been looking to retire and move to Florida since I'd met him. Nothing else opened in that space and . . ." She dropped her head into her hands. "I was naive and stupid."

Kendall reached out to pat her hand. "You're not stupid."

"But definitely naive," Sam said then yelped when Kendall swatted her arm. Chloe smiled despite the anxiety swirling in her stomach. Her friends argued back and forth for a few minutes about what it meant to be supportive, and it warmed her heart to know they were each trying in their own way. She was grateful to have both of them in her life.

Kendall was a couple of inches taller than Chloe and way more pulled together. Her shoulder-length honey-brown hair and symmetrical features made her a perfect fit for broadcast television. Chloe could barely keep her curls in check, but Kendall never seemed to have a hair out of place.

As the anchor of a popular morning program in Denver, Kendall favored conservative suits, but her style had relaxed a little since she'd started dating local landscaper Ty Bishop, who she'd met while covering a story that exposed his family's shady business practices. Falling in love had made everything about Kendall soften. Chloe knew her friend had been forced to reevaluate everything she'd worked for in life to claim a future with Ty, and Chloe couldn't be happier for her.

Sam tapped a finger on the table in front of Chloe. "I thought business was good since you took over?"

"It's getting there," Chloe said, not meeting her friend's knowing gaze. "Stan Butterfield was dedicated to the store, but he hadn't updated the merchandise or the way he did business since he'd first opened. It's taken a while for people to rediscover the shop. We're making progress, slow but steady."

"Then what's the problem?" Sam leaned forward. "Do you have a secret gambling addiction?"

"What? No, of course not."

"She knows that," Kendall said quickly then added, "but what's really going on?"

"A lot of money is tied up in payroll," Chloe admitted after a moment. "I have more employees than I need, and I pay double compared to most retail jobs, plus offer benefits when I can. Honestly, it's bleeding me dry."

"Then fire some people," Sam suggested. "Clean house."

"I can't," she said simply. "They need me. Could you cut your summer camp staff so easily?"

Sam started to respond then shook her head. "No, but I understand what you're going through. If I didn't have my savings, it would be a different future for Bryce Hollow Camp."

Despite Sam's baggy jeans and shapeless T-shirt, nothing could disguise her world-class beauty. She'd been a model for years, gracing the covers of major magazines and fashion-week runways and had several lucrative cosmetics contracts under her belt. Now she used the money she'd made to run a summer camp west of Denver for disadvantaged kids.

Kendall held up a hand. "There's more to the story. What are you not telling us?"

Kendall was a great reporter, so it shouldn't have surprised Chloe that she'd dig deeper.

It was time to share why this was so important to her. If she had any chance at saving the store, she'd need the support of everyone in her life. "I hire women who are referred to me by Denver Safehouse, the local battered women's shelter. They've left abusive relationships and are trying to create new lives for themselves but often lack the confidence and skills they need to reenter the work force." She took a deep breath and continued. "Domestic violence is more than just physical abuse. It's emotional, verbal, and often isolating. These women have been beaten down, sometimes literally but always figuratively, until they're afraid of everything, especially their own judgment."

"You give them a fresh start," Kendall said, admiration flashing in her bright hazel eyes.

"And try to bolster their confidence. A toy store is about as non-threatening as it gets as far as customers. I understand that it hurts my profits, but it helps in more important ways."

"Like your own healing," Sam whispered, her voice uncharacteristically gentle.

Chloe nodded. "I'm embarrassed at what I let happen to me, that I let Jonathan break me that way."

"But you know," Kendall offered, "that the victim of domestic violence is never to blame."

"It wasn't . . ." Chloe started to say then stopped. Her ex-husband had abused her and she needed to own that. It was easier to act like she was different from the women she tried to help. But even if he'd only hit her a few times, Jonathan had worn away her confidence to a pathetic nub. She may not have ended up in the hospital, but who knew what would have happened if she'd stayed.

"I know that in principle," she told her friends. "But reality is different. I understand what these women are going through and I can help them."

"But not if Ben Haddox won't renew your lease," Sam said, throwing up her hands when Kendall shot her another sharp look. "There's no sense in avoiding the obvious."

There was a lot of love among the three of them, but Kendall and Sam both had strong wills. Normally Chloe played the role of mediator between Sam's straightforward manner and Kendall's professional reserve. It was almost funny to see her two friends trying to manage without her in the mix.

"You're right," she said when her friends continued to glare at each other. "That's why I asked him to give me the chance to earn back the store. If I can find a way to pay the rent I owe."

"I'll give you the money," Sam offered immediately.

Chloe smiled but shook her head. "The money has to come from the store's profits. I need to prove that The Toy Chest is a viable business."

"But you want to do that without downsizing employees."

"It's a long shot." Chloe pulled off another piece of croissant. "My most profitable month was last December, so I gave everyone five-hundred-dollar bonuses. They work hard and deserve to share in the success when it happens. I don't want to disappoint anyone."

"You're the most caring person I know, but you won't be any help to them if there's no store," Sam told her, repeating the same sentiment Karen had shared. "I've been working on making camp more profitable throughout the year so it will be self-sustaining and I can focus my resources on the kids who can't afford it on their own. What you need are ideas for bringing in more customers. If you don't want to cut expenses, the alternative is increasing profits."

Kendall nodded. "I can feature the store and the kids' crafting programs you do on the show's weekly segment on hidden gems in Denver."

"I can't ask you to—"

"You're not asking," Kendall said at once. "I'm offering."

"We're in this together," Sam agreed. "You give support to everyone around you, Chloe. Now it's time to let us return the favor."

"Thank you," Chloe whispered, the ball of tension that had been weighing on her since she'd received the lease letter beginning to ease.

Kendall took her hand. "We're going to make this right for you."

"Enough with the Hallmark moment," Sam interrupted, taking a pen and notepad from her purse. "Let's make a plan. How about a sidewalk sale or an open house to draw in more customers? We'll work on getting publicity for the programs you do with my campers. Anything that helps get people through your front door."

Chloe sat up straighter, for the first time feeling hopeful that she might have a chance of making her crazy scheme work. "There's the big neighborhood festival over Fourth of July weekend. Normally I shut down the store because the crowds make some of the women nervous. But if I explain to them why we need to stay open, I'm sure they'll support it."

"What you do for those women is wonderful," Kendall began.

"But you need to start acting like you're running a business and not a charitable foundation," Sam finished. "Your heart is in the right place, but that won't mean a thing to Ben Haddox."

Chloe winced but had to admit her friend was right. She'd bought the toy store on a whim, needing something to anchor her life when her marriage fell apart. But it had become much more to her, and she refused to give it up without a fight. She had to prove to Ben, and to herself, that The Toy Chest was worth saving.

CHAPTER FIVE

Ben got out of the car in front of his dad's house Friday afternoon, tipped the driver then waved to the women gathered on the front porch of the house across the street. This section of the city had a few young professionals but consisted mostly of families that had been there for decades. The area was bordered by the Highlands neighborhood, where The Toy Chest was located, to the north and Sports Authority Field at Mile High to the south. His dad's house was a boxy brick home built in the early 1900s and hadn't changed much since Ben was a kid. It was in need of a fresh coat of paint and some major landscape upgrades, both of which he'd offered to pay for. Of course, his dad had told him where he could shove his new money. Stubborn ass.

"I never thought someone could get paid for being as mean as you are, Ben Haddox," one of the women shouted to him, her voice carrying in the still summer air.

"Nice to see you, too, Mrs. Peterson."

The other ladies on the porch snickered, but another one came to the edge of the dilapidated house's front steps. "My Angie's getting married in two weeks," she called. "We were going to order platters from

Marcelli's deli, but if you want to try out some of your newfangled recipes, I'll pay you the same per-person rate."

He held up a hand and turned to make his way toward his father's house. "I'll keep that in mind, Mrs. Donata. Appreciate the offer."

Before they could give him any more grief, Ben pushed through the front door and slammed it shut behind him. "I'm home," he called, waiting for the thunder of Zach's footsteps on the stairs.

When the house remained silent, he dropped his duffel bag and headed for the kitchen. Ben had lived alone for years, but in the last month he'd gotten used to the sound of the kids' voices, the bickering and joking and the noise that followed them everywhere.

He'd only been away twenty-four hours, one night of tossing and turning in a swanky Vegas hotel suite after he'd made his appearance at the tasting event sponsored by *bon appétit* magazine. Those events were a normal part of his life, even though he'd come to dread them almost as much as he did taping the show that had made him famous.

Last night had been no exception. The party was filled with D-list celebrities, socialites, and people with money looking to snap a selfie with someone famous. The food served was pretentious, more style than substance, which had an unsettling similarity to his life.

A woman he'd known when he'd worked in Vegas had dropped less-than-subtle hints about an invitation back to his hotel suite, at one point groping his junk under the table. A year ago he would have welcomed the bottle service at the event in the exclusive VIP section and a mindless liaison to cap off the night. For so long he'd let his circumstances define who he was, which had left him at the end of the day sitting on a big throne of hot air.

Now he just wanted to hear what he'd missed—how many diamond swords Zach had collected in his favorite video game and if Abby had eaten sugary cereal for all three meals yesterday. Hell, he wanted to cook for the kids and his dad, barter with Zach to try to get him to eat something green from the plate. He was in deep.

After working at La Lune, he'd made a point of only cooking on the clock. It was his job and he was well paid for it. Why did anyone else deserve his time and effort? Now he understood why he'd held that piece of himself back from the so-called friends in his life. It was the part that mattered most, and he only wanted to share it with people who really meant something to him.

None of whom he could find anywhere in the damn house, which was royally pissing him off.

He yelled for the kids and his father, stomped up the stairs, and barged through closed bedroom doors, but no one was around. As he came back down the steps, he heard a noise from the back patio and stalked out there. Sure enough, his father sat in the midday sun on a worn lounge chair with frayed edges. He was wearing the headphones Ben had sent him for Christmas, noise-canceling Beats plugged into the iPod balanced on his stomach. One hand loosely gripped a tumbler of iced tea, but Ben could tell by the rhythmic rise and fall of his chest that his dad was fast asleep.

In one movement, he kicked the side of the chair and snatched the headphones off his dad's head. "Wake up, old man," he growled.

"What the hell?" His father sat up sputtering, and the drink tipped onto the concrete, dark liquid spilling everywhere. "Christ, Benny, you about gave me another heart attack."

Ben tossed the headphones toward the chair. "Where are Abby and Zach?"

"I dropped them off at the toy shop this morning. First day of work for those two." Harry plopped his feet on either side of the chair. "I told Abby to call when they were ready. I haven't heard anything. Maybe they're walking home. This is a safe neighborhood. They have friends around."

"Friends who are likely getting up to the same sort of trouble as Cory and me when we were that age. Abby's fifteen and, in case you haven't noticed, she's a pretty girl. The boys around here—"

At this, Harry shot out of the chair. "If any boy so much as looks at her, I'll dust off my old boxing gloves." He made fists with his meaty hands. "Or maybe I'll go bare-knuckled. I've still got moves, you know." Harry did a few seconds of footwork that left him panting.

Ben pressed his fingers to his temples. "You didn't think to pick them up? It's possible they've been stuck at The Toy Chest all day."

"It's a toy store, not boot camp."

"Fine," Ben muttered. "I'll go get them."

Without waiting for his father's response, Ben slammed back into the house, grabbed his keys from the counter, and headed toward the Range Rover parked in the alley behind the house. Within minutes, he wedged the hulking vehicle into a spot around the corner from the toy store. He needed to get Abby a cell phone. She'd asked for one shortly after he'd arrived, but it had seemed unnecessary at the time. Now he was kicking himself. Maybe he was overreacting, but these kids were *not* going to get into trouble on his watch. He'd done a crappy job of keeping his brother on the right path and was determined to do better this time around.

The store was filled with more customers than he'd seen before, and a couple stopped him as he came through the door.

"You're 'The Beast,' right?" the woman said, whipping out her cell phone as she asked the question. "Can I get a selfie with you?"

Ben narrowed his eyes. "I'm busy," he snapped.

The woman only laughed. "You sound just like you do on TV. That's awesome." She threw an arm around his shoulder, held out the cell phone in front of her, and snapped a picture.

She was gone before Ben could even reply, which was a good thing since his response wouldn't have been appropriate for a toy store. He saw Zach's dark head peeking over an aisle on the far side of the store and made his way past several other groups of shoppers.

The older hippie woman from his first visit to the store was crouched next to his nephew, and they appeared to be in deep conversation. Ben released a breath, some of his worry easing. Maybe his father was right and he needed to release his anxiety. He had no doubt they were safe with Chloe, but it felt right to confirm it.

"Ninjas should go on the shelf above dragons," Zach said, pointing to the display of building sets.

"But the dragons are more colorful, so—"

"Doesn't matter," Zach argued. "The ninja boxes are smaller so you can fit more of them on one shelf and they'll be easier to spot up high."

"That makes sense." She nodded then noticed Ben standing behind them. She straightened and held out a hand. "We didn't actually meet when you were here before. I'm Karen Henderson."

Ben shook her hand before turning to Zach. "Where the hell have you and Abby been all day? Your grandpa was worried sick."

"Language, Mr. Haddox," Karen said with a soft tsk.

Zach actually scoffed as he stood, a mature sound coming from the skinny kid. "The Rockies are playing this afternoon and Gramps is off work. He's outside sleeping in a chair while he pretends to listen to the game." Zach glanced at Ben. "He doesn't care where we are."

Ben opened his mouth to argue, but the words that came out surprised him. "I care," he shouted.

"Inside voice," Karen added.

Ben narrowed his eyes at the woman, but she only shrugged. "What was it like in your family? Did you have to raise your voice to be heard? Sometimes there are psychological reasons why people become loud talkers."

"My grandpa is always shouting," Zach told Karen. "He's not angry all the time like Ben—"

"I'm not angry," Ben said then gritted his teeth when he realized he'd yelled the words. Both Karen and Zach gave him a pitying look. "I'm not angry," he repeated in a quieter tone. "But I will be if you don't explain why you never called Harry to pick you up."

"We're working," Zach said, as if that was the most natural thing in the world. "Chloe bought us lunch and I'm reorganizing the merchandise."

Karen nodded. "He's got a talent for it."

"And Abby?" Ben asked, curious despite himself as to what could keep his surly teenage niece occupied in a toy store all day.

"She's in back with Chloe," Karen told him, "revamping the website."

"What the . . ." He cleared his throat at the older woman's raised brow. "What does Abby know about websites?"

"A lot more than the rest of us." Karen glanced over his shoulder toward the front of the store. "Looks like a family needs assistance with the puzzles. Want to take care of them with me, Zach?"

The boy nodded eagerly. "You've got some cool 3-D puzzle balls up there. I bet we can make a quick sale." He looked up at Ben, his bright blue eyes innocent. "I've made almost a hundred dollars in sales today. We're going to help Chloe save her store."

Ben felt his mouth drop open. "From me?"

His nephew smiled. "You bet. Abby says you're going down."

"Does she now?" He glanced at Karen, who hitched her thumb toward the back of the store.

"They're in the office," she told him.

"Great. Because Abby and I need to have a little conversation about whose side she's on in this deal."

He stomped away from them, avoiding the gazes of other shoppers and ignoring the surprised yelp of the woman behind the register when he elbowed past her and through the door to Chloe's office.

He had every intention of lighting into both of them then snatching his niece away from Chloe. Ben was all for competition, but turning his family against him was playing dirty even if she didn't know what this store meant to him and his brother. In some ways he could admire Chloe for it. She didn't seem the type to have that kind of killer instinct and he had to give her props for manipulating the situation to her advantage. But if she thought—

His anger dissolved in an instant as he took in the scene before him. Abby sat in front of the computer screen at the ancient wood desk with Chloe leaning over her shoulder. As he watched, Chloe squealed with delight then wrapped his niece in a huge hug before pulling her from the chair to do some sort of bizarre dance to the soft music coming from the computer speaker.

At first Abby looked as shocked as he felt, but after a moment she hugged Chloe back just as hard then tried to teach her an intricate handshake. Chloe couldn't master it, but both of them giggled then began to spin in a circle together.

He was speechless. He'd never seen Abby so animated. The fact that this probably had something to do with the possibility of Ben losing the store wasn't lost on him, but he couldn't bring himself to care. For the first time since Ben had arrived in Denver, Abby appeared carefree. She looked her age and not like a wary worrier, always glancing over her shoulder as if she was waiting for someone to sneak up and land a sucker punch.

The happiness of his niece and nephew was the whole reason Ben had agreed to take care of the kids in the first place. To give them a shot at a normal life. How ironic that the woman who put that smile on Abby's face was the one who was frustrating him at every turn.

But right now Ben wished Chloe's soft arms were wrapped around him. He needed to be a part of the moment and the sweetness that radiated from her. Without realizing it, he took a step forward, alerting both of them to his presence. Abby's scowl returned almost immediately, and Chloe blushed such a deep pink he was surprised she didn't pass out from the blood rushing to her face. Unfortunately, the one thing both of them had in common was that neither looked happy to see him.

♦ ♦ ♦

Heat rose to Chloe's cheeks as Ben raked her with his stormy, blue-eyed gaze. But she was more worried about the other parts of her that felt like they were catching fire under his scrutiny.

Looming in her doorway, he seemed to suck most of the air from the room. Or at least all of it from her lungs. She blamed it on the dreams she continued to have about him where he was gentle and tender, so very different from real-life Ben.

Except when he glanced from her to Abby, the loneliness she'd seen before flashed in his gaze again. Then he spoke and she realized he still had no clue how to interact with his niece.

"I can't believe my brother raised you to be a traitor," he said, eyes blazing, although with obvious effort he controlled the pitch of his voice. "We're family, Abby. Why are you helping her?"

"You're not my real family," the girl spat back. "Cory didn't raise me. He hardly ever saw Zach before Mom died." She crossed her thin arms over her chest and Chloe noticed her hands were trembling.

"He's your legal guardian," Ben argued. "He loves you."

"I'm helping," Abby said with a sneer, "because you signed me up for this stupid community-service agreement. I don't care about this store. I don't care about you." Her voice caught on the last word, and Chloe wanted to throw her arms around the girl again.

But when Ben opened his big, gorgeous mouth, she stepped behind Abby and made a slicing motion across her throat. Unbelievably, the man shut up. Chloe placed a hand gently on Abby's shoulder. "You did great today, sweetie. No matter the reason, I appreciate your help. Why don't you go see how your brother is doing out front while I talk to Ben?"

The girl gave a sharp nod then hurried out to the front of the shop.

As soon as she was gone, Ben held up a hand. "You don't have to tell me how badly I screwed that up," he said on a sigh. "I'm a fucking idiot."

"No argument there," Chloe agreed. She pulled out the desk chair and dropped into it. "Come over here. I want to show you something."

Ben stepped closer then paused. "It's not your can of pepper spray, is it?"

She flashed him a smile. "Tempting, but no."

When he was behind her, she scooted a small folding chair closer and patted it. He sat as she clicked the mouse and the screen lit up. "She's set up accounts for me on all the major social media sites. Look at how she's updated the store's website." She glanced at him out of the corner of her eye. "Did you know she took a web design class at school last year?"

He shook his head, gaze locked on the screen.

"I wasn't doing much with online sales, so she's started to reengineer the functionality of the whole website—how people search, categories, the ability to review toys, my database of contacts. She's super smart about all this techie stuff, Ben."

"I had no idea," he muttered. "I sent her a laptop for Christmas because Cory said she needed one for school, but this is amazing."

"She's amazing."

He looked at her, and Chloe willed away the blush she could feel starting to creep up her neck.

"I'm glad she's working here even if it's to stick it to me," he said, a sad smile playing at the corners of his mouth. "I don't know why I went off like that. It's just . . ."

"You want the connection with her. With both of them."

"I don't know what I'm doing." He dropped his head into his hands. "I barely know Abby and Zach, and it's clear I'm not cut out to do any sort of real parenting."

"You're here." She hesitated but couldn't resist brushing her fingers over the back of his neck. Her husband had taken so much from her, and she'd thought her need for a physical connection had been wiped out for good. But despite his strength, there was an emotional frailty to Ben that made something long buried inside her spark to life once more. She massaged, gratified when a bit of tension eased under her hand. "Give yourself a break."

"I didn't get where I am in life by giving myself breaks."

"Tell me about their mother."

He looked up at her and she moved her hand away, embarrassed at how affected she was by touching him. Her breath heaved out in shallow pants, and she expected him to comment on it.

Instead he slowly took her hand, pressing their palms together as he spoke. "Chrissy and Cory hooked up a few times. She got pregnant. They were never officially together, and she already had Abby. I guess Abby's dad was a true one-night stand, so he was never in the picture. Chrissy got clean for a while after Zach was born; then for several years, she wasn't. Cory had his own problems, so like Abby said, he didn't see Zach much. But two years ago their mom fell off the wagon and left town. She dumped both kids with Cory, and they got word shortly after that she'd died. She might have had problems, but she was still their mom so it was a terrible blow to both kids. Abby and Zach are devoted to each other, and I don't think there was ever a question of splitting them up, but I know the thought of it scares Abby to death."

His honesty was startling, but at the same time, it made her want to be closer to him. His defenses were down, and for the moment, she felt safe with this burly beast of a man and the damage he was trying to undo for his niece and nephew. "That's an awful thing to have hanging over your head as a kid," Chloe murmured.

Ben nodded. "Cory talked about adopting her but hasn't done anything about it. He was in no shape to take care of them. He and my dad had been at odds for a while, so Cory wouldn't take help from him. I should have done more, but I was too wrapped up in my own life."

Chloe laced her fingers with his. His hand was warm and callused, and the connection made awareness prick all the way up her arm.

"If you don't want them here with what's going on between us, I understand."

"What's going on between us?"

She tried to laugh, choked a little instead, and tugged at his hand. "You're trying to steal my space."

Ben didn't let go. "You're months behind on rent, but that's not what you were talking about and we both know it." He dropped her hand and swiveled her desk chair so she was fully facing him. "I want to kiss you," he whispered, and his soft voice and the wicked intentions it carried made her ache for more. "But only if it's what you want, too."

She swayed closer, caught in the intensity of his eyes. After her reaction to him reaching for her in the store and that first night when she'd maced him, he must understand that she wasn't a good bet. "I don't think I know how to be with someone like you. I like things ordered, soft and gentle."

"I can be gentle."

She almost laughed at that. "Right."

"Give me a chance to show you, Chloe." He ran his hand along her arm, higher to her shoulder then to her neck. She knew he was giving her a chance to become accustomed to his touch and found herself melting because of the thoughtfulness behind the gesture. "Tell me you want this."

As his rough fingers caressed her jaw, she leaned forward with her heart beating double time and whispered, "Yes."

Chloe squeezed her eyes shut and waited for his mouth to slam into hers, but his lips were featherlight as they brushed first one eyelid then the other. His thumbs skimmed her skin and his mouth followed then finally found hers. They took turns breathing each other in, making her heart quicken. It was the sweetest thing she'd ever experienced with a man, and embarrassment washed over her as a tear tracked down her cheek.

She didn't break their connection, though. It felt too good. He felt too good. The kisses were languid, as if he had all the time in the world to enjoy her. Heat began to build low in her stomach. Parts of her she'd ignored for years yawned and stretched awake then snapped to attention. She leaned closer, wrapped her hands around the muscles of his biceps to ground herself. He was so strong yet she felt safe with him. The knowledge freed up something inside her that had lain dormant for too long. As she deepened the kiss, he moaned softly—or maybe that was her. Then he pulled away, his eyes searching her face as if looking for an explanation for the fiery attraction that linked them together.

"That was . . ." he started.

She drew in a shaky breath. "Wow."

One side of his mouth kicked up. "Right. Wow."

"And a mistake," she added, because one of them had to acknowledge it.

His eyes clouded over at her words, and she wished she'd left them unsaid.

"Chloe—"

"Don't." She held up a hand. "A kiss doesn't change anything."

"I disagree."

"I need to get back out front." She stood, surprised to find her legs a little shaky. She was pathetically out of practice at being with a man.

Ben circled her waist with his hands, his long fingers pressing into her hips. Didn't that just make her want to climb into his lap right here and now? Yep. Pathetic.

"I'm going to look at some properties tomorrow," he said. "Different restaurant spaces. Come with me."

"Why?"

He shrugged, looking up at her with his eyes full of boyish innocence. She had to remind herself there was nothing innocent about this man. "Maybe you can convince me there's a better location for my restaurant than here."

She knew he didn't believe that but couldn't let go of the opportunity. "I need to be here in the morning to open."

"Do you ever take a day off?"

"This is my life," she answered, shaking her head. "Pick me up after lunch."

"I'll pick you up and take you to lunch."

She would have argued but he seemed both hopeful and unsure. The truth was she did work too much. Her friends had told her that more than once. But other than hanging out with Kendall and Sam, Chloe didn't have a life outside the store. It had never seemed to matter before now.

When she nodded, he grinned. Releasing her slowly, as if reluctant to let go, he stood. His height allowed him to tower over her, but still she didn't step back. "You need to apologize to Abby, explain to her why you overreacted."

"Apology, yes," he told her. "Explanation, no."

"She needs both."

"Those kids need a lot of things I can't give them."

"Ben."

He shut his eyes for a moment. "Fine."

"Really?" She couldn't believe he would bend to her will that easily.

"You're very persuasive." He reached out and traced the seam of her lips with one finger. "Especially when your mouth is on me."

"I'll remember that."

She smiled when he laughed then turned for the front of the store. Chloe knew she was already in over her head with this man and those kids, but for the first time in forever she welcomed the rush of adrenaline and uncertainty that made her feel alive. Although her attraction to Ben didn't change her mind about wanting to earn back the lease to the shop, she was more than a little curious to see where the rest would lead.

CHAPTER SIX

This had been a stupid idea, Ben thought as he parked the car in front of the toy store the next day. The nerves dancing through his stomach annoyed the hell out of him. He hadn't felt nervous with a woman in years. He hadn't cared enough about any of the casual flings or hook-ups he'd had for any emotion to play into things.

He'd be smarter to turn around before this went any further. Just an innocent kiss with Chloe had knocked him for a loop. The sweetness of her skin was at total odds with the raging desire her touch had triggered in him. Hell, he'd had to wait a good five minutes before following her out of the back office after their kiss, and the looks the two women working with her had thrown him said they knew exactly why. Of course they did. He hadn't been the only one affected, and everything Chloe felt was written all over her—from the flush in her cheeks to her swollen lips to the way her body practically hummed with satisfaction. If she had that reaction from kissing, Ben could only imagine what more he could make her feel.

The funny thing was he wasn't in a hurry to get to the finish line. For so long his life had been in overdrive, from his career to his schedule to his sex life. It had all become a fast-moving blur, and he barely had time to be in one moment before he was onto the next. He wanted to savor Chloe, like he would a perfect meal, enjoying each bite with all of his senses.

Maybe it was because he knew there was a built-in end date for the two of them. The suggestion to look at other properties had been a whim, the only thing he could think of as an excuse to spend more time with her. Of course Michael had been thrilled to set up Ben with the commercial realtor. To his publicist, time was money, and Ben had been wasting both since he'd gotten to Denver.

But he had to open his restaurant in the toy store's location. He'd made a promise to Cory, and it was more important than ever that he keep it. Even if he still wasn't any closer to an original concept or ideas for a menu. So many of the best chefs had a style that defined them, their brand, and the food they cooked. Ben hadn't cooked anything but other people's recipes since the start of his career. His brand was attitude and anger, neither of which would help him come up with an original concept.

The only food on his mind now was the kind he could convince his nephew to try. Last night he'd felt like he'd won a James Beard Award when Zach had actually eaten the entire burger Ben grilled for dinner. The kid had begged all afternoon for fast food, but Ben refused. Instead he'd gotten organic ground beef from the local meat market then added shredded smoked mozzarella and cardamom into the burger.

Zach had been dubious but, with Abby's prodding, finally took a bite. To everyone's surprise, the kid loved it. Paired with homemade slaw, sweet potato fries, and a garlic aioli dipping sauce, the food he cooked for his family was the simplest he'd made in ages. Yet he took more pride in their enjoyment of his creations than in the ratings and status the show had brought him over the past two years. He just wished there was a way he could reconcile what he needed to do with the kids for his brother with supporting Chloe in her attempt to save The Toy Chest.

He opened the door to the toy store and came face-to-face with both Karen and Tamara. Although a few customers milled about, the women gave him their full attention, both staring at him narrow-eyed, hands on hips.

"I didn't do anything," he said immediately, raising his hands.

"Keep it that way," Tamara answered, pointing a fiery-red-tipped finger at him.

"Chloe hasn't been out with a man since her divorce," Karen added, flipping her thick braid over one shoulder.

"Her ex-husband . . ." Tamara began, but Karen shook her head.

"That's not our story to tell," the older woman said. "But I don't give a flip about your reputation, Ben Haddox, or this business with the store. You need to take care of her. Promise us that."

"It's only lunch," Ben argued but nodded when the two women continued to glare at him. "She's safe with me. I promise."

At that moment he heard Chloe's laughter ring out and saw her behind the register, smiling at an older man holding a toddler. An unfamiliar emotion sliced across his chest and he rubbed absently at his shirt as he watched her.

"Yeah," Tamara said, patting him on the shoulder. "He'll take care of her."

The two women turned just as Chloe's gaze crashed into his. She flashed a smile and held up one finger before disappearing into the back of the store. Ben pretended to study an arrangement of remote-controlled cars, not wanting her to think he was impatiently waiting for her. Which he was, of course.

A minute later she was next to him, clutching a purse under her arm. She'd taken off her store apron and her mouth glistened like she'd just put on some sort of gloss. For him. Not that she needed makeup. With her dark curls and creamy skin highlighting wide hazel eyes, she was perfect just as she was.

Without the apron, her curves were easy to appreciate, although her flowing skirt and pale blue button-down were demure to the point of being school-teacherish. She dressed like she was eighty, which didn't explain his body's reaction every time he was within ten feet of her.

Nothing about Ben was understated, from his expensive loafers to the flashy watch he wore. He should have taken it down a couple notches for today. Next to Chloe he felt like a pompous show-off. He'd wanted a chance to be seen as something more than his on-screen image, and this afternoon was his chance to prove it.

"What's wrong?" She smoothed a hand over her shirt. "You're scowling at me. Am I not dressed right for lunch?"

"You're perfect," he told her, forcing himself to relax.

He'd had Michael call one of the trendier downtown restaurants and request a private room for their lunch, but now that seemed like an unnecessary bit of pretension. Was he that far removed from who he used to be that he couldn't even manage a lunch date without having his publicist involved? Chloe had a store full of people who cared about her, and Ben's only friend in the world was on his payroll. Somewhere between Vegas and EatTV, Ben had lost himself to the trappings of success. His family didn't care about his money or fame, and he doubted Chloe would either.

"Are you sure everything's ok?"

The gentle pressure of Chloe's hand on his arm brought him back to the present. "Give me a second," he said and took his phone from his pocket, punching in a text to Michael. As soon as he hit send, relief washed through him. He glanced up, but his smile froze at Chloe's narrowed eyes. "Sorry. I had to change our lunch plans."

She tucked her hair behind her ears. "Because of me?"

"Yes."

She took a step away from him.

"No," he said quickly. "I have a different place I want to take you."

He put his hand on her back and steered her out into the warm afternoon sunlight.

They hadn't taken two steps when she stopped and shrugged away from his touch. "Maybe this wasn't such a good idea after all."

He shook his head. "No. It's a great idea. A brilliant idea. The best I've had in ages."

Her head tilted as she studied him, and he could still read the uncertainty in her eyes.

"I'd made a reservation," he said with a sigh and realized not many people in his life expected an explanation for his irrational behavior. They just chalked it up to celebrity quirkiness. But Chloe wanted more, and Ben found himself wanting to give it to her. "To a trendy, expensive restaurant."

"Where I wouldn't fit," she finished, pressing her lips together.

"Where I don't want to belong," he corrected. "I want to take you some place that means something to me. I need someone to understand that I'm more than flash and attitude."

She tilted her head, considering him. It was like she was deciding whether he was worth the effort of pushing past her walls and edges. Ben had never wanted to measure up so much in his life. After a moment, she gave him a shy smile. "I can try to be that someone," she said and lifted onto her tiptoes to kiss his cheek. Her scent enveloped him, soft citrus that was fresh and clean, just like her.

He tucked her arm into his and led her the half block to his car. She covered her mouth and failed to stifle a giggle. "No flash and attitude?" she choked out, pointing to the black Ferrari.

The car was the first thing he'd bought when he got the EatTV contract. He kept it in Los Angeles but rarely had the chance to drive it due to his travel schedule. He'd had it shipped to Denver right after he moved in a lame attempt to impress Zach. It had worked, of course, because a car with close to six hundred horsepower awarded universal cool points with boys of any age. Ben preferred the headroom and height of the SUV and he felt like a tool driving the expensive sports car through the streets of his dad's middle-class neighborhood.

But it was a beautiful day and the thought of Chloe on the rich leather seats, well . . .

"We can stop at the house and trade it for the SUV if it makes you uncomfortable." He hit the unlock button on the key fob and a couple of teenagers who'd been ogling the car from across the street snapped photos with their phones.

"Are you kidding?" Chloe hopped off the sidewalk. "This is amazing." She ran her hand along the hood of the car toward the front windshield. It was so much like a caress Ben's body reacted as if she were touching him instead of the carbon-fiber panel. "Can I drive it after lunch?"

Ben never let anyone, not even a valet, get behind the wheel of his baby. "Sure."

With a happy squeal, she opened the passenger door and climbed in.

Maybe he'd hold on to a little flash and attitude.

He got in and eased into traffic then gunned the engine a little and took a tight turn onto the major thoroughfare leading out of the neighborhood. Chloe threw back her head and laughed, the sound making him grin with pleasure. The Ferrari was a status symbol, and what had been important was what it represented—that he was a success and had risen above the struggles of his childhood. For the first time, driving through Denver's northwest side, the car made him happy.

Scratch that—Chloe made him happy.

He headed south down Federal Boulevard toward the neighborhood near Mile High. "How long have you been in Denver?"

She shifted in the seat. "Over three years. I visited and ended up moving here a few months later."

"Visiting from where?"

"Chicago."

"Did you move by yourself or . . . ?"

She was silent for so long he wasn't sure she was going to answer. He glanced at her fingers, which were clutching the door handle, her knuckles white.

"I'm only making conversation." He gave her what he hoped was a reassuring smile. Ben didn't have a lot of experience with reassuring. "We can talk about the weather if that's better."

"My ex-husband had business here," she said on a rush of breath, "so I came for the first time with him. One morning when he was in meetings, I had a cab drop me off near the site of the old Elitch Gardens." Ben remembered when the amusement park had been located north of the Highlands neighborhood before moving downtown. "My mom had taken a trip out here as a kid and always talked about coming back to visit. I ended up walking most of the neighborhood and stopped at The Toy Chest. Mr. Butterfield was so nice and welcoming. I felt at home, you know?"

Ben nodded, even as his jaw clenched. The Stan Butterfield he knew was the opposite of welcoming, but he wasn't going to argue the point now and risk Chloe not finishing her story.

"I fell in love with the energy of the neighborhood and lost track of time. It was almost dark when I made it back to the hotel. My husband wasn't happy, and I decided at that moment that I was leaving him."

"Because he hit you?" Ben felt his own fingers tighten around the steering wheel.

"Because I was done letting him hit me." Chloe's words were soft, but he heard the steel in her tone.

He reached for her hand. "I'm—"

"Don't say you're sorry," she said, squeezing his fingers. "I don't want pity from anyone. Shame on me for letting it happen, for staying after the first time."

"Chloe."

She shook her head. "I want to keep my past in the past, Ben. But with whatever this is . . ." One corner of her mouth curved. "You need to know going in that I'm a little . . ." She paused, looked out the window. "Broken."

He turned onto a side street just west of the stadium. The neighborhood was as shabby as he remembered, and Ben knew it like the back of his hand. He drove past houses with groups of kids playing in patchy front yards or running down the sidewalk. His car drew a few whistles and catcalls as he slowed at an intersection. He pulled to the curb and waited until she turned to him. "My dad had some problems with alcohol back in the day, and when he got a good drunk going, he and my mom got into it pretty hard. I tried to stay out of it, but my brother was a year younger and Mom's favorite. He got knocked around a few times when he got between the two of them."

Her grip tightened on his hand.

"She took off when I was thirteen," he said, lifting his gaze to hers. "There were a few rough years in there before Dad got his shit together. Cory blamed him for driving her away, and he never forgave Harry." He barked out a rough laugh. "I never forgave her for deserting us."

"She never came back or contacted you?"

He shook his head. "Cory tried to find her for a while, but it's like she never existed. Dad won't talk about it, and I just want to forget every shitty thing that happened to us. It's no accident that I left Denver as soon as I could. I hear you about leaving the past where it belongs. But you need to know that I'm more than a little broken. I'm loud and I've got a temper, so I understand if you can't deal with it. I'd never touch you in anger, Chloe. Not you or any woman."

"How do I know I can trust you?" There was a hitch in her breath as she whispered the next words, "I've just started to trust myself again." She stared at her fingers, which played with the fabric of the seatbelt, flipping the edge of the nylon back and forth.

"Chloe." He waited until she looked up at him before he said any more. When she did, the uncertainty in her eyes made him want to track down her ex-husband and see how tough the scumball was when facing a man instead of a tiny sprite of a woman. "You can trust me," he said and placed his hand on top of hers.

She started to pull away then stopped, lifting her fingers to his cheek. They were cool against his heated skin and he let himself be drawn toward her until their mouths met. He should have been comforting her but instead relaxed under the sweetness of her touch. He wanted her closer, to pull her into his lap, but he understood that he needed to take careful steps with this woman. There was also the problem of the seatbelt cutting across his chest and the console between them and then . . . "Was that your stomach?" He pulled back just enough to look into her eyes.

"I guess I'm ready for lunch," she said with a small smile, but didn't let go of him. Her eyes were shining and bright as she pushed away the hair from his forehead. She didn't look at him as she whispered, "I can deal with all of you, Ben."

His heart swelled at the words and he kissed her again before straightening. She added a complication on top of all the other complications in his life, but he didn't care. All that mattered right now was how alive he felt with her next to him, how the darkness and anger he'd lived with for so long seemed to fade away when they were together. Her stomach rumbled again. "It's a good thing you're hungry," he said, shifting the car into gear. "Because this food will blow your mind."

◆ ◆ ◆

The food wasn't the only thing blowing Chloe's mind. Although it was as good as Ben promised.

They sat on a dilapidated picnic table next to the brightly painted food truck where they'd ordered sandwiches. The sun was shining, but, thanks to a few passing clouds and a gentle breeze, the temperature was perfect for lunch outdoors. Denver had its share of trendy food trucks around the city, but the white-haired man who owned the place proudly told her he'd had the business for almost twenty years.

To Chloe's surprise, the man, Artie, had greeted Ben like a long-lost son then made both of them step up into the trailer to proudly point out the updated deep fryer and cooking surface he'd recently installed. There'd been a line of people waiting to order the melty sandwiches, but Artie had ushered them to a table and promised to bring out something special. That had ended up being one chicken and one steak sandwich, filled with meat, cheese, and onions and slathered in a homemade sauce.

She'd taken one bite and moaned with pleasure, making both Artie and Ben smile. When she'd thanked the older man for the best lunch she'd had in ages, he'd told her he couldn't have done it without Ben's help.

Ignoring Ben's suggestion that Artie get back to the customers still waiting, the man had explained to Chloe how a small grease fire a year ago had damaged the interior of the oversize vehicle, but Ben had paid for all of the equipment to be replaced, as well as Artie's insurance deductible. Ben tried to shrug it off, but Artie clearly believed Ben responsible for the fact that the food truck was still in business.

"Remember the deal," Ben said when Artie finally stopped singing his praises. "I get all the recipes after you finally retire."

The old man laughed. "I'll retire when I'm dead."

"Leave 'em to me in the will," Ben shot back.

"I'll do that, Benny." Artie clapped Ben on the shoulder and headed back to the small kitchen.

"You can't be finished already," Ben said, pointing with his sandwich at the half she'd placed on the table. "You only took a few bites."

"When was the last time you either saw Artie or ate here?"

Ben shrugged. "Not since I left for New York when I was eighteen."

"How did you know about the fire?"

"My dad keeps me updated on the neighborhood."

"Why did you pay for the repairs?" She sipped her iced tea.

"I want the dipping sauce and spice recipes," he answered but didn't look at her.

"You could figure it out if you tried." They were sitting across from each other at the table and she nudged his leg with her foot. "Why?"

"Like I told you, after my mom split, things were a mess. I felt guilty, like I hadn't given her enough of a reason to stay. I was angry and it made me stupid."

Ben finished the last bite of his sandwich and wiped his mouth with a paper napkin. "That first summer, I was hanging out with a bad group of kids, getting into trouble. We ran by here one day and knocked over Artie's big garbage can out back. He grabbed me and made me clean up the mess then put me to work. I wasn't old enough for a real job, so he'd slip me a few bills at the end of every week. The money didn't matter as much as having a place to go. I don't know what made me different from any of those other boys. He'd give me the leftover food at the end of the day." He wadded up the yellow paper the sandwich had come wrapped in. "Cory and I had grinders for dinner every night for almost three months."

"This was your start with food," she whispered.

His eyes flicked to hers. "His setup isn't fancy, but Artie always bought fresh ingredients from the local market. After a while, he let me go with him. The smells and colors of everything . . . yeah, it made an impression. Even when my mom was around, she didn't spend much time in the kitchen. I learned to cook for Cory and my dad. It was one of the few things I could do to make our house seem normal. Artie had a friend who owned an Italian restaurant about a mile from here. When I turned sixteen, he helped me land a job as a line cook."

A small smile played at the corner of his mouth. "My first real kitchen. I busted my ass there, and the owner, an old-school Italian who could have been cast on *The Sopranos*, still had a lot of friends back in New York. After I graduated from high school, he set me up with one of his buddies in the city and away I went. None of what's happened to me would have been possible if Artie hadn't taken a chance on me."

"No wonder he's so proud." She flipped her sunglasses onto the top of her head and studied him. "Ben Haddox, are you blushing?"

"Hell, no." He grabbed her chicken sandwich and took a bite.

"Hey," she protested with a laugh. "I'm not done."

Still chewing, he held it out to her. She wrapped her fingers around his and leaned forward to bite off an edge then grimaced when sauce dripped down her chin. Hard to make eating look sexy when the food was messy.

Before she picked up her napkin, Ben ran a finger over her chin then brought it to his mouth. Scratch that. Messy food was sexy as hell. Her chest tightened. Ok, not just her chest. Her nipples pulled taut under her blouse, making her squirm, and from the way Ben's gaze darkened, he knew it.

She pressed the napkin to her mouth and stood, stumbling as she slid off the bench. "What time are we meeting the realtor?" she asked.

He glanced at his watch. "Fifteen minutes in downtown. The first building is two blocks from Union Station. Plenty of time."

Grabbing her tea, she gulped it as she made her way to the rubber trash can near the side of the trailer. What she really needed to do was dump the leftover ice over her head and cool herself down. The attraction she understood. The man was too gorgeous for his own good.

Today he wore a crisp white button-down shirt rolled to his elbows and tailored trousers. She'd guess his shoes cost more than her monthly grocery budget. But it was his complexity that drew her to him. The flashes of kindness and the understanding of what he'd overcome to get where he was. Despite his reputation, he obviously cared deeply for the few people who'd been in his corner from the start.

She still didn't understand why opening a restaurant in the space occupied by The Toy Chest was so important to him. Yet she had a feeling there was a reason for it, a deeply personal reason and one that might influence how hard she worked to win their bet.

Chloe couldn't afford that. The store was all she had, and she didn't want to start over somewhere else. She had to remember that at the end of the day Ben was the enemy, although the more time she spent with him the harder that was to believe. Since her marriage to Jonathan ended, Chloe had kept herself walled off emotionally and physically from intimate relationships. Other than Kendall and Sam, no one knew the full extent of her history. Not even the women who worked for her at the store. It hadn't always been that way, but her desire to be loved and to devote herself to the happiness of the people she cared about had led to bad decisions—both with relationships and life in general.

She'd shared more with Ben today than she had with any man since her ex-husband. Although Ben warned her about his temper, she believed him when he said he wouldn't physically hurt her. But Chloe had been so focused on the emotional scars that came from abuse, she'd forgotten about good old-fashioned heartbreak. If she wasn't careful, Ben might be dangerous to her in a whole different way than her ex-husband.

She took a deep breath and shook off those ugly thoughts. She'd spent too long hiding out, and it felt good to be out with a man. With this man. The important thing was to remember that this was temporary. Either way, at the end of the month, things between them would be over. It would give her a way to dip her toes back in the water of relationships. As long as she remembered not to dive in head—or heart—first.

Ben finished off the last of her sandwich, waved to Artie, and they headed back toward the car.

When they got closer, he took her hand and pressed the keys to her palm. Anticipation revved in her for an entirely different reason as she grinned up at him. "You trust me to drive?"

He closed his eyes, took an exaggerated breath, and nodded. "Be gentle with her."

Without giving him a chance to change his mind, Chloe rushed to the driver's side. She'd heard the expression "purred to life" before and now she understood because that's exactly what the engine did when she pushed the button to start the car. She ran one hand along the dashboard as she adjusted the seat so she could better reach the gas pedal. "Hi, baby," she whispered. "You and I are going to be fast friends."

"Not too fast," Ben said as he climbed in next to her.

"You trust me," she reminded him and threw the car into reverse. It took a minute to get used to how the car handled, but once she did, adrenaline raced. She wished she were on the interstate but still had fun maneuvering such a responsive car through the city streets.

A few blocks later she stopped at a red light, glancing at Ben from the corner of her eye. "How'd I do?"

"Where did you learn to handle a car like that? Is your father a NASCAR driver?"

She smiled at the surprise and appreciation in his tone. "My dad died when I was a baby, but we'd visit my mom's family in Nebraska every summer. My uncle fixed up old muscle cars as a hobby, and he taught me to drive out on the dirt roads and county highways the summer I turned sixteen. He made sure I wouldn't drive like a girl."

"I need to thank him," Ben said, his voice rough. "Because that was hot."

She smiled at the flirtation, but a little of her excitement dimmed at the thought of her extended family. "I haven't seen him since Mom died a few years ago."

"Was she still alive when you got married?" he asked softly.

The light turned green and she hit the gas pedal harder than she meant to then slammed on the brakes when the car lurched forward. "Sorry," she whispered and took off again at a steadier pace. "We were married by the hospital chaplain a week before she died. She had pancreatic cancer and it had spread by the time they found it. She was in and out of the hospital for a few months and eventually we brought in hospice. Jonathan was her oncologist."

"It was a whirlwind courtship."

"More like heavy-duty matchmaking on my mother's part. It made her happy to think my future was secure. As much as she loved me, she never believed I could make it on my own. In turn, I didn't either. It made both of us an easy target for a man like my ex-husband. He played the part of a white knight perfectly—right down to his lab coat. I didn't notice what was under the surface until it was too late and I was left alone with him."

"Do you have brothers or sisters?"

She shook her head, easing into a turn as she headed toward downtown. "It was just the two of us. What's the address?"

Ben glanced at his phone then gave her the street and building number.

"Is this the first location you've looked at other than the toy store?"

"It is, and you're changing the subject."

"Do you want to tell me why *my* store is the space you *must* have for your restaurant?"

His shoulders stiffened. "Are you a baseball fan?" he asked, ignoring her question. "My dad loves setting people up with Rockies tickets."

She found a place to park around the corner from the building and opened the door to climb out. "I guess both of us want to keep our pasts behind us," she said over her shoulder.

He grinned at her as he came around the front of the car. "We're quite a pair." His tone was so sweet she couldn't help but return his smile.

Chloe had forgotten how much she liked being part of a pair until she'd met Ben. "Promise you'll keep an open mind," she told him as she handed him back the keys.

"My mind's open to all kinds of arrangements involving the two of us," he answered, pulling her closer for a kiss. It was still gentle and controlled, and while Chloe appreciated him taking things slowly, her body craved more.

Her flight instinct was strong, but being held by Ben felt good enough to tamp down the fear that usually rose in her chest, hot and suffocating. She wrapped her arms around his neck, nipping at his bottom lip and exploring his mouth with her tongue when he let out a surprised gasp. He recovered in an instant, threading his fingers through her hair.

They stayed like that for minutes that felt like hours, until Chloe heard a throat clear nearby.

"Um, Mr. Haddox?" The voice was deep and more than a little amused. "I'm Mark Chevers, the realtor."

Chloe tried to pull away, embarrassment washing over her. She'd just been caught in a PDA. Maybe Ben was used to that, but it was a first for her. He held her against him, strong but not forceful, and looked over his shoulder at the realtor. "Give us a minute. We'll meet you inside."

"Of course," the man said and disappeared past them.

"I can't go in there now," Chloe said, wrenching away when they were alone. She glanced both ways down the street. "Do you think anyone else saw us?"

Ben reached out to straighten her clothes. "Who cares?" he said, skimming his fingers under the loose hem of the cotton shirt.

"Stop that." She smacked his hand, earning another grin. "I'm serious."

"I'm serious, too." He pulled a few coins from his pocket and dropped them into the meter. "If you're not going in there, I'm sure as hell not either. In fact, that's a great idea. My dad took the kids to a movie so the house is probably empty." He scrubbed a hand across his jaw. "Or better yet, your house is empty. Let's head there."

She shook her head. "You have an appointment."

"He'll get the idea." Ben reached for her, his eyes a mix of passion and boyish hopefulness that made her forget about her own mortification. Maybe a PDA was worth it if she had this kind of effect on him.

Still, she sidestepped his grasp. "That's rude and not how my mother raised me."

He made a face. "One advantage to not having a decent mom. No expectations."

The truth behind his careless words made her heart ache for him. "I expect more from you," she said quietly, wondering how he'd respond.

She watched as he absorbed the comment, could almost see his brain working as he decided how to respond. Finally he nodded. "Open mind," he said and led her into the building.

CHAPTER SEVEN

Ben not only had trouble keeping his mind open, he could barely focus on anything except Chloe standing next to him. They were at the third building on the realty tour, this one just a couple of miles from the heart of the Highlands where the toy shop was located. It was a prime spot on the corner of a busy intersection near the bridge that connected the hip Lower Highlands neighborhood to downtown.

The sidewalks were bustling with shoppers moving in and out of the stores along the treelined streets. The building had a huge dining area and a state-of-the-art kitchen. According to the realtor, it had been renovated only a few years ago, when a sushi restaurant had opened in the space. Ben appreciated the wide-plank floors and neutral walls as much as he did the double-capacity refrigerator in the back. The sushi bar would have to be reconfigured, but this was the type of space that would be simple to convert.

"This one is good." Chloe glanced at him. "Even you have to admit it's good."

"The space isn't as bad as the first two," Ben said with a shrug. "But I'm not convinced it's right for what I have in mind."

"Which is?" she prompted.

He crossed his arms over his chest and stared at her but didn't offer any clarification on his plans for a restaurant. She'd prodded him for information most of the afternoon, but he'd deflected each of her questions. He knew she and Mark thought he was being purposely evasive, and Ben wasn't about to admit he had no idea what type of restaurant he wanted to open.

She huffed out a breath at his continued reticence and turned to the realtor. "Why did the previous restaurant go out of business?"

Mark Chevers leaned closer, as if imparting a state secret. "An outbreak of salmonella linked to their fish. Twice." Ben watched the realtor's gaze meet Chloe's. "Do you like sushi?" he asked with a wink.

"Mainly the rolls," she answered with her usual sweet smile. "But maybe I should think twice?"

"I know a great place in the Tech Center that serves top-quality sushi. We should check it out some time."

Ben blinked, certain his realtor hadn't just asked Chloe out on a date with Ben standing there. Especially after the guy had caught them playing tonsil hockey only a couple of hours ago. He felt Chloe stiffen next to him and placed a protective arm around her waist, gratified when she stepped closer. "I left my phone in the car," he told her. "Would you mind grabbing it for me? I want to get a picture of the kitchen area."

He understood why she looked at him curiously. He hadn't asked one question or shown any interest in any of the spaces they'd seen until now.

"Um, sure." She walked out the front door, and Ben's blood pressure shot through the roof as Mark's eyes followed her backside.

As soon as she was out of sight, he gave the realtor a hard shove, sending him back against the bar. One of the high chairs crashed onto the floor, echoing in the silence.

"What the hell, man?" Mark straightened, his bright yellow tie askew. He adjusted the tie and smoothed his hands over his expensive suit. Ben could see monogrammed cuffs peeking out from the sleeves of the tailored jacket. The guy was young and eager, and up until this point Ben had actually felt sorry for him trying so hard to make a sale that would never happen.

"You tell me," Ben shot back, keeping an eye on the front door as he shouted. "You think I'm going to let you make a play for my girl in front of me?"

Mark's jaw dropped. "I'm sorry, Beast. I—"

"Don't call me that."

"Right." The realtor nodded, his head bobbing up and down. "I didn't realize you two were together."

Ben crossed his arms over his chest.

"I mean, I saw you so I knew something . . . I've seen photos of you in the tabloids, heard stories that you don't do second dates." He flapped his hands in front of him, as if he couldn't catch a breath. Probably because he was afraid of getting his ass kicked, which Ben was mentally trying to determine if he could manage before Chloe returned. "She's cute and seems fun. I assumed things weren't serious between the two of you so . . ."

They're not, Ben thought.

"They are," he answered. "She's definitely with me." He had the urge to threaten the panicked realtor, but Ben hadn't actually been in a physical fight in years and he'd definitely never done more than exchange a few punches. The producers of the show edited episodes to make his outbursts seem more explosive than they were in real life, so Ben understood Mark's reaction to him. That didn't mean he liked it.

The other man nodded. "I'm going to turn off the lights in the kitchen. Take your time getting pictures and holler when you're ready." He sidestepped toward the edge of the bar then made a break for the hallway leading to the commercial kitchen.

Ben picked up the overturned chair and slid it back under the bar, gripping the back of it hard. It killed him that the realtor was right. Ben was almost as well known for his penchant for one-night stands as he was for his temper in the kitchen. Over the years, there'd been plenty of photos of him with various beautiful women who were little more than shallow arm candy.

The fact that he'd treated Chloe like that, practically mauling her on a public street, made his gut tighten with embarrassment. She was beautiful inside and out and deserved to be treated like it. He'd meant to do that today. By taking her to Artie's, he shared more of himself with her than he had with any other woman in his life. Then he'd screwed things up. Anyone who saw her with him would assume she was just a casual fling because that's all he did. But his feelings for Chloe were way more than casual. Reason enough to end things now, to go back to being rivals and to life as he knew it.

That life held little appeal at the moment, and, if he admitted the truth, it hadn't in a long time. The problem was he didn't know how to live any other way. He was afraid if he tried, all he'd do was fail. Even making plans for a restaurant scared the hell out of him. That was another part of the reason the toy store location was so appealing. It would take a long time to renovate the space into something that would work as a restaurant, buying him the time he needed to develop a concept and menu for the space. Sometimes it felt like all the unimaginative food he'd cooked for the show over the past couple of years had sucked the culinary creativity straight out of him. Or maybe he'd never had it to begin with. That was his biggest fear, not being able to live up to his larger-than-life reputation. What if flash and attitude really was all there was to him?

"I couldn't find the phone."

He whirled as Chloe spoke behind him. "It was in my pocket the whole time," he said with a sheepish smile. "Sorry."

"Where's Mark?" She handed him the keys and he pulled her in for a hug, resting his chin on the top of her head.

"Making sure we turned off all the lights in the building."

"It felt like he asked me out. That's weird, right?"

"It's not weird," he whispered into her hair. "It's downright stupid."

"Are you deliberately being an ass?" She pulled back and glanced up at him.

It took him a moment to understand her meaning, then he framed her face with his hands. "Any man would be lucky to be with you, Chloe. But not while I'm around."

She actually laughed at that.

"I'm serious," he said, his voice coming out a rasp. What if she wanted to go out with the realtor? What if this afternoon had only been about getting him to look at other restaurant spaces? Of course it had. Why would he think it was anything more for her?

"Come on, Ben." She dropped her hands from around his waist, but he didn't let her go. "I've heard enough about your reputation to know you don't do exclusive and we're not—"

"We are," he countered, smoothing his thumbs over her cheeks. He wanted to touch her all the time, to lose himself in the softness of her skin, in her sunshiny scent. "I want to know you better, Chloe. I want to know everything."

Her gaze shifted to his shoulder.

"We can take things slow," he said quickly. "As slow as you need, but as long as we're together, it's only you and me."

She took a step back and he let her go. This was her choice. He wouldn't pressure or force her. She had to choose, both for herself and him.

"Did you get your photos?" she asked, moving away from him to study the bar area.

"Yes," he lied, holding up his phone when she gave him a disbelieving stare. He opened the camera app and snapped a few pictures of her before she realized what he was doing.

"Enough," she said with a laugh, holding up one hand. "I need to check in at the store."

He nodded, tamping down his frustration that she'd avoided sharing more about herself once again. He understood her hesitation and
why he needed to give her time to get used to the idea of being with
him. But impatience was one of his worst traits, especially when he
wanted something as badly as he wanted Chloe.

Which was almost as much as he wanted The Toy Chest. He'd have
a better chance with her if he let that go. The stupid deal. His insistence on that location. But he couldn't shirk the promise he'd made to
Cory. He'd decided when he was just a kid that when he made it big,
he'd put that store out of business. He hadn't given it much thought
over the years, except for the times when Cory had reminded him of
that long-ago vow.

Cory had been the one to call Ben after the old man died and prod
him to buy the building. At that point, Ben had moved past their teenage plan for vengeance. He'd had his management team handle the
whole deal and had almost forgotten he owned the building until Cory
had pushed him on shutting down The Toy Chest. He'd been so upset
about his brother's conviction, he would have done anything to offer
Cory some happiness. The fact that it coincided with the renewal of
the shop's lease worked in his favor. At least that was what he'd believed
at the time.

It would have been easier if Stan Butterfield still owned it. If the
old man were alive to watch Ben ruin his beloved toy shop, there would
be no question, no hesitation. Chloe complicated things, but he had to
believe he could have her and his plan, too.

He called to the realtor then followed Chloe outside. Mark said a
quick good-bye, not even making eye contact with Chloe. Ben smiled
to himself, but made his face blank when she narrowed her eyes.

They drove in silence the few blocks to The Toy Chest. "Don't
bother parking," she told him as he rounded the corner. "I can jump
out if you pull over."

"I'll walk you to the door," he said, parking in a spot across the street.

She didn't say anything but allowed him to take her hand as they waited at the crosswalk.

"Thanks again for lunch." She waved to one of the neighboring shop owners as they crossed the street. "I know you didn't like any of the locations Mark showed us."

"They were fine," he answered noncommittally.

"Right." They were in front of the store now, and she pulled her hand away. "But I'm not giving up. Either on our deal or convincing you that this isn't the right place for your restaurant."

"Then come for dinner tonight," he suggested, the words spilling out before he had a chance to think about them.

By the look she gave him, it was obvious the invitation came as a surprise. It certainly shocked him. His reputation, annoying as it was, was accurate and . . .

"We spent most of the day together," she said, "So . . ."

He started to run a hand through his hair then realized he was sweating. He felt as nervous as a teenager asking his first girl to a dance. Christ, he hadn't been this nervous *as* a teenager. "No problem if you don't want to. The kids and my dad will be there, so it's nothing fancy. Half the time, Zach moans and groans about whatever I put on the table anyway. More than half. All the time." Now he was having a bad case of verbal diarrhea? Even better. "I shouldn't have—"

"What time?" she asked, reaching out to touch his arm with one finger. The contact was delicate, barely there, but he felt it shoot all the way through his body.

He swallowed. "Six?"

"Text me the address," she said with a smile. "I'm excited to have the great Ben Haddox cook for me."

No pressure there. Still, he couldn't help his smile. "I'll see you later." He leaned forward quickly and kissed her cheek, and not just because he could see Tamara and Karen staring out the front window of the toy store. Screw his reputation. Chloe deserved more, and he was going to give it to her.

She seemed as stunned by his restraint as she had been by the invitation. He opened the door to the store for her and after a moment she walked through. "Thank you for a lovely lunch," she whispered.

He was slightly mollified to realize she was as reluctant to leave him as he was to have her go. "Good-bye, Chloe."

As the door closed behind her, he turned and sprinted across the street to his car. He only had a couple of hours until she'd arrive for dinner, and his stomach was as jumpy as it had been when the food critic for the *New York Times* had come to Vegas to review his menu.

Ben had the suspicion that tonight there was even more on the line.

♦ ♦ ♦

Chloe adjusted the collar of her blouse as she walked toward the front porch of Ben's house a few minutes after six. The Toy Chest closed at five on the weekend, and by the time she'd shut everything down and locked up, it hadn't left her much time to get ready, especially since she'd decided to make the short ride over on her bicycle.

When she'd left her duplex, the bedroom looked like a hurricane had gone through it twice in one day. Between the outfit changes she'd done earlier and finding the right thing to wear for tonight, she'd tried on almost every article of clothing she owned. Silly of her.

As Ben had said, this was simply a casual family dinner. That hadn't stopped her from changing multiple times before settling on a black silk shirt and a pair of dark jeans. She fingered the delicate silver chain around her neck and tugged at the shirt again. The choice had probably been a mistake. Chloe might be short, but she was curvy and now worried that the deep V-neck was too revealing. She was meeting Ben's father, after all.

Zach came through the chain-link fence on one side of the plain brick house as she put down the kickstand of her bike at the base of the porch steps. "Hey, Chloe, come on around back," he called then disappeared again.

"She's a guest, Zach," a scratchy voice bellowed. "It's rude not to greet a guest at the damn front door."

Chloe hid her smile at the man who stared at her through the screen door. He was built like Ben, although a couple inches shorter with a round stomach covered by a Colorado Rockies T-shirt.

"You must be Ben's dad," she said as she moved forward.

He pushed open the screen. "Harry Haddox," he answered, holding out a beefy, suntanned hand.

"I'm Chloe Daniels." His handshake was surprisingly gentle.

"I know. Ben told me you don't like yelling so I should keep my voice down." He gave her a sheepish grin that reminded her of his son. "But the truth is I like to be heard. No offense."

"None taken," she answered, both touched and embarrassed that Ben had made the request on her behalf. "I brought this for you." She handed him the small bag with the bright purple bow tied around the handles.

"You didn't have to do that." Two spots of color reddened his cheeks, and he studied the bag as if the bag were the gift.

"There's something inside," she said gently.

"Right." He untied the bow and reached inside, pulling out a scuffed, signed baseball.

"Ben told me you're a big Rockies fan. The man who owned the toy store before me was a memorabilia collector. He took most of it with him when he retired, but I found this in a box in the storage room a few months ago. Mr. Butterfield's relatives weren't interested in anything he left behind, and I don't know much about the game so . . ." She said the words quickly, and it crossed her mind that bringing a used baseball as a gift might not have been the best idea.

Harry held it in his hand, turning the ball around and around as he studied it. "This is from the 1995 season."

She cringed. "I know. It's old. Is that bad?"

He laughed. "It was the first season they played at Coors Field after it was built. You say this belonged to Butterfield?"

She nodded then glanced over his shoulder as Ben walked into the entry. "Zach said you were here. You look amazing."

Chloe felt warmth seep through her.

Ben's gaze flicked from her to Harry. "Everything ok out here?"

"It's damn near perfect," Harry yelled, pumping his fist in the air.

Chloe jumped back a step.

"Christ," Ben muttered, reaching out a hand to steady her.

"I'm fine."

"Sorry, sweetheart." Harry threw his arms around her and planted a wet kiss on her cheek.

"Dad, what the hell?"

"Do you know what this ball is?" Harry asked, holding it up in front of Ben's face. "It's part of Stan's prized collection. He guarded those damn balls like . . . well, you know, Benny."

"There's more stuff in the box," Chloe offered then noticed that Ben had gone rigid. "If you want to come take a look."

"No," Ben growled at the same time Harry shouted, "Hell, yes."

"Butterfield would roll over in his grave," Harry said with a wink, "to know part of his prized collection now belonged to a Haddox. You've made my night, Chloe."

"Dad, don't be an ass."

"As if Stan wasn't," Harry shot back.

Ben shook his head. "Not to Chloe."

The two men squared off, neither giving an inch as they glared at each other.

"There's something I'm missing," Chloe whispered into the tense silence. If Harry had known Stan Butterfield, Ben probably did, too.

Whatever the reason he wanted the toy store location, this confirmed her suspicion that it was personal.

Harry lifted his hands then turned his attention to her. "I've already said more than Ben would want me to, but thank you for the gift." He flashed a wide grin. "I'm going to show it to Zach. That boy doesn't appreciate America's pastime half as much as he should. Despite my best efforts, neither of my sons is a baseball fan."

He trotted off down the hall, leaving Chloe and Ben alone in the front entrance. She couldn't see much of the house from where she stood—a staircase leading up to the second floor and a darkened living room to one side of the hall. While many of the houses around the neighborhood had been updated in the past few years, the ones on this block remained a bit shabby around the edges. She guessed there were hardwood floors original to the house under the well-worn beige carpet, and the architectural details of the house would come into focus if the wall color was freshened, but in a way she liked stepping back in time.

It reminded Chloe of her mother and the lace doilies and old-fashioned tchotchkes that had decorated their small apartment when she was a girl. The overflowing coatrack and stacks of newspapers on the floor under it gave the house a homey feel that appealed to her, yet it was hard to imagine Ben being happy here. Based on his choice in vehicle, clothing, and watches, he liked things modern and expensive. This house was neither, and she guessed the childhood memories of the home did little to welcome him back.

"Did I mess up with the baseball?" she asked, making her voice light.

Ben had tipped his head up, staring at the ceiling, and she could almost see him silently reining in his reaction to his father's comment. "You made his whole fucking night," he said after a moment. The words were soft, but she flinched at the anger in them.

"But ruined yours?"

"I loved playing ball with my dad in the backyard, but Harry's relationship with baseball is complicated." He ran a hand over his face, as if he could wipe away any emotions the memories brought to the surface. "He started working at Mile High as soon as the Rockies came to town then moved to Coors Field when it opened. There was almost always a pit stop on the way home—for a drink or twelve after his shift. The area wasn't as gentrified as it is now, but Mom would send me down to retrieve him. Those streets in LoDo scared the crap out of me when I was a kid."

"You'd walk a couple miles downtown when you were a boy?"

He nodded. "Eight or nine."

"Oh, Ben." The thought of a boy younger than Zach being sent out on his own late at night and saddled with that kind of responsibility made her heart ache. She reached for him, threaded her arms around his waist, and pulled him close. She pressed her cheek against his chest, felt his heart beating like crazy under the dark green T-shirt he wore. He let her hold him but didn't hug her back. He was like warm concrete against her. "I'm sorry," she whispered. "I didn't know."

"Of course not," he said in a hoarse voice. "It was a nice thing to do, and he loves it."

She waited a moment then said, "It's not just because he likes baseball. It has something to do with it being Stan Butterfield's baseball." He shifted, but she didn't let go. "Are you going to tell me why?"

"No."

She lifted the hem of his T-shirt, smoothed her hands up his back.

"Are you trying to make me change my mind?" he said with a rough laugh.

"I want to make you feel better."

He took a shuddering breath and scooped her up, burying his face in the crook of her neck. "God, you smell so good."

"I doubt that." She wiggled as his nose tickled the sensitive skin below her ear. "I rode my bike over here and it didn't cool down as much as I expected tonight. I probably smell like sweat."

"You smell sweet," he whispered then ran his tongue along the column of her throat. "And you taste better."

She could so easily lose herself in this man, in the moment. When he touched her it was easy to forget the bet, her past and his, and the fact that there were so many things she didn't know about him. All that mattered was how he made her feel. Alive and desired in a way she hadn't been before. "Speaking of taste, you invited me for dinner."

He chuckled, the vibration skimming along her heated skin. "You with the appetite."

She blushed, thinking that food wasn't what she was craving at all. But his family was waiting, so Chloe forced herself to step away. "I'm sorry I made this evening tough on you."

He leaned forward and dropped a tender kiss on her mouth. "You also made it better."

She smiled. "Then mission accomplished. Now it's your turn. I'm ready to be impressed."

At that he swallowed, looking almost nervous. "Like I said, it's a casual dinner and the options are limited with Zach."

"I'm joking, Ben." She followed him down the hall. "Mostly I heat up soup or spaghetti for myself. Whatever you serve is better than anything I could make." As they came into the kitchen, she saw Abby bent over a laptop at the Formica table, her back toward them. She wore colorful headphones and so didn't turn at their entrance.

"Working on your website and social media presence," Ben explained, pointing to his niece. "It's become her mission to make sure this is the most profitable month in the history of the shop."

"I'm sorry," she said automatically.

"You shouldn't be," he answered with a wry smile. "I like a good figh—" He paused, took a breath. "Competition."

It was easy to return his grin. "Then let the best woman win."

At that he laughed so loudly that Abby spun around in her chair. Her eyes softened when she saw Chloe. "Hey, I've linked the website to your social media accounts and posted the new specials you told me about on all the Denver parenting websites I could find."

"You two plot my demise," Ben said with a wink. "I'm going to check on the food."

Chloe stepped closer to the table. "What you're doing for the store is amazing, Abby, but I don't want it to take up all of your time."

The girl shrugged, pulling the headphones from around her neck and setting them on the table. "I don't mind. It's summer so I've got plenty."

"Less if you'd actually do any of the chores I give you." They both turned to see Ben pointing to the trash can.

"Cory never made me do work around the house."

"He should have," Ben countered.

Chloe held up a hand before the two of them could really start in on each other. "Chores first," she told Abby. "But take some time for your friends, too."

Abby closed the computer. "I don't see many people over the summer."

"Aren't there kids around the neighborhood?"

"I don't know any of them. My school's on the other side of town."

"You don't attend East?" Chloe asked, referring to the neighborhood high school.

The girl shook her head. "I go to Summit Hills Day School. Zach and I both do." She pointed at Ben. "He pays for it."

Chloe recognized the name of the most exclusive high school in the city. A few of her wealthier customers sent their kids there. It was nestled in the exclusive enclave of Cherry Hills in south Denver. She didn't know what tuition ran per year, but it gave her another insight into just how rich Ben must be to pay for both Abby and Zach's education.

Ben kept his attention trained on whatever he was stirring in the bowl on the sink. "It's not the biggest hardship you've ever faced. Where do you think all that techie training came from?"

"I hate wearing a uniform every day." Abby picked at the tattered edge of her denim shorts. "And the girls there are bitches."

"Language," Chloe said.

"I told you," Ben yelled, now chopping a ripe tomato, "that once we figure out where we're going to live for good, you can look at the district high school."

"Volume," Chloe called to him, exchanging an eye roll with Abby. She was quickly realizing that Ben didn't even notice when his voice rose. "You won't stay in the Highlands neighborhood?"

He shrugged one big shoulder. "I haven't thought that far ahead, but I'm not going to be in this crap shack indefinitely."

"This is the nicest house we've ever lived in," Abby said with a sniff. She picked up her laptop and tucked it under one arm. "Maybe you should leave all us crap behind. It's what you want, anyway."

"That isn't true and it's not what I said." Ben turned and stalked forward, still gripping the knife.

"Don't point a knife at me," Abby shouted.

Ben dropped it to the counter immediately. "Abby—"

"Zach and I don't need you." She wiped at her cheeks with the back of a hand. "I can take care of him. It's what I've always done. *I'm* the one he needs."

Ben threw a helpless glance at Chloe.

She put a gentle arm on the girl's shoulder. To her surprise, Abby leaned into the embrace instead of pulling away. "Your uncle knows how important you and Zach are to each other."

"He's not my uncle," Abby mumbled with a sniff. "I'm not even a real part of this family."

That's what this outburst was about. Chloe gave Ben a pointed look, hoping he'd understand what she was trying to tell him.

He gripped the edge of the counter, and from the set of his jaw Chloe knew this was the last conversation he wanted to have. "Of course you're a real fucking part of this family," he yelled.

"Language *and* volume," Chloe ground out but saw one side of Abby's mouth curve.

Ben returned the girl's small smile, and Chloe realized that in his own way he'd managed to lighten the mood and the tension. His voice was softer as he continued. "You're as much my niece as Zach is my nephew, Abby. Not because you take care of him or he needs you. You just are. I'm no prize and neither is Harry, but you're stuck with us for the long haul." He was standing in front of them now and tipped up Abby's chin. "Are we square on that?"

She nodded. "Summit isn't that bad, I guess. They have a sushi bar on Fridays."

"Seriously?" Ben asked. "In a school cafeteria? What happened to tater tots and mystery meat?"

Abby made a face. "Disgusting." She glanced around his shoulder. "Do you need any help with dinner?" she asked, almost shyly.

Ben's mouth dropped open before he snapped it shut. "Sure. It's almost ready, but you can whisk the vinaigrette for the salad."

"I'll see what Harry and Zach are up to out back," Chloe said quickly, feeling another wave of affection for this big, bumbling brute of a man who was trying so hard to make his family whole again.

"About fifteen minutes until dinner is served," Ben said, offering her a grateful smile that warmed her heart even more.

She headed for the back door off the kitchen as Abby placed her laptop on the counter and moved next to Ben. Watching him with the girl made it even harder for Chloe to remember why he wasn't the right man for her.

CHAPTER EIGHT

"Did you always want to own a toy store?" Harry asked around a mouthful of food.

"Gross," Abby muttered. "Don't talk with your mouth full."

"Then how am I supposed to carry on a conversation?" Harry shot back and opened his mouth wide to display the half-chewed food inside.

Abby groaned while Zach dissolved into a fit of giggles.

Ben shook his head and Chloe couldn't help but laugh. His family was loud, boisterous, and often brash. She loved being a part of all the commotion, although normally it would make her nervous. For so long her life had been quiet and contained, especially after her divorce, when keeping control of her world had been the most important thing on her priority list. Now she realized how much it had cost her to keep up all of her walls for so long. She was ready to let some of them down.

"Not until I walked into The Toy Chest," she told Harry. "I had no background in retail."

"Definitely none in e-commerce or marketing," Abby added.

Ben shot his niece a glare that she gleefully returned.

"Don't you two start at each other again because of me." Chloe took a sip of her beer. "Abby's right." She kept her gaze on Harry. It was easier to concentrate her attention on him than think of how much she was revealing to Ben with this conversation. "I was a social worker in Chicago."

"Like you took kids out of their homes?" Zach asked, his face going pale. "A social worker came to see us after Dad got arrested. She had really red hair."

Chloe made her smile gentle. "No, I worked in a small private practice. That means I met with families who needed a little extra help in life."

Zach stabbed at a sweet potato fry. He'd almost cleared his plate, and Chloe had noticed Ben watching with obvious pride several times during the meal as the boy took bites. "Maybe we should get a social worker."

Ben and Abby spoke at once. "We don't need help."

Zach rolled his eyes.

"Besides," Harry added, "we've got Chloe now."

That comment gave her a start. She'd walked away from her career after getting married, partly because of the shame of allowing herself to be bullied and manipulated by her husband.

How was she supposed to help anyone else when she was stuck in such a dysfunctional relationship herself? Yes, she informally counseled the women who worked for her, but that almost felt like penance for failing so miserably at her own life. She'd loved her career in social work but had made that a part of her past when she came to Denver.

"I think the four of you don't give yourselves enough credit," she announced to the table.

"At least we all agree that Ben is the one with the most problems," Harry told her.

"Excuse me?" Ben dropped his fork to the table while Abby snickered. "*I'm* the one with problems?"

"His cooking is getting better, anyway." Zach dipped another fry into the aioli sauce.

Chloe laughed at the look of pure disbelief that crossed Ben's face. "Your uncle is famous for his cooking," she told Zach. "I'm sure everything he makes is fantastic."

Zach shook his head. "No way. He tried to get us to eat fish balls with soggy lettuce."

"It had the texture of cooked snot." Abby shuddered. "It was like we were eating somebody's leftover boogers."

"It was seared scallops and wilted kale," Ben roared as Harry and Zach nodded their agreement with Abby's assessment. "That dish is one of La Lune's signature menu items. It's been recommended in every food critic's review of the restaurant."

"It still sucked," Zach said.

"Language," Ben, Harry, and Abby said at once.

"You three say way worse words than suck." Zach looked at Chloe. "They say bad words all the time. We need help."

She tried not to smile at the boy's angelic face and mischievous eyes. "I'll keep that in mind."

"But not with the food if you keep cooking like this." Abby speared a piece of chicken. "It actually beats Pop-Tarts."

Harry nodded. "For the first time, I see why people think you're such a big deal in the kitchen, Benny. This is the best chicken potpie I've ever had. Way better than that complicated crap with the ingredients I can't name that you usually try to feed us."

"I can't believe it." Ben ran his fingers through his hair. "I'm glad everyone is willing to actually eat something that doesn't come from a box and have a two-year shelf life, but anyone can make a potpie."

"Not like this," Chloe added. It was true. In addition to the tender chunks of chicken, the dish had caramelized onions and fresh spinach encased in a flaky crust with just a hint of nuts.

"You too?" Ben asked, a vein throbbing on the side of his forehead. "I've worked for years in some of the most prestigious kitchens in the world." He was yelling again, but it didn't bother Chloe at the moment.

It was all volume, no heat. She knew he was glad to have made his family happy with this meal, even if he didn't understand why. It was almost like shouting was easier for him than dealing with the real emotion of how it made him feel to bring his family together around the table. "This is food someone's mother could cook."

Harry barked out a laugh at that. "This is not your mama's cooking, Ben, and you know it."

"Not ours either," Abby added.

Ben looked at Chloe. "Or mine," she confirmed. "I loved my mom very much, but she was more the macaroni-and-cheese-type chef."

"Did you have the kind from the blue box?" Zach asked her. "That's my favorite." He glanced at Ben. "Could you make mac 'n' cheese better than that?"

"Yes. I. Could."

"Awesome." Zach nodded, as if making a decision in his mind. "I guess I could try more of what you cook if it's good like this. Can I be excused?"

Ben gave a curt nod. "Take your plate to the sink."

The boy did, and Abby stood as well. She looked at Ben and, for the first time, Chloe didn't see an ounce of teenage snark in her eyes. "One time Zach ate nothing but bagels and peanut butter for a month. Breakfast, lunch, and dinner for four weeks. Mom didn't even notice, but I figured he was going to get some kind of weird bad nutrition disease. It was all I could do to get him to take the chewy vitamins every day."

"You shouldn't have to worry about what he eats," Ben said through clenched teeth. "It's not your responsibility."

Abby rolled her big eyes. "My point is it's a big deal he's willing to eat real food, Ben. I know you want us to like all your fancy stuff, but this is way better." She didn't wait for an answer but picked up her plate and glass, placed them in the sink, then followed Zach out of the kitchen.

"That girl is wise beyond her years," Harry said, rocking back in his chair. "She gets it from me."

"She's not related to you," Ben answered.

"She's still right." His father stood. "I'm going to catch the last couple innings of the game. I'm happy to clean up the kitchen if you leave everything."

This seemed to shock Ben more than anything else. "You never offer to help."

"You cook, I clean," Harry said, as if it were the most natural setup in the world. "We're a team here, Benny. I've grown up enough to do my part. I would have done more for Cory if he'd let me, you know?"

"I know, Dad," Ben said softly.

Chloe watched the two men, knowing she could add nothing to whatever this moment was between them. After a few long beats, Harry nodded, as if their silent conversation was officially over. He took his plate to the counter then headed for the door that led to the backyard.

"I bet this dinner makes you grateful the DVR is still waiting at your house," Ben said, standing abruptly from the table but not meeting her gaze. "We've got so many issues, there isn't a topic of conversation we can't turn toxic."

He stalked to the sink and flipped on the water, porcelain clattering as he loaded the dishwasher like the appliance had wronged him in some way. It felt like a dismissal, and Chloe wasn't sure what she was supposed to do next. That had always been part of her problem, letting life happen to her. In her own way, she was as uncomfortable as Ben with deep emotions.

While he responded with his temper, her fallback was just to slink away, retreat deeper into her private shell. Her mother had taught her that, to hide away instead of facing trouble. Judy Daniels' life had been ruled by fear, mostly the worry of a single mother. She didn't want to risk losing her job or the apartment they could afford, so she'd been a doormat to the people in her life and had inadvertently taught Chloe to do the same thing.

It was tempting to slip out of the house now and pedal back to her quiet home. But she didn't want to just yet. It wasn't about this family needing her, although Zach was right that they could use some help coping with what the kids had been through. She stood slowly and cleared the rest of the table, stacking everything on the edge of the counter. By this time, Ben had given the plates and glasses a reprieve. He stood gripping the edge of the stainless steel sink, steam rising around him from the water still pouring from the faucet.

Her desire to touch him outweighed her fear of reaching for someone so obviously filled with anger and frustration. She placed her fingers on his T-shirt, the lightest weight on his back. She prepared herself for whatever response it would elicit, him whirling or jerking away or shouting at her to leave him alone.

The muscles twitched under her hand, but otherwise he remained a living statue. She drew closer until the front of her was pressed to the back of him. She reached forward with one hand and shut off the faucet then wrapped both her arms around his waist and rested her cheek against his spine.

After a minute of standing silent together, she felt his head slump forward. "I'm fucking lost here," he whispered, but instead of anger, his tone was filled with misery. "Nothing that I've worked for, all the things that make me a success, mean a damn to them. Where does that leave me?"

She lifted his arm and slipped under it, easy enough with his height advantage, but she knew she was only able to move him because he let her. With her back to the sink, she looked up at him. His eyes were dark, intense and distressed in a way that spoke to her hidden fears. "It leaves you here, in this kitchen, this house, and this town. It leaves you trying, Ben, which counts for more than you could imagine with both of those kids. Even if none of you realize it yet."

He blew out a breath, lifted his hand, and wound one of her curls around his fingers. "What if I can't make it right?"

"You don't have to make it right," she told him and he quirked a brow.

"Is that your experience as a social worker or a toy-store owner talking?"

"Both," she acknowledged. "You heard Abby. Zach is eating real food, probably for the first time in his life."

"I bought a pineapple at the grocery last week. He'd never seen one that wasn't already chopped before."

"You'd be shocked at how little fresh food kids have access to, especially ones with backgrounds like Abby and Zach."

"I shouldn't be shocked. It's how I grew up." He squeezed shut his eyes. "It shouldn't have been that way for them. If I'd intervened before things got this bad . . ."

"You came when they needed you. That's important. *You're* important to them."

"Thank you," he said softly. "Sometimes I feel like I'm climbing a mountain and the summit keeps getting farther away."

"Baby steps," she whispered. "That's what all of you need."

But what Chloe found to be a bigger revelation was that *she* needed them. Somehow the healing of this family was tied to her own, as was the future of the toy store and the women who worked there.

"I'm going to trust your professional judgment, Ms. Toy-Store Owner slash Social Worker. Sometime you're going to tell me the details of who you were before Denver, right?"

Someone I don't ever want to be again, she thought to herself. "I'll tell you about me when you figure out who you're going to become now that you're in Denver."

"Apparently I'm going to be someone who cooks family dinners." His mouth kicked up a notch. "That's a first, but I like it. It's a challenge to figure out recipes with ingredients that bore the hell out of me but that Zach will eat. The people who worked for me in Vegas and on the show would have a field day with that." He threw a look over his shoulder. "They wouldn't believe any of this. I swear this kitchen hasn't been updated since the seventies. If you knew what I was used to . . ."

"That doesn't matter to Zach and Abby," Chloe reminded him. "Kids have different standards than food snobs. I can't speak to your gourmet snot recipe, but tonight's dinner was some of the best food I've ever had."

"Do you know how long and hard I worked for my success?" He huffed out a laugh as he spoke the words.

She leaned over his arm and scooped her finger in the sauce left over from the chicken. "I know it was worth it if you learned how to make something this delicious." She licked her finger without thinking about it then stilled at the look of raw desire he gave her.

"You made a noise."

"What noise?"

He flashed a sexy grin. "A food noise. When you took a bite. You did the same thing at dinner. Little moans and sighs. Because it was *that* good."

Embarrassment flooded her, and she tried to step away, but his hands clamped down on the counter on either side of her.

"Did not," she mumbled. "I think your ego is making you hear things. Dinner was amazing, but I didn't make noises."

His smile widened. "Did so. Like this," he said and pressed his lips to her ear, sucking the lobe into his mouth.

She kept her mouth shut, but even with her teeth clamped together a sound erupted in her throat that wanted to be a moan.

"I bet you make sex noises, too," he whispered against her skin.

She jerked back, arching over the edge of the counter, and glared at him. "Rude of you to comment on my noises—food or bedroom or whatever." She pushed at his chest, but now he didn't budge.

"Bedroom or shower or pressed up against the wall." The deep timbre of his voice did wicked, hot, melty things to her insides. "They're sex noises because I want you way more places than just on a bed, Chloe."

She bit down on her lip as tremors rippled through her at those words. Ben's gaze flared in response. "We're talking about food," she said, trying to keep her mind on anything but how much she wanted to attach herself to this man like a barnacle.

"Food and sex." He inched his hands closer to her sides, his thumbs hooking into the waistband of her jeans. "My two favorite subjects."

She tipped up her face as his mouth lowered. But just as his lips grazed hers, a loud curse and crash came from the backyard. Chloe jumped, the top of her head banging against Ben's chin.

"Sorry," she mumbled, feeling like an idiot. First she shot him with mace and now tried to break his jaw. No wonder her only standing date was with her television. She couldn't be normal with a man even when she tried.

Ben stepped away, rubbing his chin. "Rockies must have lost."

She started to turn away, but he caught her again, crouching so that they were at eye level. "A bump on the chin doesn't make me want you less." He gave a strangled laugh. "Hell, I wish something could make me want you less. I feel like I could die from it."

"Really?" She felt a smile tug the edge of her lips.

"You have no idea."

"Maybe you should walk me home tonight," she suggested before she could think better of it. "If you want to . . ."

He tugged her away from the counter. "Let's leave now."

She laughed, digging in her heels. "Your dad will wonder where we went."

"He'll guess."

"That's worse."

"Nothing's worse," he said, wrapping his arms around her, "than how much I need you and not being able to have you." He lifted her, and his kiss was no longer gentle. It was hot, demanding, and promised so much more than Chloe had imagined.

"Delayed gratification," she said as she broke the kiss. "Right now, we're cleaning the kitchen."

He looked at her like she was crazy, and maybe she was. But this feeling, the anticipation of what was to come, was new for her. It was meant to be savored like the first bite of a delicious meal. She wanted to go slow so she could notice every nuance of it. This might be the only time she'd experience a man like Ben Haddox, and she wasn't going to waste any part of the moment.

◆ ◆ ◆

Darkness had fallen by the time Ben and Chloe headed toward her house. True to his word, Harry had come into the kitchen after the baseball game to help clean. Both Abby and Zach wandered in and, to everyone's surprise, Abby had suggested they play a game of baseball in the backyard. One of the few purely happy memories Ben had from childhood was the hours his dad spent pitching a baseball to Cory and him.

Apparently his brother had done the same thing because both Abby and Zach had great form. Chloe tried to refuse, but Harry demanded she be on his team with Zach. When she finally connected bat with ball and rounded the bases, her excitement had been contagious. As awkward as so many moments with his family had been, a summer evening playing ball felt weirdly normal and right.

"You missed that ball on purpose," Chloe said, giving his fingers a squeeze.

They held hands as they strolled along the sidewalk. He balanced her bike with his other hand and listened to the click of the wheels as he walked it.

"You earned the home run, Chloe. I'm a competitor. Why would I let you win?"

"Because you're a nicer guy than you want anyone to realize," she answered simply.

He laughed. "You might be the only person in America who thinks I'm a nice guy."

"Then maybe I'm the only one who really knows you."

The thought wasn't as scary as he would have expected. "I'm still the loud-mouth jerk who's going to shut down your store. Don't forget that."

As soon as the words were out, he waited for her to pull away. He wasn't sure why he'd reminded her, except that if this night was going to lead where he wanted it to, he needed Chloe to have her eyes wide open as to the man he was.

For so long, people had only seen the parts of him they wanted to, whether his temper or the trappings of his success. Women were interested in the Beast persona, especially in the bedroom, but Ben had long ago tired of angry sex and jockeying for power between the sheets.

If this was going to happen, Chloe had to choose all of him. At least that was what his head understood. His body was telling him to shut the fuck up and be grateful for this chance with her. He hadn't wanted anyone this much in a long time.

"I haven't forgotten," she whispered but kept her fingers laced with his. "My house is at the end of this block."

This time of night was quiet, the muted sounds of the nearby busy streets only adding to the intimacy. Although she only lived a mile from his dad's place, most of the houses here looked as though they'd been updated and remodeled. It was a nicer section of the neighborhood, with only an occasional car driving by. The temperature had cooled a few degrees, which was one of the few things he'd missed about Colorado. Summer in Vegas was scorching morning, noon, and night. The hiss of sprinklers filled the quiet, rhythmic and soothing as they sprayed mist over the lawns they passed.

"Here we are." She pointed to a redbrick duplex. It was one story, each side the mirror image of the other. "I'm on the left." Her porch was tiny, but planters of brightly colored flowers sat on the steps, and there were two whimsical plant stakes of flowers and butterflies in front of the row of shrubs that bordered the foundation. "The woman I rent from owns the house. Her daughter just had a baby, so she's up in Wyoming for a month helping." She let go of his hand and reached for the handle of the bike. "I can move this to the shed out back. I know this house isn't much. It's really small but—"

"Are there two kids plus an old man who likes to walk around in nothing but ratty boxers inside?"

She huffed out a laugh. "No."

He placed his hand over hers on the bike. "Then it's perfect."

"Hardly."

He wanted to pull her to him and prove her wrong. The idea of making her his, of how close they were to that moment, made lust stab through him, short-circuiting his brain until it could handle only primal emotions. But Chloe deserved more, and he was going to do this right, even if it killed him. "I'll take the bike around back and meet you inside."

"There's a lock on the shed," she told him and gave him the combination.

He saw lights flicker on in the house as he undid the latch on the privacy fence that surrounded the backyard. By the time he'd put the bike away and turned, she was standing on the small concrete patio. His chest hurt at how beautiful she looked framed by the glow coming from the open doorway behind her. But she also seemed to be standing guard, as if letting him into her house was crossing some threshold that had more meaning than he realized.

Being with Chloe was something he needed to earn, and the way his heart was pounding with more than lust—with a feeling that was tender and new for him—made him realize that she was worth whatever it took. He wanted her trust, her secrets, and to make her feel safe. As he walked toward her, he almost laughed at the irony. Despite his warning to her, damn if he didn't *want* to be a hero right now.

She wrapped her arms around her waist and gave him a smile that was all nerves. "Ok, well, this is it, then."

This is it, goodnight? Or this is it; let's go inside? Ben didn't wait to find out which she meant. Hell, he doubted she knew.

He folded his legs and took a seat on one of the concrete steps leading from the house. "Join me," he said and couldn't help but trace one finger over the delicate bone of her ankle. The feel of her skin made him want to tug her down onto his lap, but he patted the cool cement next to him.

She plopped down, covering her face with her hands. "I'm sorry," she said for the second time that night. "I'm terrible at this."

"At what?" he asked casually, resisting the urge to reach for her.

"Being with a man."

"Being the man in question, I disagree." He shifted toward her. "Before this goes any further, Chloe, I need to know what's going to work for you. I told you I wouldn't touch you in anger, and I meant that. But—"

"Jonathan always wanted to have sex after he hit me," she said, the words coming together so quickly he wasn't sure he'd heard her right. "He said it was how he knew I forgave him, because we could be intimate again." She held her hands fisted tightly together in her lap.

He could imagine how difficult it was for her to share that detail with him. Although anger ripped through him, he stayed silent, giving her a chance to finish what she'd started.

"But I hadn't forgiven him, and the sex ended up being the worst part. I was angry and humiliated, and that heaped more onto it. It was the lack of control, the feeling of him having that power over me." She shook her head, pressed her knuckles to her eyes. "I should have let you drag me out of the kitchen earlier. That's how it needs to happen, fast and mindless so I don't have time to think. Thinking about it kills me."

"No way," he answered, and her hazel eyes shot to his, shining in the shadows that surrounded them. "Not fast. Not mindless." He shrugged. "Not that I don't like those options, too, but we're not going to force you through this, Chloe. I won't force you to do anything."

"It wasn't like that," she explained. "I never said no. It wasn't . . . he didn't force me."

"From what I gather, you also didn't feel like you had a choice."

She shook her head. "I'm making this sound worse than it was. It wasn't like he hit me all the time. There were moments when his temper got the best—"

"Don't. Make. Excuses." He said the words quietly but couldn't help the venom that spilled out in his tone. "I have a temper. You know that."

"He wasn't like you. Jonathan was quiet and controlled. He'd been a long-distance runner in college." She smiled. "My hips were wider than his. It was embarrassing."

"Your hips are exactly the right size."

"Because you're huge." She waved a hand up and down in front of him. "Every part of you is larger than life."

"And that scares you."

She looked at him, hope and regret warring in her big eyes. "I just don't know that we'd fit."

There it was, he thought. The point where he should cut his losses and let her go. Not only did he specialize in casual sex, Ben had always made a point of keeping emotions out of his liaisons. Chloe was nothing but feeling, damaged and battered and still dealing with the emotional scars left by her ex-husband after the physical bruises healed.

But he didn't want to give up. Not now. Not for as long as she'd let him try. It was like tonight's dinner. In the end all the work had been worth it when Zach took that first bite. Maybe Ben had built his career on fancy recipes in Las Vegas then flash-and-dash cooking on the show, but what mattered now were a simple family meal and the meaning of it. Being with Chloe held the same significance. After years of technique and politics in the bedroom, he wanted something real. He wanted to put aside his own needs and make this good for her. If she'd let him.

"There's only one way to find out," he said and stood, placing his palm out. She looked at it with wide eyes, as if she wasn't sure how either of them had gotten to this point.

The question was did she trust him enough to take the chance.

CHAPTER NINE

Chloe swallowed as she looked at Ben's outstretched hand. What was he still doing here? She'd told him the most shameful secret of her life, the humiliating detail from her marriage that not even her closest friends knew. Yet he hadn't walked away.

He could, she knew. It would be so easy for Ben "The Beast" Haddox to leave her behind. He could walk into any trendy restaurant or bar in Denver and have an immediate flock of willing women hanging off his arm. Even if he hadn't been famous, everything about him screamed that he knew how to treat a woman in the bedroom. He was still here with her, waiting with as much patience as a man like him could manage. For her.

She'd come to Denver for a new life, but had only been living half of it up until now. Ben wasn't Jonathan, and she didn't want to continue to let her ex-husband control who she was now. She could never overcome her past if she didn't let anyone into her present. Slowly she straightened and slipped her hand in his, understanding she'd made the right decision as emotion flared in his eyes.

She led him into the house, through the kitchen, and down the short hall to her bedroom. Like all the rooms, it was small, and she wondered for a moment how Ben would even fit in her tiny bed.

She turned to him and took a step closer. He continued to hold her hand, tracing a pattern on the tender skin between her thumb and first finger. She waited, expecting him to move, to pull her into his embrace like he had in his dad's kitchen. Still nothing.

"So . . ."

His eyes flashed. "So."

She took a breath. "You're the expert here."

"But you're in charge."

Her eyes shot to his at those words. "I don't know . . . I can't . . . what am I supposed to do?"

He brought her fingertips to his lips and kissed them tenderly. "Whatever you want, Chloe."

She snatched back her hand and took two steps away before bumping into the mattress. "I don't know what I want," she said desperately. "You have to take control."

"Maybe later," he answered. "This is about you. Whatever comes to your mind, tell me."

"I want to see you without your shirt," she blurted then felt her cheeks flame. Ben didn't even blink.

He grabbed the hem of his T-shirt. "Like this, or do you want to do it?"

She thought about that for a moment then stepped forward. "Me."

Her mouth went dry as she came toe-to-toe with him, and she licked her lips, marveling that her lungs were still moving air in and out. His gaze went a deeper blue as he watched her, so she dropped her eyes to his chest, afraid she'd lose her nerve otherwise.

She grabbed both ends of his shirt, and he lifted his arms so she could pull it over his head.

Now she did stop breathing.

She knew he was big and broad. After that first night when he'd taken off his shirt in her store, she'd done some harmless Google searching and found paparazzi photos of him running bare chested. But waiting for her to touch him with heat coming off him like he was close to burning—nothing could have prepared her. His muscles were sculpted, like he did more than work out in a gym and bang around pots in the kitchen.

"I've never seen a six-pack in person before you," she told him and with one finger traced the groove from under his ribs to his waistband.

He started to chuckle then sucked a breath, flinching but keeping his feet planted on the floor.

She glanced up at him.

"Ticklish," he said through clenched teeth.

For some reason that made her anxiety disappear. In its place a deep curiosity bloomed, new and unfamiliar. She'd been a virgin on her wedding night, awkward and shy. Jonathan had done nothing to ease her nerves. Then things had gone bad and . . .

No. She shut off her mind, unwilling to let her ex-husband intrude on this moment.

She pressed her palm flat on Ben's stomach, splaying her fingers across his bunched muscles. His skin was golden, with only a sprinkling of darker hair across his chest and a thin band that disappeared into his shorts. Shorts that were tented, she noticed, and felt her eyes widen.

"I can keep that part under control, too," he said, sounding both hoarse and amused.

She nodded, swallowed, and continued her exploration, so close she could feel his warm breath on the top of her head. She closed her eyes and touched the tip of her nose to his skin. "You smell—"

"Like I need a shower?" he asked on a gravelly laugh.

"Good." Like a man. Like every fantasy she'd ever had come to big, bold life in front of her. She ran her finger along the outline of his tattoo, something she'd wanted to do since she'd first seen it that night in her store. Her hands curled around his biceps then up over his shoulders, and she had to stand on tiptoe to reach around his neck and thread her fingers through the soft hair at its nape.

He groaned softly, his eyes drifting shut as her breasts, annoyingly covered, pressed into his chest. She kissed him and it started tentatively, because she still wasn't sure of herself. But he whispered her name, his voice filled with longing and need, giving her confidence to deepen the kiss.

He kissed her like he couldn't get enough of her, and she waited for his arms to come around her. When they didn't, she drew back. "Why aren't you touching me?"

"I'm waiting for you to tell me that's what you want."

"Because I'm in charge?"

He nodded. "Because you're in charge."

She felt a smile break across her face. "Do you want to touch me, Ben?" Her voice held a tone she barely recognized, full of power and a womanly knowledge she hadn't realized she possessed before this moment.

"More than I want to breathe," he whispered.

"Take off my shirt," she told him. "I want to feel your skin against mine."

Ben lifted his hands, and she noticed his fingers were trembling a little. He reached for her, his big fingers fumbling with the buttons of her blouse. As each inch of skin was revealed, his gaze darkened. He peeled away the soft fabric and slipped it over her shoulders, the calluses on his palms imparting awareness on her already sensitized flesh. His fingers hooked under the straps of her polka-dot bra and tugged them down her arms.

The shirt fell to the floor and he stared at her. "I like this," he said, tracing the scalloped edges of the bra cups.

"I'm glad."

"Can I kiss you here?" His finger dipped into the hollow between her breasts.

"Yes," she said on a ragged breath and watched as his head lowered.

But instead of a simple kiss, his tongue followed the path of his fingers, then he blew on her flesh.

She felt her nipples harden as a moan escaped her mouth.

He glanced up, his brows quirked in amusement. "Sex noises."

"You like them," she said on a breath.

"Hell, yeah," he agreed then neither of them spoke for a long time.

For a man so often loud and brutish, Ben was incredibly gentle with her, taking his time to learn every part of her body as he made love to her. He made her feel perfect, like everything she did was right. She touched him, explored his body in a way she never would have had the confidence to do before him.

It was hard to imagine that a man so at ease with the strength of his body would use it to inflict pain on someone else. And when the thought that this wouldn't last forever tried to slip in and steal her pleasure, she forced it away. She focused on the right now even as she felt every move he made deep in her soul.

When he finally ripped open the foil condom packet, sheathed himself, then entered her, she was more than ready. It was like nothing she'd ever experienced, and parts of her she hadn't even known existed sprang to life in response to Ben's touch. She climbed higher and higher until she finally broke apart knowing she was safe in the cocoon of his tender embrace.

◆ ◆ ◆

"That was the best thing that's ever happened to me," Chloe said, snuggling against him, her voice a satisfied purr.

Ben thought he'd never had a prouder moment in his life. Not when he'd first arrived in New York, or took over the kitchen at La Lune, or made his first million from the show. This moment with this woman was better than every other good thing that had happened in his life.

"Is it always like that?" she asked.

He pulled her closer, her back pressed to the front of him, and curled his arm around her waist, his fingers spreading over the soft swell of her belly. He wanted to answer yes, to make some lame joke about his prowess in the bedroom, so she wouldn't realize that he'd been as affected as she was. His mouth wouldn't form the words. "No," he answered, afraid he'd give away too much if he said anything else.

"Too bad," she murmured.

"But it will be with us," he couldn't help but add. He knew it was true even if he couldn't imagine how. Ben had experienced all kinds of sex in his life and plenty of it. Angry and acrobatic, quick and dirty, long and lasting all night. Nothing had come close to being with Chloe. He knew better than to let his emotions get involved when it came to physical pleasure, but he couldn't help himself. "I should go."

"Stay," she whispered, tangling her legs with his. "Just for a little longer." Her hair tickled his cheek, the strands soft like silk along his jaw.

He shouldn't want her the way he did. These tender moments were almost as intimate as being buried deep inside her, and even more unsettling. But he couldn't walk away, not just yet.

He shifted as a small nose bumped his back. "What the—"

Chloe stretched to look behind him. "My cat," she said with a laugh.

Ben turned onto his back but kept his arm around Chloe as the cat sniffed his arm then licked it with a rough tongue. "Friendly guy."

"His name is Mr. Rogers." Chloe reached an arm across him to scratch at the cat's ears. "He was my mom's, and I adopted him after she died. He doesn't usually like men."

Ben blew out a soft laugh as the cat climbed leisurely onto the pillow and curled up in a ball next to his head, purring like an overcharged motor. "I can see that."

"Weird." Chloe swallowed a yawn. "He hissed at my ex-husband every chance he got."

"Smart cat," he whispered and kissed the pale column of her throat. "Go to sleep now."

She sighed and pressed closer, as if she couldn't imagine any place more perfect than in his arms. Panic threatened to explode through him at the thought, because he knew he was anything but perfect and was bound to ruin everything between them. He should leave now, making sure she understood exactly how it was with him. What he could and couldn't give.

His body refused to move so he lay wrapped around her, listening to her breathe for minutes or maybe hours. It was better than sleep—more relaxing to be aware of how precious and rare this quiet was in his life. He didn't expect to fall asleep. Ever since he'd started the show, he'd had to take a pill to get even a few hours a night.

But he must have drifted off because the next thing he knew, Chloe was stretched over him, a condom between her fingers. "Some parts of you wake up quicker than others," she said with the barest smile.

He sheathed himself then brought her down onto him, hissing from the pleasure of it. "The rest catches up," he said and kissed her.

As they moved together, just as right as the first time, he understood that what he could and couldn't give would forever be divided into two distinct parts—before Chloe and since her.

This woman, small and fragile but with the strongest heart he could imagine, was changing everything.

◆ ◆ ◆

Michael showed up at the house—unannounced again—a few days later.

"Ever think of calling first?" Ben said when he opened the door then tried to slam it shut again.

Unfortunately, the publicist had wedged his foot in the doorway. "Ever think of answering my calls and texts?"

"I'm busy," Ben said over his shoulder as he stalked back toward the kitchen.

"Busy ignoring your career," Michael shot back, following close on his heels. "EatTV is freaking out because you cancelled the LA appearance."

"It's the same night as employee family day at the Rockies. My dad wants us all to go."

"Who cares? You don't do family days. I'll rent a box at the next game and we'll fly in your friends and invite local celebrities. It will be a great photo op."

"I don't give a damn . . ." Ben started to yell then took a breath and made his tone softer. "I don't give a damn about photo ops with local celebrities, and I can't name one person I'd call a real friend."

"I'm your friend," Michael said with a sniff, clearly offended.

"I pay you." Ben went to the stove, took the lid off the pot simmering, and cursed. "I need burners with even heat. This is a joke."

Michael stepped closer. "Are you cooking?"

Ben rolled his eyes. "What does it look like?"

"But there are no cameras. No restaurant critics waiting." His eyes widened. "You haven't invited a critic to your dad's house?"

"Don't be ridiculous." Ben adjusted the knob on the back burner. "I'm prepping dinner." He dipped a spoon in the sauce and held it out to Michael. "Try this."

"What is it?"

"Try it."

Michael took the spoon, studied the wine-colored sauce for a moment then ate it. His eyes drifted shut then popped open. "Holy shit, that's good."

"It's a glaze for the meatloaf."

"Did you just say meatloaf?" Michael sputtered, dropping the spoon to the counter.

"Zach's request." Ben grinned at his dumbfounded publicist. "So far this week, he's tried chicken pot pie, baked ziti, and fish tacos made with panko crumbs."

"You've turned into fucking Betty Crocker."

"I'm cooking for my family and enjoying myself in the kitchen for the first time in years."

"We need to get you out of Denver, stat."

"I'm not leaving." Ben grabbed the hunk of Gruyère cheese he planned to use for the scalloped potatoes and started grating it into a small bowl. "Yet."

"Don't be an idiot. This isn't you, Beast."

"I hate that name and you know it."

"Then why aren't you yelling at me? I know I'm pissing you off. Where is the temper that made you rich and famous?"

"I'm working on controlling it."

"That temper is who you are."

"Not all of who I am," Ben said, more to himself than to Michael. He smiled at the memory of Chloe saying those words to him. Of her soft skin and the sounds she made when he was holding her. Of how he felt and what he became when they were together. How for the first time in forever he actually liked himself.

"What about the restaurant plans?" Michael tapped an impatient finger on the scratched Formica counter. "Mark—the realtor—told me you didn't like anything he showed you."

"They were all crap," Ben said even though that wasn't true. "I want a different realtor."

"He's the best commercial guy in the city."

"I don't care."

"Why should I bother when you're determined to waste your money on that dumpy toy store location?"

"I'm not sure that's going to work out, either," Ben said, voicing the words for the first time. His stomach rolled in response. With Chloe working so hard to get the money for the back rent and his niece and nephew by her side, the thought of exacting his revenge no longer held much appeal.

"Seriously?" Michael looked stunned. "That's all you've talked about since you bought the building. What's going on with you?"

"I don't know," Ben yelled, his temper finally getting the best of him. "I don't know what the hell I'm doing here, ok?" His hand slipped and the bowl of cheese went skidding along the counter before crashing to the floor, cheese and shards of glass spilling in every direction. "Damn it," he roared then glanced up to see his publicist grinning.

"It makes me nervous when you're quiet," Michael said. "Where's a broom? I'll help clean up."

Ben pointed toward the small closet on the far side of the kitchen then cursed again when the pot on the stove started bubbling over, brown glaze sizzling as it hit the stove top.

"If you don't know what you're doing here, I've got the perfect solution." Michael swept the debris into a dustpan as he spoke. "Perfect enough to get your attention in the midst of all this homemaking bliss."

"I told you I'm on a break."

"James Wyatt wants you. He's ready for a new project and wants you to develop the menu for it."

Ben turned off the heat on the stove then used a potholder to nudge the saucepan onto a cool burner. James Wyatt was famous in the industry. His investment company held a majority interest in more five-star restaurants than any other group in the world. "I told you I'm not working in someone else's kitchen again."

"He's going to give you an ownership percentage. Obviously, he likes what you did at La Lune. But this is about you. Your concept, design, and menu. You call the shots here, Ben. He provides the space and the financial backing."

"What's he getting in return?"

"Do you know how difficult it is to launch a top-tier restaurant in the current market, even if you are as well known as Wyatt? He gets your name and star power, plus a stake in the profits, of course. You didn't ask me the location." Michael practically jumped up and down. "That's the best part."

"Where?"

"It will be the flagship restaurant at The Pointe. Can you believe it? It's all yours, Ben. This is it. This is the dream right here and now."

The sudden anticipation roaring in his ears drowned out the publicist's voice. The Pointe was the new hotel being built in Las Vegas, with a construction budget that almost doubled what had been spent on the Bellagio. He'd seen the preliminary design plans a few months ago and they were mind-boggling. The hotel was set to be the shiniest, fanciest star on the Vegas strip. Having his name on the restaurant would silence every critic who'd called him a sellout after he left for EatTV. It would prove he could create a world-class menu, and money would be no object.

"I've got to think about Abby and Zach," he said automatically.

"They're kids," Michael countered. "Move them to Vegas with you if you're so dedicated."

Ben had talked to Cory last Sunday on the phone, and his brother had made him promise that he wouldn't bring either of the kids to see him in prison. Cory didn't want them to see him in the beige jumpsuit or experience the trauma of having to come through prison security for a visit. Zach had cried openly after talking to his dad, and Abby had spent the rest of the night with her bedroom door closed. He could, he reasoned, relocate them to Las Vegas. It wasn't as if they had hordes of close friends in Denver.

Other than Chloe.

He glanced at the clock, realizing he was due to pick them up from the toy store in fifteen minutes. "When does he want an answer?"

"You mean it's not an automatic yes?" Michael shook his head. "Living at this altitude has messed with your head. You're not going to get a better opportunity than this. Ever."

"How much time do I have?" Ben asked, crossing his arms over his chest and glaring at his publicist.

"They want to make an initial announcement by the end of the month," Michael answered, his jaw clenched tight. "Negotiations on specifics can happen after that."

Ben gave a sharp nod. "You'll have my decision by then. Send me whatever details you have."

"You're making a mistake if you don't take this. Plus I talked to the people at EatTV. They're willing to compress the shooting schedule and change the format to work around the build out of the restaurant."

"Damn it, Michael, I want an excuse to be done with the show and you know it."

"Did you hear what I said? Wyatt wants you because of your celebrity-chef status. We need to capitalize on your relationship with EatTV, not piss them off more than you already have." He leveled Ben with his patented "I know what's best for your career" stare.

"I'm sick of being 'The Beast.'"

"You need it."

"I need a break." Ben tossed a handful of spices into a mixing bowl.

"To make meatloaf?"

"To do whatever the hell I want."

"Including a curly-haired toy-store owner?"

Ben's fingers tightened on the edge of the stainless steel bowl. "What do you know about Chloe?"

"Mark mentioned that she was a distraction when you looked at properties."

"She was the reason I agreed to meet with a realtor in the first place."

Michael shook his head. "You're losing focus—the kids are one thing, but if your dick—"

"Stop." Ben held up a hand, unexpected rage pulsing through him. "You've been with me from the start of this, Michael, but no one is irreplaceable. Before you say one more word, you need to understand that."

"I'm looking out for what's best," the publicist argued.

"For me or you?"

"Both of us. We're a team."

"Then take a time-out." Ben dumped the sauce into a metal bowl, placed it in the refrigerator, and then washed his hands. "You'll hear from me by the end of the month. Right now, I'm going to pick up Abby and Zach." He grinned at Michael. "You're welcome to stay for meatloaf."

The other man made a gagging sound. "I haven't choked down a bite of meatloaf since my mom served it every week. Meatloaf Mondays. The smell still makes me nauseous."

Ben only smiled. "This is not your mother's meatloaf. Trust me."

"I'm going to take your word on that. Besides, I have a flight booked in a couple of hours. Taking the red-eye back to New York. The fresh air out here really bugs me." He stepped forward as Ben laughed and held out a hand.

Ben shook it and Michael smiled. "I'm sorry I came down hard on you. I know it hasn't been an easy time, and I'm on your side. The right side."

As Ben got in the Range Rover after locking the front door behind himself and Michael, he realized he couldn't blame the man for pushing him. Ben had worked with single-minded determination since he left home to make himself a success, and Michael had definitely helped him get to where he was now. He'd accomplished everything he'd ever dreamed of, and the final jewel in his crown was closing down Butterfield's store. Only it wasn't Stan Butterfield who was going to be devastated by his plan. It was Chloe.

He knew that closing the store wouldn't exact the same revenge he and his brother had planned as kids, but Cory's insistence that The Toy

Chest was the root of his problems made the situation impossible. Ben was going to hurt someone who genuinely seemed to want to help him make his life better. The irony of it burned at his gut and made his skin feel like it was being peeled away one strip at a time.

What if she didn't raise the money she needed? What if she did and he put her out of business anyway? He hadn't thought past ruining The Toy Chest to what he'd actually do with the space. He knew what was expected of him if he returned to Las Vegas. He could find the most expensive, exotic ingredients and turn them into works of art for the rich and sometimes famous to dine on. In Vegas, image was everything. Ben's bad-boy reputation coupled with a good dose of attitude, James Wyatt's deep pockets, and the right amount of skill in the kitchen would all but ensure success. He knew how to make it work.

What did he know about opening a restaurant in a family neighborhood, where Saturday night meant a bicycle ride to the nearest pizza place and ice cream store? Maybe Michael was right and Ben should stick with what he knew. The question was, what would it cost him to walk away?

CHAPTER TEN

"You can't be serious about this dress?"

Chloe and Sam exchanged a look as Jenny Castelli held up the magazine to the page Kendall had bookmarked. Jenny had grown up with Ty Bishop, and she and Kendall had formed an unlikely friendship since Kendall had started dating Ty. Chloe liked the fiery redhead, who made Sam seem almost demure with her blunt manners and comments. Until Jenny, Sam had been the least reserved person Chloe'd ever met. The two of them together would make a good stand-up comedy act.

The four women were sitting around the kitchen table in Ty and Kendall's cozy, Craftsman-style kitchen. Ty was out of town at a conference for a few days, so Kendall had invited her three bridesmaids for drinks, takeout, and brainstorming on wedding plans.

"I like it," Kendall said, tilting her head to stare at the dress. "It's fresh."

"It looks like the grass my dog eats and pukes up," Jenny said, adding in gagging sound effects, "when he has an upset stomach."

"Ty loves nature," Kendall answered with a delicate sniff, "so I wanted you guys in a dress that reflected his tastes."

"Why not just put us in empty manure bags with sticks in our hair?" Jenny took a long pull on her beer then wiped the back of her hand across her mouth.

Kendall grimaced then glanced at Chloe and Sam. "What about you two? Do you both hate it?"

"Sweetie, it's your day," Chloe said carefully. "All eyes will be on the bride, so we'll wear whatever you want us to."

Sam plucked the magazine from Jenny's fingers. "It's not that bad."

"Hell, no." Jenny shook her head. "Models don't get a vote. When your legs stop at your armpits, everything looks good."

"I want to elope," Kendall said with a sigh, scooping up a forkful of pad thai. "This is too hard."

"Great idea," Jenny agreed. "We can book you a package tonight. Tahiti? Bora Bora? Pick your poison."

"My poison," Kendall mumbled. "Thanks, Jenny."

Sam pointed at the redhead. "When was the last time you wore a dress?"

Jenny bristled, crossing her arms over her chest. "Last week at an event I went to with Owen." She paused and grabbed a spring roll from the plate on the center of the table. "Right before I broke up with him."

"You didn't," Kendall said.

Sam muttered something that sounded a lot like, "Idiot."

"It was going to happen eventually." Jenny took a halfhearted bite of the spring roll. "Better to make a clean break now than postpone the inevitable. It wasn't like we were a real couple."

Chloe felt a sharp pang of sympathy for the other woman. Those were practically the same words she'd said to herself when she thought about ending whatever was going on between Ben and her.

"Don't talk with your mouth full," Sam said then held up her hands when Jenny glared. "Sorry, I'm used to correcting the kids at camp."

"That's just . . ." Jenny paused, finished chewing then threw down the uneaten half of spring roll. "That's just it. My manners are horrible and I know it. After last week, so do Owen and all the fancy-schmancy people he hangs out with. I will never fit into his world."

Chloe had only met Owen Dalton on a couple of occasions, but had immediately liked the high-tech entrepreneur-turned-philanthropist. He might be one of the richest men in the country, but Owen seemed unconcerned with his wealth and status. He had a passion for technology, and that was what kept him working and grounded. Earlier that year, he'd been one of the men selected to go out with Kendall as part of an online dating feature sponsored by the station she worked for at the time. Of course, off camera Kendall had been falling in love with Ty, but she and Owen had become friends. From everything Kendall had said, Owen had been smitten with brash and beautiful Jenny the first time he'd met her.

"I doubt he cares about your manners," Chloe offered.

"He cares that he caught me kissing another man in the coat closet," Jenny said, almost defiantly.

Kendall gasped. "Jenny, no. Why? You care about Owen."

Jenny bit down on her lip. "And now I've publicly humiliated him." She pointed to Sam. "You can pull your eyebrows out of your hairline, Cover Girl. You'll need Botox sooner than later if you keep wrinkling your face that way."

Sam rubbed her fingers over her forehead. "Take shots at me all you want, Jen. It won't change the fact that you're a cheater."

Jenny bristled for a moment then her expression crumpled and she dropped her head into her hands. "It wasn't like that," she said on a sob. "I never wanted to hurt Owen."

"Were you wasted?" Sam asked, and Chloe nudged her. "It's a fair question," Sam whispered.

"I wasn't . . ." Jenny paused, sniffed then shook her head. "I was a little drunk. Those events make me so nervous. All the uppity people staring at me like I should be parking their cars instead of polluting their air with my presence."

"Nothing wrong with parking cars," Kendall said. Chloe knew Kendall's father had worked most of his life as a country-club valet. "Don't let them make you believe they're better than you." Kendall stood and grabbed a roll of paper towels from the counter. "Here, hon," she said, handing a few to Jenny. "Tell us what happened."

"What happened is I lo—" Jenny blew her nose into a paper towel and struggled to catch a breath. Chloe had never imagined the tiny, tough-as-nails woman could ever be so emotional. "I liked Owen and I screwed it up. I told him things would never work between us, but he wouldn't listen. He just kept saying he liked me the way I am."

"Very Bridget Jones," Sam murmured, earning a confused glance from Jenny. "Do you watch anything but horror flicks?" Sam asked her.

"The *Fast and Furious* series," Jenny answered.

Sam rolled her eyes. "Next girls' night, we're doing a chick-flick movie marathon."

"Why would you want to hang out with me ever again?" Jenny sniffled.

"Because we like women who ugly cry worse than we do?" Sam offered.

Jenny flipped her the middle finger, but one side of her mouth curved.

"Don't mind her." Chloe scooted to the seat next to Jenny and gave her a gentle hug. "Sam's idea of support is to berate you into feeling better."

"It actually works." Jenny honked into another paper towel. "I've never had friends before." She glanced at Kendall. "Other than Ty."

"You're like a sister to him," Kendall confirmed with a gentle smile.

"So we were at the part where you made out with another dude in the coat closet." Sam balanced her wineglass between two elegant fingers, taking a small sip. "And then . . ."

"Owen found us."

"That sucks," Sam murmured.

Jenny stared at the table. "I knew he would. We were getting ready to leave and he had to say good-bye to a few people. I told him I was going to the bathroom and asked him to grab my shawl and meet me by the entrance. There was a guy who'd been giving me the eye all night, so I grabbed him and pulled him into the coat closet."

"You planned for Owen to discover you in someone else's arms?" Kendall sounded as confused as Chloe felt.

"He believed that we could be together," Jenny said, her voice hoarse. "He told me our differences didn't matter."

"Did Owen use the L-word?" Sam took another, longer drink.

Jenny nodded. "It was stupid and cowardly. I'd just met the guy, and I couldn't have cared less about him. But in case you didn't realize, I'm the queen of self-sabotage. When life is good, I'm always waiting for it to turn bad, and most of the time I screw it up because that's what's going to happen anyway. The only thing I've done right in my life is Cooper." Chloe knew she was referring to her ten-year-old son. "I never let anyone get as close to me as Owen did. As much as I hate to admit being a chicken, it scared the hell out of me. I broke his heart before he could break mine."

All three women nodded. There was no shortage of man hang-ups in this room.

"I threw up in the bathroom after Owen was gone. I didn't come out until everyone else had left and the cleaning crew came through. Owen was with a group of people when he discovered me." She shook her head, and her voice clogged a little. "He looked so stunned, like he couldn't believe it was me. I humiliated him, and do you know what he did?"

"Called you a low-life slut?" Sam suggested.

Kendall slapped her on the arm. "What did he do?"

"He had a car waiting for me." Jenny's mouth pinched hard. "I came out of that building and his driver insisted on taking me home. Said Owen wanted to make sure I made it there safely."

Kendall and Chloe sighed.

Sam wiped under her eyes with two fingers then pointed at Jenny. "You need a shot." She stood, her chair scraping against the hardwood floor as she went to one of the cabinets and pulled out four small glasses. "Where do you keep the liquor?"

Kendall moved to the pantry door and opened it. "Tequila or Jäger?"

Chloe gathered the used paper towels and brought them to the garbage can. "Your call, Jen."

Jenny stared at the three of them. "Got any limes?" she asked Kendall.

"Tequila it is," Kendall answered. "Sam, grab the limes from the fridge."

Three shots later, they were back to flipping through magazines. "Some of these aren't bad," Sam said then looked at Jenny. "Are you going to try to fix it?"

"Kendall's taste in dresses?" Jenny asked, digging her spoon into a pint of Ben & Jerry's. Kendall always had ice cream on hand.

"Your relationship with Owen," Sam clarified and poured them each another finger of liquor.

Jenny shook her head, and Chloe noticed the redhead seemed to have a fuzzy golden aura around her hair. Maybe Chloe should refuse any more tequila. "It's better this way. We were too different. There were too many things that had the potential to pull us apart."

"In addition to you being a coward?" Sam cut another lime and placed a wedge in front of each woman.

"Enough support from you," Kendall said, giving Sam another poke.

"I think I've had enough to drink," Chloe said as she looked at another magazine. The bride on the cover seemed to wink at her. That was impossible, right?

"One more," Jenny told her. "Don't make me say Cover Girl is a better friend than you."

Sam shook her head. "I did Maybelline, never CoverGirl."

"Would it offend you if I didn't know the difference?" Jenny giggled, and the sound was so ridiculous coming from the tiny spitfire that it made Chloe giggle, too. Then Kendall started laughing and pretty soon all four of them were doubled over. Tequila and ice cream—a cure-all combination.

As they tipped back the final shot, Chloe, who didn't mind her reputation as a lightweight, thought the alcohol went down smoother the more she drank. "This one." She pressed her finger against a page in the magazine and tapped it a few times. Funny, she couldn't feel the tip.

"That's a tux," Kendall said, squinting to focus on the photo.

Chloe looked again then adjusted her finger to point to a woman wearing a cocktail-length, sage-green dress. It had thin straps, a fitted bodice, and an A-line waist that would flatter each woman's figure. Chloe was pretty sure she had a winner.

A loopy smile broke across Kendall's face. "Oh," she breathed. "I love it. I'm going to be jealous of my bridesmaids."

Jenny snatched the magazine and held it above her head, leaning back as she moved it closer then farther from her face. "It might work." She seemed to try to wink at Chloe but couldn't quite reopen her eye. "We won't look like total dog meat next to Maybelline over there."

Sam burped in response, making all of them laugh again.

"Unless," Jenny suggested, "you reconsider eloping. I've heard Vegas can be quite romantic."

Kendall held out a hand. "Give me the photo so you don't end up puking all over it."

"I'm not a puker." Jenny sounded affronted.

"Even if I really wanted to elope, I can't disappoint my mother that way." Kendall hiccupped then sniffed. "She's been calling every week with ideas and is already working on my veil."

"You haven't set a date," Chloe said.

"Doesn't matter," Kendall said, although to Chloe it sounded like "cousin splatter."

"Speaking of Vegas," Sam said, slamming her hand onto the table. "How's Chef Hottie?"

"Are you 'loping?" Jenny held out her fist. "Don't leave me hangin', sista."

Chloe gave the redhead a tentative fist bump. "I'm not eloping with Ben. Or anyone." She shook her head. "Marriage and I did not agree."

"Because you were married to a jackass," Sam interjected.

"I thought Ben Haddox was a jackass." Jenny held out her hands, wiggling her fingers as she gazed at them.

"He's not," Chloe said.

"We *know* he's hot," Jenny told her.

"I said he's *not*. A jackass." Chloe picked up the lime, stuck out her tongue, and touched it to the tangy pulp. "But he's different. Like you were saying with Owen. We come from different places and it can't last."

"Ty and I are different, but that's part of what I love about him."

"Not everyone is built for love," Sam said, staring at the ceiling. "Some people don't have it in them." She lifted a finger in front of her face then turned it toward her own forehead. "Like me."

"And me."

"And maybe Ben," Chloe whispered.

"You three are the most maudlin bridal party I've ever met." Kendall sighed. "I can't wait for my bachelorette party."

That comment made them laugh again. "The new season of *Downton Abbey* is available On Demand," Sam said. "Who's with me?"

Kendall and Chloe raised their hands while Jenny blinked. "What about *Pawn Stars*?" she asked.

They made their way, with only a few detours into walls or doorways, into the family room. Within minutes of watching the period drama, Sam and Jenny were snoring. They sat shoulder to shoulder on the couch, Jenny's head propped against Sam's shirtsleeve.

Chloe knew she should be tired, but energy revved through her. She shifted on the leather chair where she sat, pulled her phone out of her back pocket, and automatically checked the store's Facebook page. Ever since Abby had made herself the moderator, she'd been posting content to boost engagement on the social media fan page. Two customers had made positive comments about a picture from the most recent story-time event. Chloe started to post a status update herself but thought better of it. At least she wasn't that drunk. Next she typed Ben's name into the Internet search bar and pressed the "images" tab.

"Let me see." Kendall, who was sitting on the floor, her back against the leather chair, reached up a hand.

"See what?"

"You must be Googling Ben because you whimpered."

"I didn't whimper," Chloe protested but handed over the phone, almost dropping it on Kendall's head before making contact with her open palm.

Kendall made a noise that was somewhere between a whimper and a groan. "I don't blame you. He looks like he knows how to turn up the heat, and not just in the kitchen."

"Mmm . . . hmmm." The sound left Chloe's mouth before she realized it. Her gaze flicked to the other two women who were still sleeping soundly. In fact, it looked like Jenny might be drooling on Sam's arm.

"Your secret's safe with me." Kendall tilted up her chin to look at Chloe upside down but immediately dropped her head between her legs. "Is the room spinning?"

"I don't think so, but I know you guys are the best friends I've ever had."

"That's true even though it's the alcohol talking right now." Kendall massaged her temples for a minute then slowly turned. "Two words of advice."

A few months ago, Chloe would have laughed at Kendall giving anyone man advice, but now she was the only one of them who'd managed to have a healthy relationship. "Lay it on me."

"Booty call."

Chloe stared at her. "Seriously?"

"You're drunk, he's hot. That equals a booty call." She cocked her head to one side. "Or maybe now it's called drunk texting." She grabbed at the phone. "Want me to send it?"

"No!" Chloe clutched the phone to her chest. "I can't. I shouldn't."

"You want to." Kendall wiggled her eyebrows.

"What would I say?"

Kendall was quiet for a moment then whispered, "Do me, big guy."

Chloe felt her eyes widen. "Is that what you say to Ty?"

"Um . . . not exactly. It's more—"

"Hush." Chloe tapped Kendall's shoulder with her foot. "I don't want to know. Ok, I'm texting." She punched in two letters.

Hi.

"What if he ignores me?" She glanced at the time on her phone. "It's late. What if he's sleeping? I can't stand this." She felt dizzy, all the alcohol she'd consumed churning in her belly. "I need to take it back."

Kendall laughed and Chloe kicked at her, none too gently by the way Kendall fell over.

"How do I delete—" Her phone chimed and her hand jerked. The phone flipped to the floor.

"I'll get it," Kendall said with a devious laugh, but Chloe dove for it, grunting when her chin connected with the hardwood first.

She rolled onto her back, pushing Kendall away.

How was your night?

Her thumbs raced across the keyboard, and she pressed Send before she could think better of it.

I want to have sex.

"No beating around the bush for you." Kendall scooted closer, her head tilted so she could read the screen.

The reply was almost instantaneous.

Can you be more specific?

Kendall giggled. "I like him."

"Me too," Chloe said, smiling as she typed.

With you.

"That's the problem." She hit Send again and waited.

You should do girls' nights more often. Text me the address.

She glanced at Kendall, who nodded. "You go, honey. I'll watch over Thelma and Louise."

"I'm going to grab my purse, and I'll come by tomorrow for the car." With some effort, Chloe managed to get to her feet. "Need a hand up?"

Kendall's eyes drifted shut. "How about a pillow?"

Chloe grabbed one of the decorative pillows from the couch and tucked it under her friend's head then draped a blanket over her, having a hard time resisting the urge to sink back down to the floor. It was sleepy in the quiet living room, so after retrieving her purse from the kitchen, she let herself out the front door. Maybe the cooler night air would help her wake up. Otherwise, she was going to be the worst booty call in the history of mankind.

◆ ◆ ◆

Ben smiled as he knocked on the door of the address Chloe had texted him. He'd made record time getting to Kendall's house, although things seemed weirdly quiet compared to the drunken revelry he'd imagined from four intoxicated women. When no one answered his second knock, he checked his phone, wondering if he was at the wrong address.

Then he heard a soft snuffling and turned to see Chloe sleeping on a wooden swing at the far side of the porch. Her legs were curled up in a fetal position, her curls covering most of her face as she slept. So much for the suggestive text, he thought, but it didn't matter. She'd wanted him and whether it was for bedroom adventures or holding her hair back when she got sick, he was uncharacteristically happy to be that man.

He brushed away her hair from her cheek then sucked in a breath.

"Chloe," he said, lifting her to a sitting position as he knelt in front of her. "Are you ok? What happened?"

She blinked several times. "Hey, Chef Hottie," she slurred. "Come to have your wicked way wif me?"

"You're bleeding," he told her, pressing his thumb to a cut on the inside of her bottom lip. There was dried blood all over her chin and her already-full mouth was swollen.

Her eyes crossed as she tried to look down her nose. "I fell."

"On your face?"

She lifted her hand and after several tries, pointed to her jaw. "Here."

He dipped his head and in the dim light could see a faint bruise forming. "Were you ladies wrestling?"

She smiled then winced as the cut on her lip split again. "Ouch. Must have bit my lip. I didn't notice the cut before. Too busy propositioning you."

"I'm a sure thing," he told her, leaning in to drop a kiss on her forehead. He scooped her into his arms and stood. "But we need to get ice on that cut."

"Then we gonna have the sex?" she asked, wrapping her arms around his neck.

"I think you need a strong cup of coffee more than you need the sex." He strode toward the car and opened the passenger door.

"You're not the boss of me," she said with a pout, wriggling in his arms.

"Don't I know it." He dropped her to her feet but kept his hands on her upper arms, afraid she might tip over if he let her go.

"I'm sorry," she said, listing away from him. It was more like she was shrinking away, and a bad feeling curled around his stomach when she asked in a smaller voice, "Did I make you mad? I didn't mean to make you mad."

Her eyes had clouded over and he wasn't sure if she even realized what she was saying or who she was talking to. She seemed far away, almost as if she was reliving another time. One that held bad memories. One he didn't want associated with him.

"Chloe, look at me." She continued to stare at a space over his shoulder, and he felt a tremble course through her. "Damn it," he muttered and she twitched. His heart twisted in response. "It's ok, sweetheart." He opened the passenger-side door and maneuvered her in as gently as he could.

She was stiff but didn't resist him. Still, he was afraid she might actually bolt, so as soon as he was in the car he hit the automatic locks and started for her house.

"How much did you have to drink?" he asked as he stopped at a red light.

She shook her head, a tiny movement. "Too much."

"No doubt. Take some breaths, Chloe. I'm not mad. No one is mad. Everything is good."

At this she rolled her head across the back of the seat, her anxious gaze meeting his. "I'm not good," she whispered. "I'm sorry."

"Stop apologizing," he shouted then immediately regretted it. She jumped several inches and he heard her head knock into the window. Shit. He hadn't meant to yell at her. It was the frustration of feeling so helpless, of having to watch her deal with the repercussions of what that asshole ex-husband had done to her. "You don't have anything to apologize for," he said in a gentler tone.

"I want to go home," she said, her voice miserable.

"Almost there." He wanted to reach for her but was afraid he'd freak her out more than she already was. A few minutes later, he pulled to the curb in front of her duplex. He was out of the car in a heartbeat, sliding across the hood to land on the sidewalk as she scrambled from the passenger's side.

"Chloe."

She slammed the door then turned and held onto the edge of it. "This isn't about you," she muttered. "I know that. I just . . . it reminded me . . ."

"It's ok." He placed a hand, the lightest touch he could manage, on her shoulder. "Let me walk you inside."

She didn't move. "I'm so embarrassed."

"No need for that in front of me." He drew his fingers down her arm and wrapped them around her elbow. "Let's go."

He thought she might wrench away from him again, but after a few weighted moments, she took a step onto the sidewalk and started up the path toward her front porch.

Ben didn't say anything, simply grateful that she let him stay. Christ, this night had gone to hell. When she'd texted, he'd been asleep on the couch with his dad snoring in the recliner next to him as reruns of *Everybody Loves Raymond* played on the TV in the background. There'd been a moment of half-asleep bliss at the thought of holding her in his arms again. And while he hadn't factored in how much she'd drunk tonight, he was still grateful to be the man at her side right now.

Although he'd never been one for messy scenes or alcohol-fueled emotional meltdowns, he would have no sooner left Chloe's side than cut off his right hand. He wanted to be the one to get her through whatever long-buried issues were brought to the surface by the booze.

He wanted to be a man she could depend on even in her darkest moments.

As they approached the door, she fumbled in her purse, taking out a set of keys then dropping them to the concrete. Before he could stop her, she reached for them and fell forward, almost face-planting again before he caught her around the waist.

"I'm going to carry you again," he said, holding her tightly to him as he unlocked the door and opened it. "Is that ok?"

It was a ridiculous question since her balance was precarious at best. Still, he knew it was essential to have her permission on this.

"Ok," she murmured and once again, he lifted her into his arms. She weighed next to nothing and it felt exactly right when she buried her face in his shoulder.

He moved into the darkened house, where Mr. Rogers waited to curl around his legs as he fumbled for the light switch. After depositing Chloe onto the sofa, he took ice from the freezer, dumped it in a plastic bag, then wet a paper towel. He found her coffeemaker and started a fresh pot before returning to the living room.

Chloe remained where he'd left her, eyes closed and head tipped back against the couch cushions.

"I'm not passed out," she said, blinking at him as he drew closer.

"How do you feel?" He smoothed the hair away from her face and pressed the ice to her lip.

"Like I'll never do tequila shots again." She grimaced. "I may not be able to stomach a margarita either."

"A crying shame," he murmured.

"I'm sorry," she said again.

He shook his head. "No need. We've all had nights like this."

She frowned. "I don't have nights like this."

"You were right earlier, Chloe. I'm not the boss of you and I'd never try to be."

She gave him a long look.

"Ok," he admitted, "I'm overbearing by nature. But not like that. Do you want to tell me what happened back there?"

"No."

"Will you tell me anyway?"

She covered his hand with hers, moved it away from her mouth, and touched her tongue to the cut on her lip. "The first time Jonathan hit me was a shock. We weren't even having a big fight. It was inconsequential. He wanted me to wear a certain dress to the hospital Christmas party."

He felt his hand curl into a fist and forced himself to relax, handing her the wet paper towel.

She dabbed at the blood crusting her chin. "I thought it was too short, and I'd bought something new, a sparkly sweater that went with a pair of pants I loved. He kept pushing, holding the dress up to me like he could change my mind. I told him he wasn't the boss of me . . ."

"And . . ."

"He backhanded me."

It killed him that her voice was matter-of-fact, as if they were discussing traffic patterns instead of domestic abuse.

"He seemed as upset as I was. It came out of nowhere. He'd never even raised his voice."

"What did you do?"

"Nothing. He apologized right away, talked about the stress at work and making a good impression on his colleagues. He brought me ice . . ." She trailed off and they both looked at the freezer bag Ben still held. "I put on extra concealer and we went to the party."

"What did you wear?"

Her wary gaze caught on his, as if she hadn't expected the question. "The dress he wanted."

"I'm going to get you a cup of coffee," he said, knowing his voice sounded tight. He was furious at everything that had happened to her, but his anger wouldn't help her now.

She shook her head. "I don't need it. That trip down memory lane killed any buzz I had."

"I'm sorry."

"You didn't do anything, Ben. It's me. Like always. I ruined a perfectly good drunk-text booty call."

One side of his mouth curved, even though she seemed totally serious. "Come here, sweetheart."

She slid closer and he tucked her against him, massaging his fingers along the delicate bones of her spine. He thought about his parents, all the yelling and fighting they'd done for years. Most of it had been fueled by alcohol. Alcohol and anger. It was why Ben had stopped getting drunk a few years ago. He'd come close to too many bar brawls, making him feel like his dad on a bender. He never wanted to turn into a man he could easily hate. "You didn't ruin anything," he told her.

"But no sex," she murmured, her breath warm against his throat.

"A rain check," he told her. "Are you ready for bed?"

She tipped back her head to look up at him. "Will you stay?" Her eyes were big and vulnerable.

"As long as you need me to."

She kissed his cheek and stood, still swaying a little.

"Need help?"

"I think I do," she said, and it felt like the words were hard for her to say. He liked that she said them anyway.

He draped an arm around her waist and led her to the bedroom. She plopped onto the edge of the bed and her fingers fumbled with the buttons of her shirt. "PJs on the hook behind the door."

They were soft cotton and smelled like Chloe, fresh and sweet. He helped her out of her clothes and into the pajamas, careful to keep his hands from wandering too far from the task at hand. Her eyelids were drooping already as he slid back the quilt and sheets and tucked her under.

"You're a good guy," she whispered, and he wanted to believe the words. Wanted to be a better person than he knew himself to be. For her.

So when he climbed into the bed next to her, he didn't take off his clothes and made sure to lie on top of the covers. She snuggled into him, and although his body reacted, he simply enjoyed the feeling of her relying on him. He stayed with her most of the night, only slipping out as the first tendrils of light appeared in the eastern sky outside her window.

For a night of getting very little sleep himself, he felt more rested than he had in ages.

CHAPTER ELEVEN

"Rough night?" Karen looked up from the computer in the back office as Chloe walked in the next day. The store didn't open for another hour, but Karen had volunteered to check the online site early each morning so they could process and ship the orders placed without delay. This was also the morning of the weekly employee meeting. The rest of the women would arrive shortly to discuss store business and also for a support session and updates on their new lives. Chloe had found that the meetings helped keep them focused and committed to the changes they'd made, but today she wished she'd been able to stay in bed.

"Does it show?" Chloe thought she'd done a pretty good job of cleaning herself up, at least compared to how she'd looked this morning. It had been close to seven when she'd stumbled into the bathroom, mouth full of cotton and head pounding. Her reflection in the mirror was almost unrecognizable. The eye shadow and mascara she'd applied yesterday was smeared halfway down her face and her curls had turned to frizz, plastered to one side of her head while sticking up wildly on the other.

Is this how she'd looked last night with Ben? Mortification had flooded her, sharp and heavy. She'd texted him for sex and ended up being a sad, sloppy drunk. The worst part was that she'd freaked out on him, letting her memories of Jonathan overshadow the present once again. Her hot mess of a face ran a pretty close second.

If only she'd passed out on the couch along with Sam and Jenny.

Kendall had texted her earlier asking about the night. She'd sent a photo of Sam and Jenny spooning on the couch. At least Chloe hadn't been the only one to act out of character last night. Too bad hers was with Ben.

"You don't look great," Karen said, pushing back from the desk, "but the delivery you received this morning was a bigger clue." She picked up a white grocery bag and large plastic cup from the bookshelf. "Ben brought this by a few minutes ago."

Unexpected warmth shot through Chloe's veins at the same time her face heated. She inhaled as she took the bag. "It smells delicious."

"He said you might need something substantial this morning and swore he makes the best breakfast burrito in town." Karen handed over the cup. "He also brought a vanilla milkshake."

"A milkshake?"

"It's a hangover cure," Karen told her, one eyebrow raised.

Chloe nodded. "Girls' night at Kendall's."

"Ben was at your girls' night?"

"I texted him at one point, and he picked me up."

"Booty call," a voice sang out behind her.

She whirled then groaned as a wave of dizziness tore through her. Tamara stood with three other women in the doorway of the office, all of them grinning from ear to ear.

"Chloe's got herself a hot man," Tamara called, bumping hips with Sally, one of the store's newest hires.

"Nice going, boss. I'd tap that beautiful piece of beastly man in a heartbeat," Sally said with a wink at Chloe.

"Wait one minute." Tamara took a step closer to Chloe. "Your lip is busted. You've got dark gloss on to hide it."

Chloe touched her tongue to the thin cut. "It's nothing."

"Of course it's something," Karen said, coming around the counter. She placed a hand on Chloe's chin and tipped her head back toward the light. "He promised you were safe with him. And now this. We're going to—"

"Do nothing," Chloe interrupted, twisting away from Karen's grasp. "It wasn't Ben."

"Of course not. We've all been there, girlfriend." Sally shook her head. "Damn men."

"I mean it. I was drunk at Kendall's and I fell." She held out her cell phone. "Call and ask her. Ben didn't touch me. We didn't even . . ."

The women stared at her, their expressions ranging from disbelief to sympathy.

"I didn't tap anything," she said quickly, her voice sharp. "Nothing intimate happened between Ben and me. I was too drunk. He took me home and put me to bed. Ben was . . ." She broke off, gave a strangled laugh. "He was a perfect gentleman and far kinder than he needed to be." Chloe shook her head. "End of story. I promise. We need to start the meeting."

As if sensing the topic wasn't up for discussion, the women filed into the office and took their normal seats around the room. The ends of Tamara's hair were now colored a dark shade of purple, which matched her brightly painted nails. Sally was the youngest of the women, barely twenty-one. She was still full of youthful attitude despite having spent four years in an abusive relationship with her high-school boyfriend that only ended after Sally spent several nights in the hospital.

The final member of their group was Laura, a soft-spoken woman in her mid-thirties who'd moved to Denver from southern Wyoming with her two kids six months earlier. She was shy and sometimes skittish with adults but loved to help with the weekly classes. Chloe hoped to give her enough experience that she could apply as a teaching aide at a preschool or day care in the fall.

They discussed the sales for the week, upcoming classes, and the employee schedule. Then Chloe asked for a personal update from each woman. While most of them received support from the local shelter, Chloe knew the community they'd created at the store felt like family to each of them.

After congratulating Tamara on her decision to apply to a local cosmetology school, Chloe glanced at her watch. "Ten minutes until we open. Is there anything else we need to discuss?"

The four women glanced at each other. "You haven't given us an update," Karen said after a moment, clearly the de facto spokesperson for the group.

Chloe blinked. "I talked about myself at the beginning of the meeting."

"No," Tamara countered. "You talked about how the Beast took care of you because you can't hold your liquor."

"There's nothing else—"

"What about your feelings for Ben?" Tamara asked.

Karen nodded. "If you're starting a relationship with a man, you should explore the emotions around it. It's part of the healing process."

"I don't need healing," Chloe snapped then cringed. "What I meant was that I've gone through the process already. I left my abusive relationship four years ago."

"I got rid of the last loser who beat on me almost ten years ago." Karen crossed her arms over her colorful peasant blouse. "I still have issues that come up." She pointed at Chloe. "Not once in the time I've worked here have you had a boyfriend. Ben Haddox is the first."

"Ben isn't my boyfriend. It's obvious he's out of my league. Look at him and look at me."

"You're the one who needs to take another look," Karen argued. "I'm sure your mother loved you, but she did a number on your self-esteem. You're a beautiful woman both inside and out. It's past time you honor that."

Chloe swallowed, her throat suddenly full of sand. Her mother had spent years lecturing her on what "average" women could expect out of life. She knew rationally it had been the depression talking but also understood somewhere deep inside that she'd never thought of herself as anything but average. Ben made her feel like she was so much more, and she feared she was just setting herself up for a harsh dose of reality when this month was over. "He's the last man I'd seriously go out with. He's loud and brash and his temper has made him famous. I can't be with someone like that."

"And yet . . ." Tamara raised her perfectly shaped brows. "There was a booty call."

"It wasn't a . . ." Chloe took another sip of the milkshake. "I was drunk."

Sally nodded. "Not a prerequisite for gettin' a little something, but it helps."

"I was in no state for anything."

"So did he . . ." Tamara began, her tone careful, "What exactly went down with the two of you?"

"Nothing." Chloe released a breath. "He took care of me. I freaked out, melted down, fell on my face. The epitome of a sloppy drunk. Ben got me home safely, cleaned me up, and stayed with me while I slept it off. He was gone by the time I woke up this morning."

The women let out a collective sigh. "He has a temper," Karen said, "but has only been gentle with you. In contrast to your ex-husband, who was quiet and controlled . . ."

"Until he lost it," Chloe finished. She unwrapped the burrito and took a bite, hoping the grease would calm her rolling stomach. Her pounding heart was another matter. "This is why it's easier to be alone."

"It's also lonelier," Karen said softly and Tamara nodded.

"I miss men," Tamara said. "How I feel when the right man touches me. How they smell." She looked at Chloe. "I bet Ben Haddox smells great."

"He does," Chloe admitted. He smelled like spice and man, and she thought she'd never grow tired of nuzzling into his neck and breathing him in. When she'd turned over in her bed this morning, Ben's faint scent had clung to the quilt in the same way she wanted to hold on to him and never let go.

Dangerous territory.

She took another bite and glanced toward the front of the store. "Sally, will you flip the lights and unlock the door?"

"Is that your way of saying you're done talking about Ben?" Karen asked, grabbing a stack of papers from the printer.

"Yep." Chloe didn't bother to deny it. "Plus I have a moms' group coming in this morning for a toddler class. I appreciate your support, I really do. But no matter what happens, this store and all of you are my first priority. I won't forget that."

♦ ♦ ♦

"Of course Abby and Zach are my first priority." Ben shifted in the metal chair of the Colorado Territorial Correctional Facility visiting room. He'd driven the couple hours down to Cañon City to visit Cory. The prison was situated in a wide-open valley flanked by rugged mountain ranges in the distance. But the stark brick building with barbed wire strung around its concrete perimeter held an ominous feeling of hopelessness despite the beautiful surroundings.

It had been two days since he'd left Chloe asleep in her bed the morning after her girls' night. She'd texted him to apologize again, but had otherwise avoided his calls. He didn't want her to be embarrassed, yet he sure as hell didn't want to spend another night away from her. Abby and Zach were at The Toy Chest today giving him a perfect excuse to stop by, but Ben needed to see his younger brother.

"Christ," he mumbled when Cory's expression remained surly. "I dropped everything to come to Denver and take care of them."

"Big-shot Ben saves the day," his brother snapped. Cory was thinner than the last time Ben had seen him, with dark shadows beneath his eyes. He tapped his fingers on the table between them, and Ben could tell his knee was jiggling underneath the table by the way his whole body moved. Cory had been filled with a wild energy when they were kids, constantly moving until he'd fallen asleep at night. "That's what you want everyone to believe, right?"

"No." Ben shook his head. "It's not like that. Only my publicist even knows about the situation."

"Because you're embarrassed by my kids?" Cory leaned forward. "They're both *my* kids, Benny. Don't forget that."

"I haven't." Ben realized he'd yelled the words when people from the nearby tables turned to stare. Glancing at the guard standing by the door, he smiled and nodded to show he had things under control. He *needed* to get himself under control. He'd visited Cory once before when he'd first arrived in Colorado, but at that time his brother had been contrite and grateful to Ben for his willingness to help. That Cory bore little resemblance to the angry man sitting in front of him now.

"What's going on? Are you in trouble in here? Is something bad—"

Cory gave a sharp shake of his head. "I talked to Zach last week."

"He was happy to hear your voice," Ben said with a nod. "Both kids want to see you."

"No. I don't want them anywhere near this place. But that doesn't mean you can ignore the fact that I'm still part of their lives."

Where the hell was this coming from? "I'm not trying to—"

Cory held up a hand. "Zach told me he and Abby are helping in old man Butterfield's toy store."

An uncomfortable ripple of guilt sailed up Ben's spine. He should have thought of the fact that The Toy Chest would come up in conversation when the kids talked to their father. But Cory's life in prison seemed so separate from what was happening in Denver that Ben hadn't prepared for this. He nodded slowly. "He got caught shoplifting and

Abby did some damage in the store trying to make a distraction so he could get away."

The barest hint of a smile curved one side of Cory's lips. "It's a wonder that girl isn't actually my flesh and blood. She's just like me."

"She's nothing like you," Ben bellowed. The prison guard made eye contact again. "Sorry," Ben called to the man with a wave before turning his attention to Cory. "She is smarter than both of us combined. She's helping with the online business, social media and marketing. Do you know how talented she is with web development, e-commerce, and all that technical stuff?"

Cory shifted, dropping his gaze to the floor. "Of course I know," he muttered, but Ben didn't believe him. "It doesn't change anything. I don't want her anywhere near that store."

"It's good for her, Cory. For both of them."

"What the hell happened to the plan of shutting it down? You made a promise to me."

Ben rubbed a hand across his jaw. "The plan is still there. But Chloe . . ." He stopped at the flicker in his brother's eyes. "The new owner has taken Abby under her wing, and she's not Butterfield. Our gripe was with him."

"My problems started with the store." Cory let out a disgusted snort. "You're fucking the new owner," he all but spat. "Does it make you hot to bend her over the stuffed animals when you think of my life being royally screwed?"

"Shut up, Cory. You don't know what you're talking about. The kids have nothing to do with what happened to you, and neither does Chloe."

"You promised me, Benny." Cory's voice cracked as he put his elbows on the table then covered his face with his hands. "I have nothing in here. My life is worth nothing."

"That's not true," Ben argued automatically. "Zach and Abby need you to stay strong, Cory."

"I've screwed up so many times, and all of my problems started with The Toy Chest. Everything went downhill from the moment you gave me the idea to go after Butterfield. I can still see him gloating when the cops came through the door."

His brother glanced up at him then, his eyes shining with anger and regret. It hit Ben like a punch to the gut. When he'd impulsively suggested revenge on Stan Butterfield all those years ago, it had been an empty threat to placate Cory and assuage Ben's own guilt. The promise he had made about the store was more for his own benefit than Cory's. He'd been the one who needed a channel for his anger. Or so he'd thought.

"I'm going to take care of it," he said quietly. His doubts about shutting down the store disappeared for the moment. He still understood that Chloe wasn't responsible for what had happened to Cory, but it didn't matter. He looked at his brother's slumped shoulders and resolve coalesced inside him. Yes, he'd made a promise and he wasn't going to renege on it, not when his brother was depending on him. He hadn't been able to keep Cory safe as a boy, but he wasn't going to let him or Abby and Zach down now.

Even if it ruined what he had with Chloe.

CHAPTER TWELVE

"She's a good kid." Chloe joined Sam in peering around the curtain that separated the small classroom in the back of the building from the main store.

Abby sat in the big rocking chair in front of a group of eight toddlers and their parents for the weekend story-time hour that would be followed by crafting. Chloe had learned a lot of things about running a toy store, but she didn't have a crafty bone in her body. Lucky for her, Sam did and often helped out with the projects Chloe coordinated for her customers.

Like many Saturdays when Sam was volunteering, there were more dads in attendance than normal. Sam's career as a model had been short but prolific, and she'd graced not only a few swimsuit editions but appeared on the runway as one of the most popular lingerie models. The first time she'd come into the store, Chloe thought she was going to deal with a mutiny from some of the regular moms, but Sam was so unaffected by her own image it was hard to hate her, even if she was a ridiculously beautiful woman.

"She's had great ideas for the website and is a natural with the kids." Chloe flipped closed the curtain and held out her fingers for inspection. "I've got paper cuts all over my hands from boxing up merchandise and running it to the post office this week. I'll be lucky to keep some of the toys in stock, the way they're selling."

"Is it enough to pay the back rent?" Sam asked, concern shining in her pale green eyes.

"I'm getting there." Chloe tapped her fingers on the counter. "But Laura, one of my employees, needed some help."

"Chloe, no." Sam shook her head. "You promised Kendall and me no more expenses until the store is secure."

"I know, but her son is thirteen and had an emergency appendectomy. She only has catastrophic coverage, and I'm afraid if she doesn't get the support she needs now she'll go back to her husband. This is important."

"So is your future. You won't have one if you lose The Toy Chest."

Chloe turned and greeted a regular customer who passed by the register.

"Unless . . ." Sam leaned closer. "You're ready to apply for your social work license."

"Why would you suggest that?"

"Because ever since I've known you, your focus has been more on helping and counseling the women who work for you than on selling toys."

"I sell lots of toys."

"To pay for the rest of it."

Chloe sniffed. "I'm not having this conversation. Stan Butterfield trusted me with his legacy. He loved this store, and he gave me hope at a time when I didn't have any of my own. I don't know why Ben is determined to shut this place down, but I won't let him win."

"You're fighting for what you want," Sam said with a smile.

"I'm working," Chloe answered, nudging her friend out of the way when Zach brought a young boy and his grandma toward the register.

She rang up their purchases as Sam talked to Zach. As she bagged the purchase, her skin started to tingle and her breath caught in her chest. She knew without looking up that Ben had arrived to pick up his niece and nephew.

She took her time tying a ribbon around the handles of the brown bag then took a few extra minutes to speak to the customers about their plans for the rest of the day. As if more time would lessen her reaction to Ben. If anything, her body became more aware, and by the smug grin on his face when she glanced over, he knew it.

When the customers walked away, Chloe took a calming breath and stepped around the counter. "Have you two met?" she asked, shifting her gaze between Ben and Sam and hating the fact that they looked like the perfect couple standing next to each other.

"Zach introduced us," Ben answered.

Although his short-sleeve linen shirt and cargo shorts were as casual as Sam's flowing sundress, they could have been heading out to a beach party in the Hamptons rather than crowded into her neighborhood toy store. Her mother's delicate voice rang in her head: "You're a six, Chloe. Don't try for anything above a seven or eight."

Both Ben and Sam were clearly past ten, and she waited to see some spark of awareness flicker between the two of them. Instead, Sam barely looked away from whatever Zach was explaining to her and Ben moved forward to trace his finger along the bone of Chloe's wrist.

"Not here." She jerked away even as a tremor of need rolled through her. She never thought she'd crave a man's touch the way she did Ben's.

"Everywhere," he whispered but stuffed his hands into his front pockets.

The truth of that one word made a blush rise to her cheeks. Caught in his smoldering, blue-eyed gaze, Chloe brought her hands up to cover her flaming cheeks. Ben's grin spread, then Zach tugged on his hand.

"Can I go to Bryce Hollow Camp next weekend?" He bounced up and down on his toes. "Chloe will be there. They have archery and a ropes course and canoes on the lake." The more he talked, the more he bounced. "I've never been in the mountains for real."

"What do you mean you haven't been in the mountains?" Ben asked, his brows furrowing. "You were born in Colorado."

"In *Den-ver*." Zach drew out the word as if speaking to a toddler. "I see the mountains, but I've never been in them. I think it's different."

Sam chuckled at that. "It's way different."

"What's Bryce Hollow?" Ben's gaze flicked between Sam and Chloe.

"I run a summer camp for kids from the city whose backgrounds haven't allowed them to spend time in nature. It's about ten miles outside of Evergreen as you start into the foothills."

"You went from modeling to summer camp?"

One of Sam's perfectly arched brows lifted. "Is that a problem?"

Ben shook his head. "Tell me more."

"We bring groups of kids up for a week at a time and they participate in all kinds of outdoor adventures. But more importantly, we work on self-confidence, teamwork, personal responsibility, and problem solving. The largest percentage comes from Denver, but we have a few who fly in from other cities. Most of them are like Zach. They've lived in the city all their lives. These are new experiences, new friends, and lifelong memories."

"I'll think about it," Ben offered noncommittally. "Or I can take you and Abby up to Bachelor Gulch for a few days."

As Sam groaned, Chloe stifled a chuckle at the mention of the swanky resort outside of Beaver Creek near Vail.

"Not exactly roughing it," Sam said with an eye roll.

"Roughing it isn't all that it's cracked up to be."

"It is at my camp," she shot back.

He turned to Chloe. "Why are you going?"

"I donate craft supplies each summer and head up when I can to help. This year our friend Kendall . . ." She paused, swallowed. "Well, we're both going up."

Sam leaned in closer. "Kendall is the anchor of a morning news show in Denver. She's spotlighting the help Chloe gives to the camp as part of a feature on the toy store." She gave Ben an exaggerated wink. "It's extra PR to drum up business, if you know what I mean?"

Chloe saw his jaw tighten. "I know what you mean," he answered.

"Abby can come too, right?" Zach switched his wide-eyed gaze to Chloe. "She can help teach and stuff."

"Fine with me," Sam said when Chloe's gaze flicked to her. "Zach, would you grab one of those boomerangs from the front for me? I want to try using it as part of a teamwork exercise at camp."

Zach nodded and zipped toward the front of the store. Sam nudged Ben in the ribs then poked at his stomach. "Oh, nice. Six-pack, right?" She asked the question to Chloe, who blushed again.

"How would I know?"

"You know," Ben and Sam said at the same time.

"More like a twelve," Chloe mumbled, which drew a sigh from Sam and a chuckle from Ben.

"So what do you think, Chef Hottie?" Sam asked. "From her interactions with kids in the store and how she takes care of her brother, Abby would make an excellent junior counselor. I've got a leaders-in-training program she could be a part of if she wants. She'll learn to work with other teens, and it's great for a college application."

Chloe saw Ben pale slightly. "I don't think they've gotten to the college-application stage," she said to Sam then turned to Ben. "Next weekend is Father's Day. It might be easier if the kids were away and busy."

"We'll give you a weekend off," Sam added.

"I may not be their dad, but that doesn't mean I want to ditch them when things get tough." Ben directed the question to Sam but didn't take his eyes off Chloe. "What if I don't want a weekend off?"

"You don't want to spend time at a kids' summer camp," Chloe told him.

"You have to work while you're there," Sam answered, ignoring the glare Chloe shot her. "Everyone pitches in to help. Do you have any . . . skills you can offer?" Sam's smile was challenging, and although Ben might be surprised, Chloe was used to her friend's blunt manner and innuendo-filled comments.

Ben still watched Chloe, as if gauging her reaction to the conversation. "How about a class on cooking with whole foods instead of processed junk? If Zach and Abby are representative of your campers, some of them might not be familiar with food that doesn't come from a box or bag."

"Can you handle it without swear words?"

Ben switched his gaze to Sam. "I can handle anything you throw at me."

Sam smacked Ben lightly on the arm like he was her older brother. "Nice comeback, chef. The class sounds great. We do a camp garden every year, although it's too early in the season for harvesting much. But the class sounds perfect." She turned to Chloe. "I'm going to check on Abby and talk to her about working at camp," she said then disappeared behind the curtain.

"Are you really coming to camp?"

"Does it really bother you?"

She didn't quite know how to answer since everything about him left her hot and bothered. "It's a free country," she said even as she cursed herself for sounding so lame.

Feeling her face color, she turned for the counter, but he tugged her close. His fingers splayed across the middle of her back, warm and gentle. She'd noticed that whenever they were together, he touched her. A hand on her elbow, the soft brush of his lips against her hair. It was like she was an unbroken pony and he was working to settle her, moment by moment. In a way that's how she felt around him, skittish and wild but slowly growing accustomed to him. "I won't go to camp if it's a problem for you, Chloe. Your choice."

And he had a way of slipping through her defenses with little moments of unexpected sweetness. "You should," she said, nuzzling her nose into the crook of his neck. "But only because it would make Abby and Zach happy."

He chuckled. "Only Abby and Zach?"

"Yep," she whispered and lurched away when the curtain opened. Families spilled out along with Abby and Tamara, who was supervising the afternoon's activity. Abby was excitedly talking with Sam, so Chloe knew the girl was thrilled at the opportunity to work at the camp. The change in the teen in the past couple of weeks was amazing, and if Chloe admitted the truth, it made her miss her career as a social worker.

A line formed at the cash register and she hurried over, pretending Ben wasn't standing a few feet away as she rang up purchases. Or at least tried to. He was a difficult man to ignore, both because of his physical presence and his fame. Several of the women had their pictures taken with him, and, to Chloe's surprise, he gamely smiled and posed, even giving the camera his trademark scowl when asked for it.

After a few minutes, Tamara stepped behind the counter with Chloe. "Between Ben and Sam, this place might have a second run as a singles' spot. Word gets out we've got a former supermodel and a hottie celebrity chef hanging out here on a regular basis, we could charge a front-door cover." She laughed as Ben hoisted a young girl onto his shoulder while her mom snapped photos.

"They'd make a cute couple," Chloe murmured.

Tamara's head snapped back. "Um . . . she's about twenty years too young for him."

Chloe shook her head. "I meant Sam, not the kid."

"That man hasn't been able to take his eyes off you since he walked in here."

As if to prove Tamara's point, Ben glanced over at Chloe and smiled. Abby came up to him, then, and he set down the girl, signed a few autographs and, with a quick wave to Chloe, followed his niece and nephew out of the store. Chloe continued to wait on her customers, mainly dodging questions about why "The Beast" was in her store. When things died down, Sam came up to the desk, holding the boomerang she'd asked Zach to find for her. "Would you put this on my account?" She handed the price sticker to Tamara. "I think it will work well with what I'm planning for the kids."

The other woman disappeared into the back.

"Do you need a bag?" Chloe asked, not bothering to keep the snippiness out of her voice.

"What did I do now?" Sam made a face. "It was Zach's idea that he come to camp, and it will be great for his sister."

"It will," Chloe agreed.

"Is this about The Beast?"

"He doesn't like that nickname." Chloe handed over the boomerang. "Why did you invite him?"

"Because he's totally into you, and you like him, too." Sam slipped the toy into the side pocket of her purse.

"No . . . I mean yes." Chloe threw up her hands. "Whatever's between us isn't serious."

"It's serious when the man who built his career berating people on television volunteers to teach a bunch of kids how to cook. That's called dedication."

"To his niece and nephew."

"Not only them." Sam reached across the counter and gave Chloe a hug. "You and Kendall are leaving me behind. It's not fair."

"I'm not . . . it doesn't mean anything."

"Don't bother to deny it. The chemistry between the two of you . . ." Sam fanned a hand in front of her face. "I'm happy for you, Chloe. Truly."

"It can't last," she said with a sigh. "One of us has to lose."

"Then let's make sure it isn't you." Sam's tone was uncharacteristically serious. "You've been through enough."

"The problem is, so has he."

◆ ◆ ◆

Ben couldn't believe he was willingly putting himself through the torture of a weekend at a kids' summer camp. Sure, it was beautiful in the mountains west of Denver. They were only an hour out of the city, but it felt like another world up here. From the hillsides of pine trees and aspen groves to the craggy peaks jutting up in the distance, the drive toward camp was a huge change from the city. The blue sky seemed wider and brighter as they drove up the mountain pass and turned off the paved highway.

Abby and Zach had been so excited to go they'd downloaded the packing list from the camp's website as soon as they returned home and even convinced Harry to take them shopping for supplies. Ben's grouchy, hard-nosed father had spent his day off in the upscale camping equipment store near downtown trolling the aisles for backpacks, sleeping bags, bug repellent, and the other gear the kids had insisted they needed for the weekend.

Of course, Ben had provided his credit card for the trip yet had been surprised when they brought home bags of gear for him as well. But he'd refused to wear the wide-brimmed hat Abby insisted he needed for days in the bright Colorado sun.

"Do you know how much stronger the UV rays are at altitude?" she'd asked and while her concern was sweet, he'd stick with his Rockies ball cap.

As they drove the dirt road that led to the camp, he absorbed some of their excitement, or maybe it was simply the thought of being with Chloe again. He wanted to set aside his visit with Cory and all the problems between them to simply concentrate on the way she made him feel.

She'd gone up a day early with Sam, and the time away from her had made him restless and itchy, like his skin had shrunk around him. Alone in his bed, he'd tossed and turned, and it was more than a physical need. Being with Chloe calmed him in a way that made him long just to see her again.

Then he did. She stood outside a log cabin as they approached, wearing denim shorts rolled above her knee and a simple white T-shirt that framed her sweet curves. As she lifted a hand to wave, Ben glanced at Abby.

"I texted her," the girl said with a glimmer of a smile. "Don't act like you aren't dying to see her. You've been a crabass all morning."

"Language," Zach called from the backseat.

"Maybe I'm grumpy because my idea of a perfect weekend isn't dealing with bugs and kids." He frowned at her. "Trust me, you and your brother are enough."

"Fine." Abby sniffed. "You can just drop us off and leave. We'll be fine for the weekend."

Something like panic flashed in Ben, because maybe they didn't need him the way he needed them.

"Uncle Ben has to stay." Zach lifted himself to meet Ben's eyes in the rearview mirror. "You're an official teacher. That's a big deal."

Ben smiled at the note of pride threading through his nephew's words. How had his brother not been able to get his life on track when these two were depending on him? "I'm staying," he told both kids. "And I'm nervous, not grumpy." He slowed the Range Rover as he drove over a deep rut in the driveway.

"About camping?" Zach asked.

"About teaching the cooking class," Ben explained. "I've never done something like that before."

"But you take over restaurant kitchens all the time," Abby countered. "You yell and scream, but you don't get nervous."

"I do, but I don't show it on camera. Kids are different. I doubt they care about my reputation or temper. They expect me to be a good teacher. I don't want to let them down." *I don't want to let you down,* he thought silently.

As if she could read his mind, Abby flashed a reassuring smile. "You'll be great. Zach and I will ooh and aah over the food." "Even if it sucks," Zach added then quickly said, "I know—language." The boy rolled down his window and shouted a greeting to Chloe. When Ben parked the car, both kids hopped out and ran over for a big hug. He wasn't the only one who'd been missing her.

"Nice place," he said as he ambled over, trying to appear cooler than he felt.

She gave him a brilliant grin that he felt all the way to his toes. Damn, he had it bad for this woman. "I'm glad you three are here. It's a great group of kids this week." She ruffled Zach's hair. "Lots of boys your age. They're starting at the archery range in about an hour."

"Awesome." Zach pumped his fist in the air. "Can I go check it out?"

"Unload first," Ben told him and clicked the button to open the tailgate.

As they pulled out the gear, a teenage boy approached from one of the gravel paths. Ben heard Abby suck in a breath and looked a little closer. The kid was probably her age or a year older. He had tanned skin and floppy blond hair bleached by the summer sun. He was several inches shorter than Ben and still on the thin side, but long-limbed in a way that made it seem like he'd fill out in a few years. He wore sagging board shorts, a Bryce Hollow T-shirt, and aviator sunglasses.

"Hey, Ms. Daniels," he called as he got closer. "Are these your friends?"

"Hi, Jake." She drew the teen forward. "Zach and Abby, this is Jake Masterson. He's one of the counselors for the boys' cabin this summer. Zach, you'll be in Jake's group for the weekend."

"Nice backpack," Jake told the boy, earning a huge smile from Zach.

"Abby," Chloe continued, "Jake will be doing your tour and initial orientation. The girls are on a hike this morning so he'll get you squared away and make introductions at lunch."

When his niece just stared, Ben elbowed her. "Earth to Abby . . ."

"Great," she stammered. "That's great. Fine. Wonderful."

If the kid noticed Abby's nerves, he didn't make a big deal of it. "Want some help with your stuff?" he asked.

"Sure," she said, her voice a squeak. Ben saw her shoot Chloe a look when Jake reached into the back of the SUV. Shepherding a girl through her teenage years was going to be more difficult than anything he'd faced in a kitchen.

Jake introduced himself to Ben, shook his hand, and then led Zach and Abby up the steps of the main cabin. When they'd disappeared into the building, Chloe turned to him. "Don't worry. Jake's a great kid. He's been coming to the camp since Sam opened it. I trust him completely."

"I don't trust any teenage boy," Ben said, setting the rest of his gear on the ground next to the Range Rover. "I know what he's thinking."

Chloe gave a small laugh. "Just because you got into trouble, doesn't mean all boys are going to."

"I'll be keeping an eye on him just the same." He slammed shut the rear access then turned to find Chloe standing right behind him.

"It's cute how protective you are of her," she said and reached up to brush a gentle kiss over his mouth. Her lips were soft and he smelled her normal scent mixed with sunscreen and a little sweat—the combination making the need banked inside him flare to life.

In one movement, he picked her up and stepped to the far side of the SUV. Pressing her back to the passenger door, he deepened the kiss at the same time he wedged a knee between her legs, balancing her so his hands were free to skim under her T-shirt and up her warm, bare skin.

She moaned softly, melting against him. Her mouth was as hungry and demanding as he felt, and it was several seconds before he could force himself to break away. "You missed me," he whispered, setting her gently to the ground but keeping his hold on her arms as her knees seemed to give a little.

The look she gave him as she nodded was so adorably flustered, he wanted to pull her to him once again.

"It's probably not a good idea for anyone to find us out here."

That comment must have registered with her because she jumped away from him. "No." She glanced to either side of the Range Rover then blew out a breath when she verified they were still alone. "You can't do that," she said, poking him in the chest.

"What? Say hello to you?"

"Kiss me until I forget everything but you."

He grinned at that admission. "I like kissing you, Chloe."

She straightened her shirt and readjusted the ponytail knotted at the back of her head. Ben's own knees went weak at the sight of the pale slip of skin between her shirt and shorts, which was the only explanation for what he said next. "I missed you, too. A lot."

She stilled, meeting his eyes as if trying to decide if that was the truth or if he was feeding her a line. He shuttered his gaze, not wanting to reveal how much she'd wormed her way in, as if by osmosis, and how it was difficult to imagine his life without her in it. He couldn't let her see that, because this was temporary. They'd agreed and he knew, in theory, it was the best thing for both of them.

But he hated the feeling that he'd disappointed her, the thin press of her lips as if she'd determined that his words were just part of the game they were playing. It didn't feel like a game to him, and it wasn't a casual summer fling. It felt real, which was scarier than anything else.

"They're only words," she said into the awkward silence hanging between them. "I know they don't mean anything, and I don't want them to." Her chin jutted out, like she'd issued a challenge, and he waited for the relief he knew should come. But instead frustration built inside him, reckless and hot, making him want to kiss the stupid lie right off her lips.

Except what if it wasn't a lie? What if he was the only one who needed more? Maybe what Chloe meant when she'd said she'd missed him was that she missed the sex. The chemistry that circled like a tempest whenever they were together. How could it truly be anything more with the end date stamped on their time together?

"Good," he said, feeding her his own particular brand of bullshit. He was so jumbled by all the new emotions coursing through him that he grabbed on to what felt familiar—being a jerk. Ben might not like the Beast nickname, but there was no doubt he'd earned it. "Because this isn't real. Don't pin any hopes on me, Chloe. I've been a jackass for so long, it's about the only thing I do well anymore."

Her eyes clouded even more, with hurt and unspoken recriminations. But before she could answer, he grabbed his gear from the ground and loaded it onto his back.

"I can show you where to go," she said quietly behind him.

"No need." He threw the words over his shoulder, ignoring the searing pain they caused in his chest. "I can find my own way, sweetheart. It's how it works for me."

CHAPTER THIRTEEN

Chloe zipped up her fleece jacket later that night, curling the edges of the blanket she sat on around her legs. It always cooled off in the mountains at night, and despite the warmth coming from the bonfire, the breeze off the lake seeped into her bones.

No one else seemed bothered by the temperature, so maybe the way she felt had more to do with Ben's attitude since he'd arrived at camp. Despite kissing her like he wanted her as much as she did him, since then he'd avoided her. There hadn't been one glance, one clandestine touch. He'd sat with Zach and the boys' group during dinner, and she'd even seen him giving opinions on nail polish colors with Abby and the other girls. But he'd pretended like she didn't exist, even as he joked with Sam and the other supervisors. The more he engaged with everyone except her, the more Chloe felt her heart cave in on itself.

She'd wanted him to deny what she'd said about him not meaning the words he spoke. Now she had to admit she'd hit the nail exactly on the head. Their relationship was nothing more than a fling, a bit of mindless fun made more intense by their competition over the toy store. Ben thrived on competition, and bedding her had just been one more way he'd wanted to prove that he could get the best of her.

There was no doubt she'd given him her best. Parts of her she hadn't known existed had been unearthed by him, dug out like a precious stone and polished to perfection in his arms. But it was fool's gold, she realized, and once again, Chloe had been the biggest fool.

She jumped when someone tapped her on the shoulder then relaxed as Abby folded her thin frame next to Chloe on the blanket. "How was your first day?" she asked, scooting over to give the girl more room.

"How can I have grown up in Colorado and never been to a place like this?" Abby sighed. "It's beautiful here, and everyone is nice. At my school, people think it's weird that I don't ski or climb fourteeners or go white-water rafting in the summer. No one at camp cares."

Chloe nodded. "All of the counselors are former campers, so many of them remember what it's like to spend your life in the city."

"A couple of the girls live in our neighborhood and invited me to hang out once camp ends."

"That's great, sweetie."

"Do you think Ben will let me switch schools this fall?"

Chloe couldn't imagine that Ben had thought far enough ahead to consider what he or the kids would be doing when school started again. "He wants what's best for you, so I'm sure he'll at least be willing to discuss options."

After a moment, Abby rested her head on Chloe's shoulder. "Thank you," she whispered.

"What did I do?"

"You gave me a chance after I wrecked your store when Zach took those marbles. You could have called the cops or made Ben give you a bunch of money to repay the damage."

"You've more than worked off your debt," Chloe said, slipping an arm around the girl. "And everyone deserves another chance."

"Did you purposely ask Jake to show me around camp?"

Chloe breathed a soft laugh. "I didn't, but he's a nice boy."

"And cute."

"There's that."

"I've never had a boyfriend," Abby said quietly. "He asked me to hang out after the kids go to bed tonight. Do you think he likes me?"

"I think he'd be silly not to like you. But you're young, Abby, and Sam has rules about the counselors. I hope Jake wants to get to know you better, but if he tries anything else—"

"Like making out with me behind a Range Rover?"

Chloe stiffened.

"It's ok," Abby said quickly. "No one else saw anything. I left my headphones in the car so I came back out and . . ."

"I'm sorry. You shouldn't have seen that. It didn't . . . it doesn't . . . there's nothing going on between your uncle and me."

"He's not really my—"

"Enough with that," Chloe said, lifting a hand. "Harry and Ben are your family, whether you like it or not."

Abby made a face. "I guess I like it," she admitted after a moment. "Except for Harry running around in his boxers."

"No doubt," Chloe agreed.

"I like you and Ben together, too. He's nicer since he met you. Calmer."

"I think that has more to do with you and your brother than me. Regardless of Ben and me, you're young and need to take things slowly with any boy you like." She leaned closer and pushed Abby's bangs out of her eyes. "I hope your mother told you this, but in case she didn't, I want you to know that you have value, Abby. As a person and a woman. Value and power. Hold on to those things and surround yourself with friends who respect who you are inside. Especially boyfriends. You deserve to be treated like the amazing girl you are. But you have to believe that before anyone else will."

Abby's gaze shifted to her lap then back to Chloe. "I don't think Mom realized that for herself, and she sure never mentioned it to me. She had some bad boyfriends, you know?"

"I can imagine," Chloe told her, "But I'm sure she wanted something better for you."

"Do you believe you deserve a good boyfriend?"

"I'm trying," Chloe whispered with a half smile. "It's taken a long time for me, and I've made some big mistakes."

"Ben isn't one of them," Abby said with the innocent conviction of the inexperienced.

Chloe just smiled, then Sam announced it was time for the campers to head to their cabins. Abby gave Chloe a quick hug then scrambled to her feet. "I've got to help round up the girls."

"I'll see you in the morning, sweetie."

Chloe stood as the campers disappeared down the path toward the cabins. She helped collect trash and extra blankets and made sure the fire was extinguished before making her way toward the main lodge building where she was staying with Sam.

She walked slowly, allowing the others to get well in front of her. Tonight she wasn't in the mood for making conversation and wrapped her arms around herself as she ambled down the path. Pulling in deep breaths, she tried to enjoy the quiet of the night and let the fresh smell of pine soothe her.

A hand reached out from the darkness, pulling her into the shadows of a copse of fir trees a few hundred feet from her cabin. It was a testament to how far she'd come in the past few weeks that she didn't panic or scream. Or maybe it was that she immediately recognized Ben's scent and the heat that always radiated from his body. As he pulled her against his chest, flashes of sensation zinged along her spine. It was so easy to lose herself in this man, to forget everything else but her response to him.

But she pushed away when he lowered his mouth to hers, the words she'd just said to Abby ringing in her ears. *I deserve more*, she thought to herself, and if Ben couldn't give it to her, she was going to claim it without him in her life.

"No more," she breathed, her lungs constricting along with her heart.

"You're cutting me off?" She could hardly make out his face in the darkness, but the hurt and disbelief in his tone were clear.

"This was always meant to have an end date, Ben. Don't pretend it was any other way, especially since you've been avoiding me all night."

"Maybe I'm not the one pretending," he suggested, the words soft but harsh, slicing across her heart.

"I can't play games. I don't have it in me. I thought—"

"Damn it, Chloe," he yelled, and she heard some creature rustle in the dark underbrush around them. She took a step away, but Ben followed her. "I'm sorry," he said, making his voice calmer. "This isn't a game for me. I want more." As her eyes adjusted to the dim moonlight, she saw that his eyes were shining with emotion. Her body reacted even as her skin went cold.

She didn't want to see that look in his eyes, didn't want him to draw her in, snaking past all the defenses she'd built to protect herself after having her identity shredded to bits. "I want to be the kind of man who deserves you. But you have to give me a chance."

"What happens at the end of the month?"

"You get the store or I do. Either way I want to be with you." He dragged a hand through his hair. "I'll give you the store if that's what it takes. I want to be with you. I want to take care of you."

Chloe sucked in a breath as if he'd slapped her. He couldn't know what those words meant, how her mother had always told her she was the type of woman who needed someone to take care of her. That had been her mom's biggest dream—mostly because after struggling for years as a single mother, she'd wanted a different life for Chloe.

She wished her mom were still alive so she could ask whether it was simply overprotectiveness or if Judy believed something was intrinsically lacking in Chloe that made her unable to fend for herself. Even Jonathan had used those words after he'd hit her. "Let me make it better, baby," he'd crooned as he pressed ice or a wet cloth to her scrapes and bruises. "Let me take care of you."

Ben was innocent of the pain and shame that she'd had heaped on her in her past, but he also reminded her why she'd walled herself off for so long. No one in her life had believed Chloe could handle things on her own, could make a decision. Even if the toy store wasn't her ultimate dream in life, she controlled things there. Yes, it was small scale, and the consequences were minuscule in comparison to her previous counseling work. But it was safe and easy and she'd created it on her own.

Her body longed to lean into Ben, to let him wrap her in his bulk and strength until she forgot everything else. But that wouldn't fix what was broken inside her. The parts that had only recently started to mend back together. If anything, she would put herself at risk for splintering again, and this time—with this man—she wasn't sure if she'd ever recover from that kind of pain.

"No," she whispered, her voice sounding hollow in her own ears. "It won't work."

"You don't mean that."

"I do, Ben. I've learned to take care of myself, and that's what I'm doing. It's what I have to do." She whirled away, stumbling back to the path, her flashlight making bobbing ribbons of light on the dirt trail. But even though she was doing this to protect herself, her heart felt like it was breaking anyway.

◆　◆　◆

"Does anyone recognize this?" Ben held up a bouquet of green leafy herbs in front of the group of kids standing around the perimeter of the large work island in the camp's commercial kitchen the next morning.

"Lettuce," the boy standing next to Zach called out.

Ben smiled and shook his head. The kid had guessed lettuce for every green food Ben had asked them to identify. "It's actually basil, which is an herb best known for seasoning tomato sauce and making pesto. It likes all the sun we get in Colorado, and you can even plant it in a pot." He pointed to the neat rows of basil plants on the far counter. "I've got a little basil for each of you to take home at the end of the week. Today we're going to try it in a homemade pasta sauce and pesto pretzel twists I made this morning." He glanced at Sam, who was standing behind him at the front of the kitchen.

"Nice work, chef," she said, "I'm impressed. You should be proud of yourself."

He thought about throwing out a pithy retort but settled for, "Thank you." He *was* proud of himself. This past hour in the kitchen and the prep work that had gone into it made him feel good in the same way cooking dinner for his family did.

"Any questions while we plate the food?" Sam asked the kids.

"Have you ever beaten anyone up on your show?"

"No." Ben shook his head.

"Even after they turned off the camera? Remember that time the chef in New Jersey threw a plate of food at you? You were so mad they had to beep out half of the episode. You made him cry."

Ben cringed, rubbing his hand along the back of his neck. "I remember." What he also remembered was discovering the chef, who also owned the restaurant where the show was filming, had a little girl with a congenital heart defect. His marriage was in shambles and he was struggling to pay the bills both at home and his restaurant so had taken to cutting corners in the kitchen to save money.

"Nothing happened off camera," he told the kids. Actually, what had happened off camera was that Ben had given the man a check to cover the surgery his daughter needed. That had been the beginning of the end of him wanting to live up to his Beast reputation. It was when it dawned on him, much too late, that he wasn't the only one with a past that had screwed him up or with things he was trying to work through. He glanced at Chloe, who stood in the back corner watching the class.

He'd been so angry at her rejection last night that his first impulse was to leave camp entirely, to head back to Denver and down to one of the trendy bars he'd avoided since he'd been in town. There was an almost irresistible urge to lose himself in alcohol and his celebrity status, and to seek out the bullshit hangers-on he knew would be waiting for him. The camp was too quiet, with time for him to think and reflect on why he wasn't enough for her.

As he'd stalked back toward his cabin, car keys jingling in his hand, he'd gotten a glimpse of Zach and some of the other boys through the window of the cabin. They were having a major-league pillow fight and the pure joy on his nephew's face had stopped him in his tracks. Although Abby did most of the caregiving, it dawned on Ben that Zach, as much as he seemed unaffected by the circumstances of his life, probably had never had a simple sleepover or time to hang out with friends. Bryce Hollow was truly the first time the kid could have fun without worrying about what was coming next in life.

So he'd veered off the trail into the boys' cabin, picked up a pillow, and challenged Zach and his new friends to the ultimate boy-versus-Beast pillow fight. Of course, Ben had been properly pummeled and the counselors had eventually shut down the shenanigans, but the hug Zach had given him as he'd left the cabin had made the whole weekend worth it. For once in his life, Ben hadn't walked away or let his temper get the best of him.

"Have you ever met Bobby Flay?" one of the girls asked.

"Yep. A few times. He's a good guy."

"Is he a better chef than you?" another kid chimed in.

"He has his style and I have mine." Unfortunately, Ben's style was more about proving he could best other chefs than about the food he prepared.

"Did you ever beat him up?" the same kid from before asked.

Bloodthirsty little cuss. "Never." Ben looked directly at the kid. "There are better ways to solve problems than with your fists."

"Like screaming at people and making them cry?" the boy suggested, making Ben wish he could burn every recording of *A Beast in Your Kitchen* that was out in the world.

He looked around the room for rescue, but all of the kids and counselors were staring at him expectantly. Sam was smiling slightly and Chloe's expression was blank. To Ben, the lack of emotion was worse than anything else she could have shown him.

"Like talking about problems and working them out," he told the boy. The kid rolled his eyes. "That's not what you do on TV."

"You're right," Ben agreed, taking a step forward. He knew many of these kids had suffered through upbringings similar to his, but he also knew there was a better way to cope with issues than his way. Chloe had shown him that, and even if she didn't want to be with him, he needed to make her understand that their time together meant something to him. That she *still* meant something, more than he even understood.

"Yes, I yell on camera and I've done way too much of it." He pointed to his niece and nephew. "Abby and Zach can tell you that."

"He's getting better," Zach said immediately. "He makes more sense when he's not screaming."

Ben threw his nephew a wry smile. "I'm learning to control my temper because I want people to hear the words I say, not just my temper. I grew up in a family of people who fought all the time. Maybe some of you can relate to that?" He glanced around as he said the words, his skin burning after revealing such a personal detail about himself to a group of kids. But several of them nodded and a couple just stared at the ground. Those were the ones who understood what he was saying.

"What I know now and I hope you understand way before I did is that you are in control of who you are and what you want to be. You don't need to yell or fight to have that kind of power. It's already yours, and you need to hold on to it. Don't let anyone make you believe you're less than you know yourself to be. Find people, like your friends and counselors at this camp, who like you for who you are. Who take care of you and protect you, not tear you down or force you to be someone you're not. You deserve people in your life who believe in you and your dreams."

He picked up one of the plates from the counter. "Do you know how many people told me it was stupid to want to become a chef? That someone like me had no business in a fancy restaurant? I used my anger as a shield because I was so damn . . ." He looked at Abby. "I mean so darn scared."

"What's so scary about cooking?" one of the older boys asked. "My mom cooks every night."

"Then you're lucky, and you better say thank you and compliment whatever she serves." Ben took a step forward and the boy nodded his head and swallowed. "But it was different for a big, troublemaking teenage boy. I got mad, and I stayed mad for a long time. But that's not what made me a success. What made me a success was that I love cooking. The anger fueled me, but the love made me good at what I do. Figure out what you love to do, and don't get caught up in what other people think of it like I did. Because being mad all the time isn't actually much fun." He leveled a look at the boy who'd asked the original question. "Despite how it looks on TV."

The boy stared at him for a moment then nodded. "Love is cool," he said casually. "Now can we try the food? I'm starving."

Ben laughed and the other kids cheered, but before they could start eating, Sam let out a long whistle. "I think all of us want to thank Chef Ben, for not only an enlightening cooking demonstration, but also for his very wise words." She flashed him a cheeky grin. "Nice switch from Beast to Beauty." Then as she led the campers in a round of applause, Ben found himself actually blushing.

"I didn't mean to go off on that tangent," he said quietly as the kids took their plates out to the mess hall.

"It was a good tangent," Sam said, patting him on the back. "And a helpful class. A lot of these boys don't have male role models in their lives, so to hear from someone like you that they can follow their dreams is a big deal. Even if you weren't saying it for their benefit."

Ben's gaze flicked to the empty corner of the kitchen. "Chloe left."

"A few minutes ago," Sam confirmed. "She heard what you needed her to hear."

"She thinks I'm playing games. That this is all about winning."

"Isn't it?"

"Despite what I told the kids, fighting is what I know how to do. Sometimes it seems like it's all I know how to do."

"You know how to love, too."

To his surprise, Ben didn't hear any sarcasm in Sam's tone. "Yeah, right."

"I don't believe what you said about loving to cook was a lie." She nudged his arm. "And it's clear you love those kids."

"I've only really known them for a few weeks. Before that—"

Sam held up a hand. "You don't have to know someone for a long time to love them, Chef Biceps."

Ben smiled and shook his head at her description of him.

"Sometimes it happens in an instant." She squeezed his arm. "Or in a matter of weeks."

He studied her for a moment. "There's more to you than that million-dollar face."

"Just like there's more to you than the temper and the muscles." She squeezed him again.

"I think you like the muscles."

She gave him a grin that was more a friendly leer than flirty. "I'm only human. Want to take your shirt off?"

"You don't mean that," he said, shaking his head.

"I do, but only from a purely theoretical standpoint."

He laughed. "I'm going to sit down with the kids before you molest me."

"You wish."

He was almost to the kitchen door when Sam called his name. "There's a little cabin about halfway around the lake on the east side. It would be a good place to go if you wanted some privacy."

"I don't—" He paused as realization dawned. "Do you think Chloe wanted privacy when she left here?"

"Well, I can't tell you that," Sam said with an eye roll. "But if I had to guess—"

"Thank you." Ben sat with the kids for a few minutes, answering more questions, mostly about foods that were in season and what could be grown locally in Denver. He knew community gardens were gaining popularity in most urban cities, and decided he'd try to find out more about what Denver had to offer kids who might not otherwise have access to fresh food.

After checking in with Zach and Abby, he stopped by the staff cabin to grab a jacket then headed east around the lake.

CHAPTER FOURTEEN

"She told you where to find me." Chloe said the words softly as she heard someone approach around the edge of the old fishing cabin. She sat on the glider on the back of the deck, watching the sun start to leave pink-and-gold trails across the Colorado sky.

This time of afternoon had always been her favorite at camp. The temperature had dropped several degrees as billowy clouds gathered over the mountain that rose up beyond the western edge of the lake.

The main camp was peaceful, the kids clearly having their hour of mandatory quiet time before dinner. Most of them chose to read or journal. Often one or two of the boys would take a kayak onto the lake, but today the water was still, other than the occasional bubble of a fish surfacing.

"If you want me to go I will," Ben said from her side. "I just wanted to apologize for . . . well, everything."

She glanced up at him, his hair a soft silhouette against the pine trees behind him. He'd put on a light jacket, the collar flipped up and grazing his jaw the way she wanted to with her fingers. He'd worked hard to make himself a success and overcome everything he'd been up against as a kid. She knew how important it was for him to prove wrong the people who'd doubted him. Yet today he'd given those kids—and her—a glimpse of the softness inside him she'd glimpsed only late at night when they were together.

"Sit down." She patted the bench next to her.

Ben folded his tall frame into the corner of the glider. Even though he was clearly trying to keep his distance, the heat was coming off him in waves and she wanted to curl into it, to take the edge off the chill in the air whispering through the surrounding pine trees.

"You don't need to apologize," she told him after a moment. "But I do want you to explain."

"About the recipes I made today?"

Chloe barked out a laugh. "Nice try. Tell me about how you knew Stan Butterfield."

She felt rather than saw him stiffen.

"When I gave your father the baseball that had been Stan's, he seemed almost giddy."

"My dad has a long memory," Ben muttered.

"I don't think he's the only one."

"I told the kids today that everyone has a dream."

"It was great what you said to them."

"My brother's dream was to be an archaeologist." He pressed a hand to his forehead, rubbing it as if he had a huge headache. "It seems ludicrous now, with everything that happened. But Cory was obsessed after he found an arrowhead buried in our backyard. He was constantly digging, looking for more artifacts, bones . . . anything he could find."

"That's cute."

A ghost of a smile crossed his face. "It was annoying as hell. But The Toy Chest had this geoscience digging kit on display for months before Christmas the year Cory turned twelve. Cory would walk past every day after school to stare at it. Mom had left that summer, and to say Dad was out of control would be an understatement."

He shook his head. "But Butterfield had banned both of us from his shop."

She glanced at him.

"Zach comes by his sticky fingers honestly, I guess, because Cory had gotten caught more than once stealing piddly stuff from the toy store—mostly baseball cards and Matchbox cars. Every time Butterfield called the cops and my dad. He'd give my father these long lectures about raising reprobate boys and how the apple doesn't fall from the tree, etc. Dad wasn't a saint when he was younger, either."

"That had to be difficult for him."

"It definitely made him hate The Toy Chest. He would have never bought Cory that science set, even if he had the money. But things weren't like they are today. There was no Internet, only the big chain stores and a few neighborhood specialty places like Butterfield's. I knew Cory had to have that set. It had taken on some bigger meaning for him, you know? Like it was tied to his future somehow. I told him I'd help him get the money for it and we'd hide it from Dad. All that fall we did chores and odd jobs for people around the neighborhood, raking leaves and washing cars then shoveling snow as the weather turned colder."

"What were you getting out of it?"

He took a breath and stretched his long legs in front of him. "I was angry when Mom left. I'd always been more like Harry with my temper. Cory was a total mama's boy. I'm actually still shocked she didn't take him with her when she left. He cried himself to sleep for months after she was gone. We shared a room and I'd lie there at night, my pillow crammed over my head trying *not* to hear him. He needed something to take his mind off it, and the dinosaur crap did. I guess I wanted a peaceful night's sleep."

She wanted to reach for him, to offer some comfort against the painful memories and the idea that a young boy, already wounded from his mother's desertion, would be put in that position. But she knew from her training that talking was also part of healing. It took all her will-power, but Chloe forced herself to be an impartial listener as he spoke.

"It was just after Thanksgiving that we had enough money. It was going to be an early Christmas gift since there was no doubt Dad wasn't in a position to go all out for the holidays."

"How wonderful. Your brother must have been so happy."

He threw her a sidelong glance. "Stan Butterfield wouldn't let us in the store."

Chloe felt herself frowning. "What do you mean? Why not?"

"I told you Cory had lifted a few things from the shop. Butterfield decided we were trouble and he wanted nothing to do with either of us."

"But you had the money. Did you show him the money?"

Ben's smile was sad. "He accused us of stealing it. Made a big show of berating Cory and me in front of a store full of holiday shoppers. Bad seeds, future criminals. You name the insult, he used it."

Chloe couldn't reconcile the gentle, supportive older man she knew with the grown-up bully Ben described. "What happened? Did your Dad get involved?"

"Eventually," Ben said, his voice gravelly with emotion. "Cory and I went back home, me running my mouth as usual. Yelling and cussing about all the things I was going to do to get back at Butterfield. They were just words, but not to Cory. He snuck out that night, took one of Dad's baseball bats, broke the front window, and set fire to a display of baseball cards. All the things I'd threatened, Cory actually did. He went crazy. It was like his anger over Mom and Dad, about everything, bubbled up to the surface and spilled over in one horrible outburst. The cops came, of course, and Butterfield was livid. Dad begged him to handle it privately, promised to pay for the damage. But he pressed charges and Cory went to a juvenile detention center."

"Oh, Ben. No."

"It was only for a couple of nights plus a community service sen-tence, but it changed Cory. There was no more talk of archaeology or earning money for doing chores. No more tears in his pillow. That night hardened him. It changed his relationship with Dad and his reputation in the neighborhood. I tried to keep him away from the troublemakers, but he wouldn't listen, and, for a time, I ended up right there beside him. It was the only way I could protect him."

He jumped to his feet and walked a few paces toward the lake then back again. The light was softer now and the clouds had thinned. Shades of pink and orange streaked the sky, making shadows fall across the forest. Chloe held her arms tightly against her chest to ward off the cold seeping through her fleece sweater.

"I hated Stan Butterfield."

"I understand why."

"And I hated The Toy Chest. That store represented all the things that were screwed up in my family. I vowed that I'd find a way to shut it down. Butterfield loved the place. It was his whole life, and I wanted him to see it fail. Hell, there was more than one occasion when I was tempted to burn the whole thing to the ground and the consequences be damned."

"Ben."

He turned to her. "He owned it outright so there was never anything I could do. But when he died . . ."

"You bought the building."

He nodded sharply. "I'd forgotten about the vendetta, but Cory called me right away. He'd refused all my offers of help over the years. This was the only thing he ever asked me to do. Your lease came up for renewal just as he was arrested. Shutting down the store was the only hope I could offer him."

"And now Cory's kids are helping to save it. Does your brother know the two of them are working for me?"

"Yes, but I promised I'd put a stop to it."

"Yet you haven't. Why?"

"You gave them a second chance. What if Stan Butterfield had done that for Cory? What if he'd looked past the things he thought he knew about my brother and seen a kid in a lot of pain who needed help? The story of my family might be different." He looked at her, his blue eyes so dark they were almost black. "Abby and Zach needed something, and it turns out The Toy Chest was it. They need *you*, Chloe." He started to move toward her then stopped. His voice dropped to a whisper. "Just like I do."

Her whole body reacted to his words, skin buzzing and heart pounding. "You told the cooking class that your actions had been fueled by anger. It feels like my whole life has been governed by fear."

"That's not true. Look at all you've done to make a new life for yourself."

"In a box. I love the toy store, but what I love more are the women I'm able to help by owning it. It's safe and insulated . . ." She paused, stood, and closed the distance between them. "And you aren't, Ben."

"I want to be a safe place for you."

"I don't know if I can trust you."

He reached out and traced a finger along her eyebrow and down the edge of her face. "You shouldn't, but I want you to, Chloe."

"It's not easy for me. I know what my issues are, and I've worn them like a suit of armor for a long time. But . . ." She lifted up onto her tiptoes, brushed her lips over his. "You make me want to try."

He returned her kiss, but pulled back after a moment. His hands lifted to cradle her face. "The store," he said, searching her gaze. "I don't know—"

"We'll figure it out," she said, certain she wouldn't let it come between them again. "I understand why you want the space."

"But—"

She held a finger against his lips. "I still plan to win. I don't want any handouts or for you to give up because of what's between us. We both have reasons for what we want, but if the past few years have showed me anything, it's that I need to take care of myself. You have to let me do that, Ben."

"Damn it, Chloe," he muttered. "You're putting me in a position where I'm going to hurt you."

"Not if I beat you. I'm tired of doing the safe thing, of expecting someone to bail me out like I can't function on my own. You said you thought I was strong. Let me prove it."

He kissed her as an answer, but it was no longer gentle. This kiss was hot and demanding, but Chloe still wanted more. "In the cabin," she breathed against his skin. "I need you, Ben. Now."

He lifted her easily, her legs wrapping around his waist. Darkness was quickly falling around them, yet he had no problem negotiating his way through the door.

The cramped interior was even more shadowed than outside. Chloe had spent enough time there to know the placement of the furniture. She dropped to the floor and led him to the far side of the room, pulling back the covers on the small daybed there. Turning, she pushed Ben down then crawled into his lap, unzipping his jacket and pushing it off his broad shoulders. He tugged at the hem of her sweater and within moments they were a tumble of clothes and limbs, laughing as they jockeyed for position and power. Losing herself in this man and this moment was what she needed more than anything.

It freed her, made her feel strong and powerful in a way she'd come to depend on from Ben. He pushed her boundaries, but never further than she was willing to go. As he trailed kisses along her neck then down lower between her breasts, she understood it was because she did feel safe with him. In his own rough and edgy way, he made her feel cherished but still allowed her the independence she'd never before had.

He laughed as she pushed him to his back, straddling him and moving her hands over his beautiful bare chest. "Bossy," he whispered then sucked in a breath as she traced his nipple with her tongue. A moment later, Chloe felt the clasp on her bra pop and Ben was on top of her, peeling the fabric from her skin.

"I could look at you forever," he said, as he cupped her in his big hands.

The words spiked through her, making her body heat at the same time her heart swelled. She'd never considered wanting another forever after her divorce. In truth, she thought she'd sworn off men completely in the aftermath of that awful relationship.

It felt good to feel alive and wanted. She might be damaged, but she wasn't as broken as she'd once believed.

"What do you want, Chloe?" Ben's voice was a harsh rasp. He wanted her to say the words, to tell him how she wanted to be touched and where she was willing to go.

"Your mouth," she said on a hiss. "On me."

With a wicked gleam in his eyes, he obliged her. His tongued circled her nipple, and she moaned as he pulled the tight peak into his mouth. "Here?" he asked, moving his attention to the other breast.

"Lower," she whispered and earned a husky laugh.

He licked and sucked his way down her rib cage to the curve of her belly. When he paused, she arched underneath him, lifting her hips off the twin-size mattress. "Tell me, Chloe."

"More." She was too charged to care that she was panting. "Please, Ben. More."

He eased farther down her body, pulling her underpants over her hips then moving between her legs. The first time he'd looked at her so intimately, Chloe had almost died of embarrassment, but now she reveled in the desire clouding his eyes. He felt that way for her, and it was more than she'd ever dreamed of having.

When he touched her, she nearly exploded, came even closer to dropping over the edge as his mouth followed his fingers. She was lost within minutes, stars and fireworks and a thousand meteor showers exploding behind her eyes. But still it wasn't enough, and when he reached for his wallet, she grabbed it from him.

"In a hurry?" he asked with a smile.

She ripped open the condom and rolled it over his length, her fingers trembling at how he was both hard and soft under her fingertips. She met his gaze and didn't bother to hide what she felt for him. It was complicated and confusing, but this man had changed her, and, although she wouldn't say the word out loud, she let him see the love shining in her eyes. "I need you," she whispered. What she meant was *I love you.*

He stilled for a moment then drove into her, wrapping his arms around her back and pulling her close. They moved together, Ben's face buried in her hair, and it was perfect. She felt herself rise again, her body racing toward another release. Just before she reached the ultimate peak, Ben lifted his head, cupping her face between his hands. His beautiful blue eyes held hers, then his gaze opened and for an instant he wasn't hiding either. Everything he was feeling was right there, and when they came together and he whispered her name like a prayer, it sounded like *I love you.*

◆ ◆ ◆

Later that week, Ben felt happier than he'd ever imagined as he and Chloe walked toward the Mexican restaurant in downtown Denver where they were meeting her friends. It was a celebration dinner, although his dad had thrown a fit wondering why Ben would willingly be celebrating Chloe's success at making the toy store a household name in the Mile High city.

The morning before Ben came back to town, Chloe's friend Kendall had shown up with a camera crew to film campers having fun with merchandise from The Toy Chest. Kendall talked to Sam about the camp, the toys she'd donated, and the volunteering Chloe did with the kids. Then the reporter interviewed Chloe about the shop, the classes and family activities she sponsored, the store's history in the neighborhood, and why it was important for people to support local businesses.

She'd also interviewed some of the kids, including Zach and Abby, about the toys and about their experience at the store. Despite Ben's negative feelings about the store, he couldn't help but share in their excitement. The kids felt like they were part of something, probably for the first time in their lives. He discovered that Chloe hosted several mini-reunions for campers throughout the year. It was another reminder of her dedication both to The Toy Chest and to the community she served.

Overall, it had made Ben feel like the biggest ass on the planet for trying to shut it down. He'd tried to talk to Chloe again, but she brushed aside his concerns. Yesterday the feature story had aired on Kendall's highly rated morning show, and families had flooded the store looking for toys and activities to entertain their kids during the last weeks of summer vacation. His niece and nephew had stayed at camp for a few extra days, but he knew they'd be thrilled to see the increase in business.

A few people pointed at him as they walked into the crowded restaurant, and the hostess asked for his autograph and a photo before she seated them. Ben would have liked to refuse, but Chloe was continually entertained by his celebrity status and had gamely snapped the picture, encouraging him to throw an arm around the young girl's shoulders.

They approached the table where Kendall sat with a tall man with lighter hair and a suntan that spoke more of working outside than a life of leisure. He stood and gave Chloe a friendly hug before Kendall grabbed her and squeezed tightly.

"It was so good," Kendall confirmed. "We've gotten more hits on the station's Facebook page today."

Chloe couldn't hide her smile. "The store was crowded all day, and sales were at an all-time high on our website."

Kendall gave Ben a tiny wave and apologetic smile. "I hope it's ok when she foils your dastardly plans for ruining one of Denver's new favorite local businesses."

"That's not how it is," Chloe said, nudging her friend.

The other man straightened and stood taller, as if he expected Ben to start screaming at the cheeky journalist.

"It's fine," Ben said, earning a doubtful stare from all three of them. "I'm proud of her."

He was rewarded with a brilliant smile from Kendall. "Then welcome to the celebration, chef. This is my fiancé, Ty Bishop."

Ben stuck out his hand and shook the other man's, which was strong and callused. "I'm a fan of your show," Ty told him as they sat back down.

"That makes one of us."

Ty laughed as a waitress came by, taking Ben's beer order along with Chloe's request for a glass of sangria. "Our chef would like to make you something special, items that aren't on the menu." When she winced as Ben opened his mouth, he understood she also expected an outburst of temper.

Instead he smiled. "This is her night," he said, pointing to Chloe. "She's in charge."

The waitress switched her gaze to Chloe, who nodded even as she blushed. "Please tell the chef thank you."

"Between everyone staring at these two," Ty said to Chloe with a wink, "you and I might as well be invisible."

"Never to me," Kendall told him and leaned over to kiss his cheek.

Ben felt Chloe shift uncomfortably next to him. He draped an arm around her shoulder, pulling her close. "You're the star tonight," he whispered against her hair and she relaxed against him.

They talked a little more about the feature, then the conversation switched to Ty's work with conservation efforts around Denver. It was obvious that despite her local fame, Kendall was just as happy to let her fiancé have the spotlight. Ben liked getting to know people who weren't impressed by celebrity status, his or anyone else's. This was also the first double date he'd ever had, and the normalcy of it gave him a strange feeling of contentment.

The waitress brought a round of appetizers to the table.

"I can see how you're useful to have around," Ty said around a bite of black-bean-and-goat-cheese quesadilla. "This is fantastic."

Ben laughed and took a bite himself. In addition to the quesadillas, there were blackened jalapeños stuffed with cheese and artichokes. They were simple, but the cheese mixture perfectly balanced the heat of the peppers. He appreciated the efforts the chef had gone to and made a quick appearance in the kitchen to personally thank him and the rest of the staff.

When he returned, Chloe excused herself to go to the bathroom. Ben continued to talk with Kendall and Ty, but when the main course arrived and she still wasn't back, he glanced toward the hallway that led to the restrooms.

"I should check on her," Kendall said, following his gaze.

"I'll go." He stood, a sick feeling trying to take hold in his stomach. He pushed it away, telling himself that he was overreacting, but had no problem brushing past the other patrons, who called to him as he moved through the crowded restaurant.

As soon as he turned the corner from the main dining area, he saw Chloe in the small room obviously reserved for private events. He released a shaky breath then noticed the man standing across from her. Everything about him was average—his height and build, his slightly receding hairline and wire-rimmed glasses. Next to him was a short, plain woman with her hair pulled back in a tight bun. For a moment Ben figured the couple had seen Chloe on TV and stopped her to chat. As he got closer he realized Chloe's posture was rigid and the man was looking at her through eyes narrowed with rage.

Ben had a feeling he knew exactly who the guy was to Chloe, and he charged forward, the door to the room rattling on its hinges as he slammed it open. Three sets of eyes flicked to him, but all he cared about was Chloe. He expected her to look relieved to see him, but instead there was a warning in her gaze. He ignored it, of course.

"Let me guess," he growled. "You're the ex-husband?"

The man's gaze zeroed in on Chloe. "This is a private conversation that is none of your business."

"I'm making it my business," he bellowed, pointing at the couple. "You need to get the fuck out of here."

The woman started to move toward the door, but the man clamped a hand on her wrist.

"Who are you?" he asked Ben.

"I'm your worst nightmare," Ben spat back and thought he heard a snort from Chloe. He ignored that, too. After weeks of keeping his temper in check, it was almost a relief for anger to coalesce inside him, to channel all his latent frustration at the man who had hurt the woman he loved.

Whoa.

He opened his mouth but no words came out as the implications of that realization zinged through him. He glanced over his shoulder at Chloe, who looked at him as if he were crazy.

Crazy about her.

"Did you hire a meathead bodyguard now?" the man said to Chloe.

Ben snapped to attention. That little pissant had just called him a meathead.

He took a step forward, but paused when Chloe curled her fingers around his arm. She moved around him, her spine straight as she faced her ex-husband.

CHAPTER FIFTEEN

Chloe stepped forward. "I don't need a bodyguard, Jonathan." She hated that her voice shook. She cleared her throat and said more firmly, "I have a permanent restraining order that you're violating."

"I don't give a damn about the restraining order. It was bullshit back then, and it still is. I thought you moved to Milwaukee."

"I lied."

Something flashed in her ex-husband's gaze, as if he was happy she'd tried to deceive him.

"Hiding out, like the mouse you've always been."

Chloe felt energy surge off Ben and was certain if it weren't for her gentle pressure on his arm, he would have launched himself at Jonathan.

"I've stopped hiding. You have no claim to me. No power anymore. I let you knock me around, destroying my pride and my heart for too long. I'm stronger than that now, and I'm not afraid of you." The woman next to him stiffened and visibly swallowed.

"Thatta girl," she heard Ben whisper behind her.

"Whatever." Jonathan scoffed. "You needed me more than I ever needed you. Hell, the only reason I married you was because I felt sorry for you. We got in some fights. It's what couples do. If you wouldn't have blown it out of proportion—"

"You hit me, Jonathan." Her tone was quiet but sure. "It was abuse, and I'm guessing I wasn't the first or last." She turned to the woman next to him. "He's an abusive man, and if he hasn't yet, he will hurt you." The woman's mouth thinned as her gaze dropped.

"He already has," Chloe whispered.

"Shut up, Chloe." Jonathan gripped the woman harder. "My life is none of your business."

Chloe ignored him, speaking directly to the woman. "You can reach me through the toy store. We have a website with all my contact information. If you need help—"

"Shut up," Jonathan hissed through gritted teeth. If Chloe had been paying closer attention to her ex-husband, she would have heard the change in his tone. Jonathan's tell before he lost it had always been his voice. He became almost preternaturally quiet before he snapped.

"It doesn't have to be like this," Chloe said quietly. "You deserve better."

Jonathan's hand shot out like a rocket, grabbing a fistful of her hair before she could step away. Her months of self-defense lessons flashed through her mind, how she should lift her knee at the same time she tried to drive her knuckles into his Adam's apple. She wasn't the same person she'd been during her marriage, when she'd been afraid that fighting back would make it worse. But somehow she couldn't move as he wrenched her forward. Couldn't breathe as the smell of his sweat clogged her nostrils, and panic finally made its way into her consciousness. Then he was gone and she stumbled back, her hip slamming into the corner of a table before she righted herself.

A woman's scream pierced the air, and Chloe shook her head to clear it, focusing on her ex-husband's limp body now sprawled along the ground. Ben was standing over him, his broad back bristling with angry energy. She caught a glimpse of his face, the fury in his gaze as he lifted Jonathan by his shirtfront. Her ex-husband moaned as his head snapped back, blood gushing from a nose that was clearly broken.

As Ben drew back his arm for another punch, Chloe surged forward. "Stop! Ben, don't."

He paused but didn't release Jonathan or lower his arm. She grabbed on to him, feeling like she was trying to wrap her arms around a tank.

"I'm going to kill him for hurting you," he shouted.

"Let him go, Ben." He remained still for a moment then took a breath, pushing Jonathan away. She heard a commotion behind them and looked over her shoulder to see several members of the waitstaff staring at them.

"He attacked me." Jonathan sounded like a congested pig, squealing about how Ben had gone after him unprovoked as his date handed him a cloth napkin for his face. "He's a fucking beast, just like everyone says."

"Shut up, Jonathan," Chloe said then gave Ben a shove toward the door to the private dining room. "We need to get out of here."

The restaurant's manager and a man in a white uniform and tall hat who must have been the head chef stepped forward. Chloe could see a few of the patrons who'd gathered outside to watch the scene holding up cell phones. How much had they gotten on camera? A sinking pit formed in her stomach.

"Mr. Haddox," the manager said, "can you explain—"

"I have a restraining order against that man," she said quickly. She pointed to Jonathan, who was now slumped in a chair, his face covered by a napkin. His girlfriend stood next to him as the waitstaff swarmed about. She glanced up at Chloe then squeezed shut her eyes and nodded, a silent communication that Chloe understood all too well.

She didn't regret offering help to the woman but now wondered what price they would pay for the endeavor.

◆ ◆ ◆

An hour later, Ben tossed his cell phone to the coffee table in Chloe's living room.

"Well?" she asked, pressing a bag of ice to his knuckles.

"A couple of my endorsement deals have been canceled, and Michael expects more to roll in as the interview with your ex-husband gains traction."

With her free hand, Chloe punched a few keys on her laptop. "The YouTube video already has a few hundred thousand views. It's going viral, Ben. How much more traction can there be?"

"Michael's working to have the content taken down."

"But it's out there. You can't take that back."

No matter how much he wanted to. Whoever had taken the video of the fight had only recorded the last several seconds when Ben had lifted a much smaller and already injured Jonathan, ready to drive his fist into the man's face for a second time. Even Ben admitted he looked wild and out of control.

Of course, that was how he'd felt at the moment, but it wasn't the whole story. Unfortunately, Jonathan had given an interview from the ER to one of the local stations, claiming that Ben had attacked him unprovoked after Jonathan had made a seemingly innocent comment about Ben's skills in the kitchen. "What am I going to tell Abby and Zach?"

"I called Sam and explained the situation while you were on your phone with the publicist. There's a strict no-electronics rule at Bryce Hollow, but you're going to need to tell them before they get down here and find out."

"I spent a weekend talking to the kids at camp about how there are better ways to deal with problems than violence." He clenched his fist, hissing out a breath as his swollen, stiff knuckles protested the movement. "I'm a total fraud."

"You're not." Chloe shifted the ice on his hand. "If I come forward and explain why Jonathan—"

"No." Ben took the bag from her and placed it next to his phone. "You shouldn't have to defend me. I was the one who hit the guy."

"Because he went after me."

"I don't want that kind of attention on you."

"There's footage from the store airing alongside the other." She turned her laptop so that he could see the screen. "This was the day you were there when the class got out. Someone took a video of you posing for pictures. There's an online article about how you're unstable with your Dr.-Jekyll-and-Mr.-Hyde personalities."

He took the laptop from her hand, closed the screen, and added it to the pile on the coffee table. "Maybe there's something to that." He forced himself to meet her hazel eyes. "Saying I wanted to kill your ex-husband wasn't just me mouthing off. When he grabbed you . . ." He trailed off, lifting his fingers to tangle them gently in her curls. "It was different from anything I'd ever felt, Chloe. Yes, I blow my top in the kitchen, but with Jonathan I felt out of control for the first time in a long time. Even when you grabbed me, I wanted to shake you off and keep at him." He ran a hand through his hair, hating to say the words. "What if it was you instead?"

"You didn't," she answered immediately. "You wouldn't."

She brought her finger to his lips when he would have said more. "But for future reference, I need you to understand that I can take care of myself."

"It didn't look like it, Chloe. You didn't fight him."

"He took me by surprise. Fighting doesn't always have to mean beating the tar out of someone. I'm not looking for a superhero to save me."

He shrugged. "I want to keep you safe."

"I want the same thing for you." She crawled into his lap, straddling his hips and wrapping her arms around his neck. Her heart beating against his chest was the most wonderful thing he'd ever felt. "You put your career and everything you've worked for in jeopardy tonight."

"It doesn't matter."

"It will if Child Protective Services gets involved."

He shook his head. "That's not an option."

"Abby and Zach have to be your first priority, and you have to be a role model for them. There are better ways to handle problems than with your fists."

"Name one."

"Your words."

He coughed out a disbelieving laugh. "You sound like a preschool teacher." He wanted it to be a joke, to forget about those awful minutes and go back to the abandoned celebration.

"You scared me tonight," she whispered, and the words sliced across him like a razor blade. "I've had enough anger and fear in my life. I need to know I've left that behind."

Ben let the meaning of what she was saying sink into him. He understood why she felt that way, and he wanted to be that man. Damn it if he hadn't been trying to change. For her. For Zach and Abby. His whole body ached with the effort of it.

What if he couldn't? The anger he'd felt today had risen up swift and strong, like a raging current, and he'd almost drowned in the intensity of it. But when he'd finally given in and let it wash over him, it had felt good. Righteous, even, although he knew Chloe didn't see it that way.

And what if he exploded again only it wasn't directed at someone as deserving as her scumbag ex-husband? What if it were Chloe or one of the kids or their friends or an annoying teacher? That was the only good thing about the Beast persona. Before he'd come back to Denver, people had expected him to be a jackass. Hell, the producers on the show had encouraged it. Now when he got mad about something real, something that mattered, it came back to bite him.

Now it was all too much. The responsibility of two kids, of keeping his family on the right track. The thought of his own restaurant. Chloe's expectations.

He stood abruptly, setting Chloe none too gently on the sofa. She shook her head, reaching for him as if she knew what he was going to say.

"I didn't mean—" she whispered, tears welling in her eyes. "I'm upset about what happened tonight, the position you're in now."

"I'll be fine," he said, his voice tight. "But that was who I am, Chloe. As much as you can't deal with my anger, I can't spend my life tiptoeing around, worried that a muttered curse or frustrated outburst will send you running."

"Tonight was more than that, Ben."

"I was trying to protect someone . . ." He stopped, unable to say the words when they wouldn't change anything. "Someone I care about," he finished.

"I know."

He shook his head. "No. You're right. You need something more than I can give you, someone different than who I am. This was never meant to last. Isn't that what you told me?"

"I was wrong and scared. It's more than that and you know it. I love you, Ben."

Nothing she could have said would have affected him more. But he hid it, put his walls back up before he could give in to what his heart wanted. He wasn't that man, and it was time he stopped pretending. "Doesn't change the reality," he told her.

"Please." She stood and took a step closer to him. "Don't go. Not tonight."

"I—" His protest died on his lips when she lifted her shirt over her head then shimmied out of her dark jeans, standing before him in nothing but her bra and panties. A matching set, pink with lace edges and transparent enough that he could just see . . .

Nope. Not going there.

"You aren't playing fair," he said on a harsh breath.

"This isn't a game." Her voice was husky, and she pressed her full lips together as she reached for him.

He was screaming at himself on the inside, knowing he had to get away. If he took her in his arms now, he'd never let her go. "You say it's not a game, but it feels like we're both losing here." He took a step back, his fists balling at his sides. "Good-bye, Chloe."

He turned on his heel, but not before he saw the heartbreak in her eyes. It didn't stop him, though, and even through the aching hurt that threatened to overtake him, he kept moving. One foot in front of the other until he was out of her life for good.

◆ ◆ ◆

Chloe dragged herself to the toy store every day that week, but it felt like her heart had been ripped out of her chest the night Ben left. She no longer felt anything. In fact, none of her senses worked right. Kendall had brought her a pint of ice cream and brownies warm from her favorite local bakery the night after she'd humiliated herself in front of Ben. They'd smelled like nothing and tasted like sawdust, making her throat dry.

"He'll apologize and beg you to take him back," Kendall had told her.

But he wouldn't. Chloe was as certain of that fact as she was about the sun rising each morning. She couldn't accept Ben for who he was, and he had no intention of changing for her. She didn't blame him. His anger was as much a part of his identity as her fear was of hers. In fact, she'd spent most of her time that week staring at the computer screen in the back office, the site pulled up to begin the application process for her social work license. Her mouse had hovered over the Apply button until her wrist cramped, but Chloe hadn't pushed the button.

It was too much to go after something she really wanted when she was still such a coward. She'd continue to unofficially counsel the women who worked at the store. But what if she failed someone who really needed her? That was a chance she refused to take.

The Toy Chest continued to flourish. Between the news stories, the online marketing Abby had arranged, and the gossip about Ben frequenting the store, business was booming. In fact, Karen had showed her the monthly accounting that morning, and Chloe had just enough to pay the rent she owed and take care of her outstanding bills and expenses.

She'd won, although it no longer felt like a victory. As Ben said, she only felt like a loser. But she had an obligation to her employees and to Abby and Zach, who'd worked so hard on her behalf. She had an appointment set for tomorrow morning at the bank to get a cashier's check to deliver to the property management company. There was no question of delivering it directly to Ben. He'd made it more than clear that he wanted nothing more to do with her.

She was packing up more orders as a frantic knocking started on the back door that led to the alley behind the store. As soon as she cracked the door, Abby burst through, tears streaming down her face. The girl launched herself into Chloe's arms, sending them both back several steps.

"Sweetie, what is it?" Chloe tried to unlatch the girl's arms from her waist, but Abby held tight, a hollow, keening sound coming from her throat. "Is it Zach? Ben? You have to talk to me, Abby."

"Mmm . . . my dad," the girl finally choked out. "I . . . I mea-mean Cory." She sputtered, drew a breath, and sobbed again.

Cold dread seeped into Chloe's bones. She didn't know much about prison other than what she'd seen on television crime shows. If something had gone wrong with Ben's brother to have Abby this upset, it had to be bad.

Slowly she moved them both toward the small love seat and drew Abby down. The girl crumpled against Chloe and they sat there for several long minutes. The only sound was Abby's soft sobbing. Chloe rubbed Abby's back, murmuring words of comfort, and waited.

Eventually her breathing slowed, and Abby lifted her head. "I'm sorry," she whispered, looking miserable. "I messed everything up."

"What happened to your dad, sweetie?" Chloe wiped the pads of her thumbs across the girl's tear-stained cheeks.

"He's not my real dad," Abby said miserably, "and now he hates me."

"I don't believe that."

"I came in today while you were gone." Abby sniffled and swiped at her nose with the back of her hand. "Karen said that thanks to me you were going to be able to save your store."

Chloe nodded. "We still need the sales from this weekend to push us over the top, but the store will survive. Did you tell—"

"Not Ben. I know you guys had a fight and . . ." Abby shook her head. "Cory. It's terrible, Chloe. How could I have—" She burst into tears again.

Chloe was trying to make sense of what the girl was saying. "Did something happen to Cory in prison? Was he hurt?"

"N-no. Maybe. I talked to him today." She drew in a deep, shuddering breath. "I told him about the store and the bet and how you were going to win."

Chloe thought about what Ben had told her of his brother's past history with The Toy Chest and Stan Butterfield. "But he already knew you were working here this summer."

"Zach mentioned it to him a couple of weeks ago but said he acted strange so neither of us have said anything else. Cory said Ben promised to shut down the store."

Chloe nodded. "I knew that, but he was going to talk to Cory and explain that things were different."

"I told him that it was because of me that the store is doing so well." Abby gulped back another sob. "Before I knew what this place meant to him. What if he makes Ben send me to foster care?"

"Sweetie—"

"I'm not his daughter," Abby repeated frantically. "He said, 'No kid of mine would stab me in the back that way.'"

"You didn't."

"Yes. That's exactly what happened. Even if I didn't realize it." She clutched the front of her shirt, as if she needed something to hold on to. "They can't separate me from Zach. He needs me." She swallowed. "I need him."

"Ben would never do that, Abby. Neither would Harry. They love you."

"Cory got so mad. He was screaming and cursing—totally flipping out on the phone. He dropped it, and I could hear a big commotion on the other end of the line. Guys were yelling, cheering, and then I heard the guards shouting. Someone hung up the phone." Her eyes were huge, terrified. "What if they hurt Cory because of me?"

Chloe tried to keep her rarely used temper under control. She wasn't going to lose it. But right now she would have liked to hurt Ben's felon brother. To make an innocent girl feel guilty for something he did long ago was appalling, especially when Abby had done so much more than right her own mistakes.

"Have you talked to Ben?"

"I couldn't tell him, Chloe." Abby clutched at her chest. "He'll flip out. It's all because of me. He'll drive down to the prison and do something stupid. It will make him too mad and worried."

"Abby," Chloe said gently. "Ben and Harry have to know. If Cory is in trouble, they need to check on him. Ben can make him understand that you didn't do anything wrong."

"I saved the store."

Chloe wanted to argue, but it was the truth. No matter how hard any of them worked, without Abby's skills with the website and online marketing, Chloe never would have made enough money to pay the back rent. She owed the girl so much, but now Abby was miserable, and Chloe didn't know how to make it better. As tough as she pretended to be, there was a vulnerability to Abby that Chloe understood all too well. Now that the girl felt a part of the Haddox family, Chloe couldn't jeopardize that security.

"We'll figure something—" Chloe's words cut off at a loud crash and yelling from the front of the store.

"Ben?" Abby asked in a miserable whisper. "Maybe he figured out what I did and is looking for me."

Anger surged through Chloe. If that was the case, she was going to go off on him, too. To scare Abby this way and make a scene in her toy store was unacceptable, even from him.

"Stay here," she told the girl, standing and adjusting her apron.

She charged through the door into the main store, for the first time in her life itching for a fight.

CHAPTER SIXTEEN

The scene playing out in the toy store unfolded before Chloe in slow motion, as if she were watching a movie played on the wrong speed. It wasn't Ben causing the commotion. It was her worst nightmare come to life.

A man stood in the middle of the store, one of his arms waving wildly. At the end of it flashed the shiny blade of a knife.

She sucked in a breath as her eyes tracked to Tamara, who was lying in a crumpled heap against the display shelves on the far side of the store.

"Bitch," the man spat out, "get up."

Her heartbeat racing, Chloe darted around the edge of the counter and moved toward Tamara.

"Don't go near her," the man shouted, pointing the knife at Chloe. She froze. "Don't any of you people move."

Chloe's gaze flicked to the one customer in the store, a mother hugging her baby and toddler close to her chest by the stuffed animals. Karen stood behind the register and as Chloe watched, Abby shuffled from the doorway to the office closer to the older woman.

"I said don't fucking move," the man roared at Abby.

"Jimmy, don't do this." Tamara was on her knees now, blood dripping from her nose. "These people have nothing to do with us."

The man's savage gaze darted around the store, as if he wasn't sure how he'd gotten to this point. "They hid you from me, baby." Sweat rolled down the forehead of the man Chloe recognized as Tamara's exboyfriend, and his eyes were dilated like he was on something. "I been looking for you for months. I drove all night from Dallas to find you. To bring you home."

They'd talked about this in meetings, made a plan for what to do if one of the men came to the store. Most of them had restraining orders in place against their abusers, but Chloe knew that was no guarantee of safety. She had a Taser gun in the drawer behind the counter but had been too intent on making sure Tamara was ok to grab it before she'd run out. They had protocols and procedures in place—who would call the cops, how to diffuse the situation, code words in case one of the women was in trouble. None of it had prepared her for the bold threat of violence facing them.

Tamara slowly got to her feet. "How did you find me?"

"There was a picture on the Internet. Some famous chef in this store. You were in the background."

The picture of Ben that Abby had posted online. Why hadn't Chloe thought of that? It was part of the reason she hadn't done much advertising before now—so the women could remain anonymous.

It had all gone out the window with her need to save the store, but this moment made it clear how irresponsible that decision had been. She glanced at the front door, praying no other customers would walk in until this crisis was diffused. Praying she could bring an end to it with no one getting hurt.

"I'm not going with you, Jimmy." Tamara threw back her shoulders, all bravado and strength.

Chloe hoped it wasn't just an act. She felt chained by her fear. The preparation and training she'd done to keep herself and the women around her safe seemed to dissolve in the face of this man's anger, just as it had that night in the restaurant with Jonathan.

"Don't say that." He shook his head, the hand that still held the knife aloft trembling. "I just want to talk to you. You have to give me another chance to make things better. I love you, baby. So much. Things will be better this time."

"Look at my face." Tamara pressed her fingers to her cheek. "You haven't changed."

"I have," Jimmy argued, squeezing his eyes shut for a moment before focusing on Tamara again. "You have to believe me. I'm tired now, that's all. It will be different once we're home."

"What's different is *me*," Tamara said, her voice steady even as a muscle under her eye twitched.

"You have to come with me." Jimmy's voice cracked then turned angry again. "Either you walk out that door with me or I'll start hurting people, Tammy. I don't give a shit what happens to me if we're not together. My life isn't worth crap if you're not in it."

Chloe saw Tamara glance around the store, then she closed her eyes and took a breath.

No, Chloe wanted to shout. She knew if Tamara walked out the door with her ex-boyfriend they'd likely never see her again. With the shape Jimmy was in he'd want to make sure Tamara remained under his control, one way or another. The majority of homicides related to domestic-violence situations happened at the point of separation or when the victim refused to return to the relationship. She couldn't let Tamara put herself at risk that way.

"First let everyone—"

"No!" Chloe shouted the word and ran to Tamara's side before Jimmy could move. "You're not leaving with him." She shoved the other woman behind her, hearing Tamara let out a muffled sob. Chloe knew she wasn't the only one who understood what would happen if Jimmy was allowed to take Tamara out of the store.

"She's not going anywhere with you." Chloe's whole body started to shake as Jimmy's fury-filled stare narrowed on her. But she didn't back down. "Walk away, Jimmy, while you still have a chance. Before the cops get here."

He threw a look over his shoulder then back at Chloe. "There are no cops."

"I called them from the back," Chloe lied. "They'll be here any minute, and it won't be good for you."

"I'm taking Tammy," he said in a deadly voice.

"No." Chloe made her voice clear, the way she'd been taught in self-defense class. She filled her lungs with air then exhaled completely, forcing her chest and abdomen to rise and fall to keep her breathing slow and steady.

"Bitch, you're going to regret this." Jimmy took one step forward and Chloe braced herself. If Jimmy's attention was on her, maybe Karen could get Abby and the customers out of the store. She had to keep them safe.

At that moment, the chimes above the door rang. Her focus had been Jimmy, who whirled toward the front of the store.

Panic gripped Chloe as Zach walked in, unaware of the drama playing out inside.

"Zach, run!" Abby's scream split the charged moment, sending the store into chaos.

Zach's eyes widened as he took in the scene, but before he could turn, Jimmy had closed the distance between them and grabbed him by the arm, yanking him toward the middle of the store. Something primal reared up in Chloe as her panic for the boy's safety overcame her own fear of the brutal man in front of her.

"Let him go," she yelled, taking advantage of Jimmy's attention being focused on Zach to give him a hard shove. When he stumbled, she wrenched Zach away from his grasp, pushing the boy toward Tamara. She didn't wait for Jimmy to regain his balance before unleashing a barrage of punches and kicks aimed at Jimmy's neck, face, and groin. Doubling over, he dropped the knife and she snatched it off the floor. Somewhere in the back of her brain she heard sirens wailing, but Chloe's focus remained on Jimmy.

He straightened and started to lunge for her, but she pointed the knife at him, gripping it so tightly her knuckles turned white.

His enraged eyes met hers. "You're going to regret this when I—"

At that moment two uniformed officers burst into the store. One of them grabbed Jimmy, hauling him to his feet as Chloe dropped the knife. It clattered to the floor and the second officer scooped it up. "Are you ok, ma'am?" he asked, his concerned gaze trained on Chloe.

Her mouth opened and shut several times as she tried to process what had just happened. She gave a jerky nod then turned to survey the others inside the store. Tamara was holding tightly to Zach as she pressed a sleeve to her face. Karen had an arm wrapped around Abby's thin shoulders.

"It's over," Chloe whispered. Both kids ran forward and she wrapped them in a tight embrace.

Through the window she saw the officer cuff Jimmy and shove him into the back of the patrol car. She released Zach and Abby long enough to check on the mother and her kids, who were shaken but not injured. The ambulance arrived along with more police. One of the paramedics checked Tamara's nose, which was not broken.

The husband of the woman who'd been shopping in the store came to pick up his family. Their reunion made Chloe's eyes water. The baby seemed oblivious to the commotion, but the young boy broke away to approach Chloe.

"You were like a superhero," he told her solemnly. "You beat up the bad guy."

Chloe crouched to his level. "Everyone in here was a hero. You were brave to stay quiet and not cry when I know it must have been scary."

"Boys aren't supposed to hit girls." He glanced over his shoulder. "That's what Mommy says."

"You're right, sweetheart." Chloe's voice caught. If only she and the women at the store had learned that lesson years ago. "I'd like you to pick out a toy—anything you want—to thank you for being so brave today."

"Can Aubrey get something, too?" He pointed to his sister. "She likes elephants."

"Of course she can."

Chloe apologized again to the parents. The woman was still shaken, and after the boy picked a toy for both him and his sister, the family quickly left the store.

"That was a close one," Karen said, coming out of the back office.

"It was more than a close call." Chloe gazed at the destruction of her store, and not just the physical mess, but also the emotional fallout this afternoon was bound to have. The Toy Chest was supposed to be a safe haven, not just for her but also for the women she worked with and the customers they valued.

This was her tie to the community, but she feared that details about the women she employed were bound to leak. Already one news crew had arrived, with a reporter stationed on the sidewalk in front of the store. As she watched, the reporter stopped the family and shoved a microphone in the mother's face.

"I need to call Kendall," she muttered.

"She's on her way," Karen said. "After I talked to Ben, I called her. I know Sam's still up at camp and thought you might need the support."

Ben. Of course he'd be coming to pick up the kids. "How are Zach and Abby?" she asked, ignoring Karen's comment about needing support.

"Ok, I think. Tamara is talking to them now in the back." Karen shrugged. "Those kids have been through way more in their lives than they should."

"I know," Chloe whispered. "I was supposed to keep them safe. I was supposed to keep all of us safe."

She heard a male voice coming from the office.

"I told Ben to come in through the back," Karen explained quickly. "If people were to see Ben Haddox arriving at the store after everything that went down—"

"It's fine." Chloe took a breath, trying to steel herself for the reaction she expected Ben to have. How could he do anything but blame her for putting his niece and nephew in danger? But no matter what he thought or said, it couldn't be any worse than the words spilling through her own head.

As she walked into the back office, Ben's steely gaze landed on her. He held both Abby and Zach in his big arms, and she wanted nothing more than to run to him and let him swallow her in his embrace as well. His mouth thinned as he took her in from head to toe. Feeling self-conscious, she ran a hand through her hair, tucked a few errant curls behind her ears. Her blouse was torn at the shoulder where Jimmy had grabbed at her, and if she looked as unsettled as she felt, she must be quite a sight.

"I'm sorry," she mouthed, and he gave a sharp shake of his head in response. Chloe felt the emotions she'd been holding back start to spill over, tears rising in her throat. She bit down on the inside of her cheek until she tasted blood. It was better to focus on the physical pain instead of the heartache of being so close to him yet with a whole world separating them.

◆ ◆ ◆

Ben watched as the two women, Tamara and Karen, came to stand on either side of Chloe. Circling the proverbial wagons around their friend and employer.

"Chloe was a hero," Tamara said as if daring Ben to contradict her. Chloe hated her friend's swollen nose and the fact that her eyes were already blackening, but Tamara ignored her injuries. "She fought off my dirt ball ex-boyfriend single-handedly." She gave Chloe a quick hug. "I'm going to check on things out front."

Ben's gaze was riveted to Chloe. "You fought him?" he choked out.

All Karen had said in her frantic call was that Tamara's ex-boyfriend had stormed the store. The police came, and the kids were shaken but fine.

Only an hour ago he'd dropped off Zach in front of the store then headed home, thrilled to have some time to himself. The kids had wanted to go to the water park today, but Ben had been too busy wallowing in his own disappointment over losing Chloe to take them.

Instead he'd lost his cool, yelling about everything from socks left in the upstairs hallway to the volume on the television. It had been stupid and petty, but he'd effectively chased them out of the house with his temper. Now he kicked himself for not walking the boy into The Toy Chest. The truth was Ben hadn't wanted to see Chloe. He'd been too worried about his reaction to her so he'd pulled to the curb while his nephew hopped out of the car. Ben's anger and cowardice had put Zach and Abby in danger, and he hated himself for it.

Chloe frowned. "I had to keep everyone safe."

Abby moved in his arms, taking a step away from him to look at Chloe. "Would he have killed Tamara?"

Chloe seemed to consider her answer. "I don't think that was his plan, but sometimes when people lose control like that, they do bad things."

"The guy had a knife, Uncle Ben." Zach tipped up his head, but Ben continued to stare at Chloe. "He grabbed me when I walked into the store."

Now Ben did look at Zach. "That man held you at knifepoint?"

Zach nodded. "Until Chloe put the karate moves on him."

Michelle Major

"It was from my self-defense classes," she murmured, but Ben barely heard her.

Ben hugged Zach to him once more. "If anything had happened to you," he said, feeling emotion rage inside him even as he kept his voice calm. "To either of you . . ." He smoothed the heavy bangs off Abby's forehead. "It's my job to protect you both. I promised Cory, and I'm sorry I wasn't here."

"We're ok."

"Because of Chloe's ka-ra-te," Zach said again. "Show Uncle Ben your moves, Chloe."

"I think your uncle has seen them already," Karen said dryly.

"It should never have gone down like this." Ben kept a hand on each of the kids but spoke to Chloe.

"I know," she whispered, and he was at once both horrified and furious. The two emotions warred within him, struggling and churning until one finally overcame the other.

She moved closer to him as his desire, worry, and frustration coalesced. "I'm sorry," she said. "We'd prepared for—"

"There's no excuse," he yelled, and her mouth clamped shut. He let go of the kids and shoved them back as anger overtook him.

Karen stepped closer, but Chloe waved her away. Brave woman. She was going to face him on her own. Stupid woman.

He hadn't felt this out of control in years. What he really wanted was to find Tamara's ex-boyfriend and annihilate him. "This is not a shelter for abused women," he roared, "although that's how you treat it. It's a fucking toy store, Chloe. A place where families with children gather."

"I know," she murmured, and the sound of her voice, sad and broken, made another wave of outrage pulse through him.

"You don't know." The words came tumbling forth like a landslide. "You're too afraid to live so you've holed yourself up here, pretending to make a difference to people, but it's nothing. This whole thing is nothing."

"Ben, stop. You're being mean." He felt Abby's small hand on his arm but shook her off.

He was worse than mean. He was a man with a black soul. The accusations his critics had leveled at him over the years, the words he'd been called—beast, monster, bastard—flooded his brain. He was each of those things in this moment, because he was lashing out at the one person who'd wanted more from him and for him. He accused her of being afraid, but it was his own fear that made the nasty words keep pouring forth. "You put them in danger." He continued to bellow the words, unable to stop. "Every person in this store."

Chloe swiped one hand across her cheeks and he saw the cuts and scrapes on her knuckles. She'd been hurt. It was more than just a threat. The man had hurt her, and it could have been worse. Ben should have been here. He'd let his pride and ego get in the way of taking care of Abby and Zach. In that moment, the anger inside him swooped and turned, almost knocking him over with its force. He wasn't mad at Chloe, he was furious with himself for failing the people he loved.

"Now wait just a minute." Karen stepped forward, tugging on her heavy braid, her gaze wary but blazing. "You don't know how much Chloe has helped us."

"He's right." Chloe put a hand on the older woman's shoulder. "You don't need to defend me, Karen."

"He isn't—" the older woman began, but Chloe shook her head.

"This is a toy store, not a community service center." Chloe spoke to Karen, who shook her head and stormed to the front of the store. Standing alone, Chloe turned her gaze to Ben. It was cold and blank. He'd done that. He'd stripped the emotion from her. He'd ruined her, like he contaminated everything around him. "Abby and Zach, thank you for everything you've done for The Toy Chest these last few weeks. It has been such a blessing to have you here, and I can't say enough how sorry I am that it's ending this way."

"It's not ending," Zach argued. "Uncle Ben, tell her you're sorry for being a jerk. Make this better."

"He's protecting you," Chloe said quietly, "the best way he knows how." She looked at Abby. "I *will* make this right."

Ben heard his niece suck in a breath but didn't understand the significance of what Chloe had just said to her. But he certainly understood the significance of his tirade.

Shit.

Why was he so messed up that he couldn't separate his emotions and allow himself to feel anything except anger?

He opened his mouth to say something, anything to stave off the panic eating away at him. Panic that he'd irrevocably screwed up the best thing that had ever happened in his life.

"No." Chloe held up a hand. "You don't get to speak anymore." A tremble ran through her and she swallowed, straightening her shoulders. "I'm doing the best I can, Ben. I'm trying to make my life better, different than it was before. Maybe it's not a total success. You're right, I'm scared, and when that happens I hide away. But I would never put Zach and Abby or any of the women who work for me in danger. Bad things happen, and we move through them the best way we can."

She gave him the slightest smile, a hint of a curve at the corner of her mouth, and it made his gut clench. "If this afternoon had one good thing come from it, it's that I get who you are now. I know what it's like to be so filled with rage that it consumes you. When Jimmy grabbed Zach, I wanted to hurt him." She grimaced. "To kill him, even. Nothing else mattered. And maybe that anger fueled me, but I won't let it control my life. Mine or anyone else's."

"Chloe."

"You should go now." She said the words without inflection. "Take the kids home and take care of them, Ben. You're a better person than you believe, and they need you to be that man."

A dull roar filled his head, and he wanted to rewind the past few minutes. Hell, he'd like a do-over of half his life. But she turned and walked to the front of the store before he'd even taken another breath.

"You really fucked that up." Abby stared at him, her arms crossed over her chest.

He couldn't deny it and didn't bother to mention her language.

"Let's go," he said and started for the door.

Zach hung back. "Are we going to see Chloe again?" His big eyes filled with tears. "You hurt her feelings, Uncle Ben. It wasn't nice."

"I'm not a nice guy," Ben muttered. He opened the door and motioned Zach out into the afternoon sunlight. "There was never any question about that, buddy."

"What about the store? Did she win the bet? It's almost the end of the month. What's going to happen to The Toy Chest?"

"We'll figure it out, Zach. If the toy store is so important to—"

"Screw the bet," Abby muttered. "You can't let her keep this place."

Ben opened the door of the Range Rover and watched Zach climb in before turning to Abby. "You spent the last few weeks working to make sure she had the money to do exactly that."

She bit down on her lower lip. "That was before I talked to Cory."

Oh, no. He'd asked his brother to keep quiet about his history with Stan Butterfield and The Toy Chest until he could resolve the situation. Clearly, Cory had given Abby an earful. "What did he say, Abby? How much does he know?"

"He flipped out," Abby said quietly. "He dropped the phone, but it didn't hang up right away. I could hear him screaming and things breaking. I think he's in trouble, Ben."

Ben grabbed the girl's thin shoulders. "Why didn't you tell me?"

"I came to talk to Chloe. I . . . I . . ."

"What?" His tone was sharper than he meant it to be.

"I was afraid to tell you."

The huge pit in Ben's stomach opened like a gaping cavern. So many things he'd messed up, and so many people being hurt because of it.

"Get in the car."

"I'm sorry," she said on a sob and started around the front of the SUV.

He caught her wrist before she got far and wrapped his arms around her. "This is not your fault," he whispered as she crumpled into him, her breath hitching. "None of it. We're going to figure out how to make it all right. I'll make it all right."

He said the words with conviction, even though he was afraid it was one more promise he'd never be able to keep.

CHAPTER SEVENTEEN

On Sunday morning of the July Fourth weekend, Chloe dipped her toes in the water of the lake at Bryce Hollow Camp. It was alpine cold; her feet went practically numb on contact. Earlier she'd watched the campers partake in the traditional final-morning swim. The air couldn't have been more than seventy degrees, with the water temperature a few degrees lower. The kids' enthusiasm for the freezing lake was impressive, and she'd happily stood on the shore to hand out towels when they were finished. Although Sam jumped in along with the campers every week, Chloe had never managed it during any of her many visits.

She hadn't bothered to pack her suit for this trip. Hell, she hadn't packed anything. Just flipped the "Closed" sign on the store, given Mr. Rogers an extra scoop of food, and pointed her car west. The drive out of Denver and into the foothills had calmed her, but by the time she'd pulled into the darkened camp, exhaustion from the day's events had caught up to her.

For all of Sam's sarcasm, she was better at taking care of people than almost anyone Chloe knew. Without asking questions, Sam gave her a clean pair of pajamas and tucked her into bed in the tiny fishing cabin. Chloe appreciated the time to think about what she was going to do next, even as memories of being with Ben at camp continued to engulf her.

Even with two full days of hiding out at camp, she still hadn't figured it out. Her emotions remained as jumbled as her plans for the future. The threat of violence at her store and Ben's subsequent tirade had stripped away the last of her barricades, leaving her wondering how to correct the course of her life. She had no answers, but as footsteps echoed on the dock behind her, Chloe knew her quiet musings were at an end.

"You had a good group of kids this week," she said as Sam sank down next to her.

"They always are." Sam wore loose sweatpants and a fleece sweatshirt, her long blond hair tucked under a knit cap.

"You're dressed for the first snow instead of a beautiful summer day."

Sam laughed. "It takes me a few hours to warm up after the morning swim." She gave an involuntary shiver. "At some point, I'm going to need to put myself on towel duty. I'm too old for the polar bear plunge."

"You love it. When does the next group arrive?"

"Day after tomorrow. The staff has the night off. They're heading to Evergreen for the fireworks, and we'll start turning things over tomorrow."

"Sorry if I'm keeping you from a night on the town."

"There's no place I'd rather be than here." Sam scooted closer, nudging her hip against Chloe's. "Kendall called this morning. She's worried about you."

"How much press has the story gotten?" Chloe asked.

"Enough. The interview with the mother has been picked up nationally. According to Ken, the most popular headline is 'Tragedy Avoided in Neighborhood Toy Store.' Tamara gave her side of things and the director of the Safehouse shelter has given a statement. A few of the reports are focusing on whether it was right to hire women with histories of abuse, but most stories are calling you a hero."

"I'm not a hero. Not even close."

"Kendall wants to know if you've thought any more about letting her interview you?"

That had been one of the millions of things going through Chloe's mind this morning. "If I do, I'll have to talk about my story and why The Toy Chest means so much to me."

"That's a good thing, Chloe. It's time."

"I wanted to forget that part of my life, Sam. To leave it behind for a fresh start."

"You have, but everything that's happened before now is a part of you."

Chloe shook her head. "I haven't left it behind or dealt with it. I ignored what Jonathan did to me—not the physical violence—but everything else that went with it. I've been counseling these women, pushing them to take chances without expecting anything of myself."

"What you do is import—"

"I'm hiding away. Hiding behind my fear. Yes, I love The Toy Chest, but it's not truly my dream. It never has been. Maybe that's why, until this summer, I was just scraping by. My focus has always been on the women, not on selling toys."

"But you've made it work, Chloe. You've helped give those women back their confidence and, in many ways, their lives."

"Because I'm too afraid of living my own."

"I think you've been doing quite a bit of living this summer."

Chloe risked a glance at Sam and saw her friend smiling.

"It's over."

"Then he's a bigger jackass than he acts like on TV. He really liked you, Chloe. I could tell."

"He's not an ass . . . exactly." Chloe was sick of the way her mind reeled and tumbled around her feelings for Ben. "But he's not the right man for me."

"Because he's not an ass?"

Sam asked the question innocently enough, but Chloe pushed her anyway. "There are two sides here. You're supposed to be on mine."

"I am, sweetie."

Chloe stood, the emotions shooting through her making her unable to sit still. She paced a few feet toward shore then back again. "There's so much anger in him."

"From what I understand, he's working on that."

"But what if it's not enough, Sam? What if I fall in love with him and he hurts me?"

"I think you're already in love with him."

Chloe covered her face with her hands and let out a low groan. "That's even worse. I'm such an idiot."

"No." Sam's voice was firm. "You're not."

Chloe felt like a fool. Not just for falling in love with Ben but because she'd allowed fear to rule her life at the same time she expected more from the people around her. She lifted her face to the bright sunshine and the vast blue expanse of the Colorado sky. A hawk glided over the treetops toward the lake then swooped down, executing a brisk dive toward the water. The bird plucked a fish out of the placid stillness of the lake before rocketing back up and disappearing into the trees. That's what Chloe wanted, to dive in and grab what she wanted from life. Without fear holding her back.

"It's a big weekend in Denver," Sam said after a few moments.

"The Highlands Family Festival to celebrate July Fourth," Chloe agreed with a nod.

"All the work you've done to prepare the store . . ."

"I've just flushed down the toilet by coming here instead."

"What about the money for the lease?"

Chloe took a breath then whispered, "I'm closing the store." She walked forward to the edge of the dock.

"I can help," Sam offered immediately.

"It's not about the money," Chloe said, shaking her head. "Ben needs that space."

"He doesn't seem to care about opening a restaurant there."

"It's not for him. He made a promise to his brother. Ben feels like he failed Cory when they were kids, and somehow turning that space into something new is going to make up for the past. I may not agree, but Abby asked me to help her make things right. This is how I'm going to do it."

"It isn't fair."

"But it's right. Not just for them, Sam. For me, too. The Toy Chest has served its purpose for me. The store taught me that I have more to give. Now it's time for me to risk more of myself. To believe in me again, or maybe for the first time ever." She glanced toward the main camp. "Is anyone around right now?"

"No. They all drove into town for the afternoon."

Chloe stripped off her T-shirt then shimmied out of her shorts. "I'm going swimming."

Sam laughed. "Are you sure? You hate being cold."

"Not as much as I hate being afraid."

"Do you want company?"

A shiver rippled through Chloe as the breeze danced across her bare skin. But at the same time the sun was warm, and there was something liberating about looking over the clear lake that made her feel like this was the start of something new and good for her. "I think I can manage it."

Sam stood and slung an arm around Chloe's shoulder for a quick hug. "Then I'm going to run back to camp and grab some towels. Trust me, you'll need them."

Chloe waited until Sam had disappeared into the trees, walked to the edge of the dock, and then leapt into the air. For a second she was weightless, then she hit the water, the cold temperature stealing her breath at the same time it seemed to wash away all of her other worries and doubts.

She surfaced with a whoop, slicking her hair away from her face as she trod water. Her teeth already chattered, but she forced herself to swim toward the middle of the lake, each stroke reminding her that she was stronger than she believed. The rippling of the water and her own breathing were the only things that filled her mind. She'd come to Denver for a new start, and this moment was another one.

Yes, the things Ben had said to her hurt. But they'd also been true. She'd lived with fear as a companion for too long.

Now was the time to shed the rest of her baggage and start fresh. Her teeth started chattering louder and she turned, swimming back to the dock. Warm up first, and then start fresh.

◆ ◆ ◆

Ben let himself into the darkened house late Monday night, exhausted from a long day in Las Vegas. He'd called Michael on Friday night after the fiasco at Chloe's store to say he was interested in James Wyatt's restaurant deal. His agent had wasted no time in setting up a meeting, so Ben had flown to Las Vegas early this morning on Wyatt's private jet. Access to the plane was one of his stipulations for the deal, so that he could get back to Colorado when he needed to for Abby and Zach.

He hadn't discussed it with the kids, but he wasn't moving them to Vegas. Denver was their home, and even though Harry was cranky, they'd be better off with him than as part of Ben's crazy-busy life preparing to open a restaurant of the caliber Wyatt had planned. There was also the unspoken fact that Ben was afraid he'd screw them up if he stayed. Just like he'd messed up things with Chloe. In a way he couldn't repair, even though he'd tried. He'd called and texted her early Saturday morning, but she hadn't answered either. He didn't blame her. As he played over in his head the horrible things he'd said to her and the look of devastation in her eyes, he couldn't imagine that she'd ever want to speak with him again.

The thought made a fresh dose of pain shoot through him. He'd been desperate enough to try to track her down, both at her house and the store. Even though he didn't deserve her, he needed her to understand that he hadn't meant the things he'd said. But no one answered at her house and the store was closed, even though that meant she was losing sales during the busy neighborhood festival over the holiday weekend.

As the details had emerged from both Abby and Zach, Ben had realized how truly out of line he'd been. Chloe had saved not only Zach, but also most likely all of the people in the store that day. And he'd berated her for it. One more reason he knew he had to leave Denver. He was poison to the people he cared about, and he didn't want to spend another moment hurting her or his niece and nephew.

He started for the steps then noticed a faint blue light coming from the family room. His father sat slumped in his recliner in front of the muted television. Harry's rhythmic snoring the only sound filling the room.

"Dad, what are you doing down here?" Ben nudged his father's ankle.

Harry let out a snort then startled awake, his eyes blinking owlishly in the dark room. "You're home."

"It's after midnight. Why aren't you in bed?"

"I was waiting up for you."

"About fifteen years too late to keep me out of trouble."

"I'm still your father, and we need to talk." Harry sat up in his chair.

"Can it wait until morning? I'm beat."

Ben turned to go without waiting for an answer.

"Sit your ass down." His father's booming voice stopped Ben in his tracks.

"Christ, Dad." Ben dropped onto the couch, rubbing a hand over his jaw. "You're going to wake the kids."

"I took them to see your brother this afternoon. Got the warden to approve it on short notice." Harry crossed his arms over his chest, as if daring Ben to react.

Ben couldn't have kept his temper in check at that news if he'd wanted to. "Why?" he asked through clenched teeth. "Cory was adamant that they not visit him in prison. You know he didn't want Zach or Abby seeing him like that."

"He's Zach's father and the closest thing Abby has to one." Harry pointed at Ben. "Although you've got way more paternal instincts than I would have guessed, Benny. You're good for those kids."

"I'm not, but I know enough to respect Cory's wishes."

"That's bullshit." Harry waved away Ben's words with a flip of his hand. "Your brother has made a lot of bad choices in his life, and he hasn't taken responsibility for most of them. Sure it's humiliating for your kid to see you in prison. Too damn bad. He shouldn't have gotten himself there in the first place. After what Abby heard over the phone, those kids needed to see for themselves that he was ok." Harry flipped on the lamp on the end table and turned off the television. "Plus your brother needed to hear that his vendetta against The Toy Chest is hurting innocent people."

Ben sucked in a breath. "You know why he hates that place."

"I know why he hated Stan Butterfield, and while the man was a jerk, Cory made his own bed by the damage he caused to the store."

"Because of me."

Harry shook his head. "Because Cory couldn't control his damn temper."

"Wonder where he got that?" Ben spat out.

"I was a crappy father," Harry said. "Your mom wasn't much better. I take full responsibility for that. But your brother is a grown man now, Ben. He's got to learn to clean up his life, or even this jail time isn't going to do him any good."

"He was innocent when Stan had him sent to juvie," Ben argued, standing to pace to the edge of the small room and back. He could still picture his brother's scared face as the police took him away.

"He did thousands of dollars in damage," his dad shouted. "That's not innocent."

"I gave him the idea." Ben raked his fingers through his hair, guilt and shame burning a hole in his stomach. "It was my big mouth that got him into trouble."

"Cory made the choice, not you."

"It might as well have been me."

"No." Harry moved so fast Ben didn't see him coming. His dad pushed him hard in the chest, sending Ben stumbling back against the wall.

"What the hell, Dad?"

"I'm not so old that I can't knock some sense into you still." Harry was panting, his eyes burning as he glared at Ben. "You've got more heart than anyone I know, but you keep it hidden behind that bullshit temper and the guilt that fuels it. You did not ruin your brother's life, Benny. He did that all on his own. Hell, if it weren't for you watching out for him—for both of us—things would have gone to hell a lot quicker than they did. You tell everyone the story of how Artie made you want to be a chef. But you were cooking long before you got that job in the restaurant." Harry pointed a meaty finger at Ben. "Do you remember? Do you remember when and why you started cooking?"

Ben shut his eyes, but that didn't stop the memories from crystallizing in his mind. "It doesn't matter," he whispered.

"It does to me, and it should to your brother. He was picky, just like Zach. You started experimenting with whatever we had in the kitchen, trying to come up with food he would eat."

"He was so skinny, especially after Mom left."

"Between you inventing new things for him to try and the breakfasts you practically force-fed me as hangover remedies, it's a wonder you can tolerate being in a kitchen."

"It was all I could do." Ben sank down onto the couch and dropped his head into his hands. He'd blocked most of the memories from his childhood other than the ones that had led to Cory's downward spiral. Now he let some of the good things trickle in, even though the pain from those was different and almost more acute than the punishment of blaming himself. "It was a challenge, you know? Trying to make things he would eat. Seeing how many new ingredients I could sneak in without him realizing it. With you it was the combination of carbs and protein that would get you out of bed the quickest."

"Two pancakes and four eggs," his father murmured, taking a long drink of the iced tea sitting on the coffee table.

"Plus bacon if we could afford it." Ben smiled at the memory. Despite what his dad thought, cooking had been one of his happiest times as a kid. In the kitchen, he was in control, and he could help his dad and brother in a way that seemed impossible otherwise.

"You took care of us," Harry said, his voice taking on a wistful tone, "even though that was my job."

"Don't make me into a hero, old man." Pressure built behind his eyes, pulsing and scratchy. "You know that's far from the truth."

"I understand why you hide behind your temper. I did the same thing for years, all through the troubles your mom and I had and for a long time after. But Chloe is not your mother and you're not me. She's someone you could trust. A woman worthy of your love."

Ben let out a harsh laugh. "I don't think the issue is her worthiness. The lack lies with me, as it always has."

"You came home when those kids needed you, and in just a few weeks you've changed their lives."

"I came home because I owe Cory, and Abby and Zach would have been fine without me. You've cleaned up, Dad. I'm not the only one who deserves some credit."

Harry shrugged. "All I'm saying is don't throw away a chance at something good because you think you might fail."

"What if I think I might hurt her?"

"You won't, Ben. Not like you're talking about. You aren't me." Harry reached out a hand and patted Ben gruffly on the back. It was the closest the old man had come to a hug in years. Ben was shocked to find it made his throat thicken.

"This is from your brother." Harry stood and pulled a folded piece of notepaper out of his back pocket, dropping it into Ben's lap. "Do me a favor and read it before you make any decisions."

As his dad walked out of the room, Ben stared at the piece of paper for several minutes. He wasn't sure what he was going to find, but somehow he knew this note was about to change everything for him.

With shaking hands that he was glad no one was around to see, he opened the note and began to read his brother's scrawly handwriting.

CHAPTER EIGHTEEN

Chloe fingered the delicate heart pendant at her throat as she stood before her four employees, who were gathered around the back counter of the toy store later that week. "Thank you for coming in today and for the extra work and hours each of you has been putting in at the store to increase our sales numbers. What you all have done here in the past month has been nothing short of amazing. Our sales are up almost forty percent, the morning and weekend workshops and classes have waiting lists, and the online sales continue to grow."

Sally and Laura patted each other on the back.

Chloe made eye contact with Tamara, who gave her a sympathetic nod. "Unfortunately," Chloe continued, "despite all that work, it hasn't been enough—"

"Then why did you close the store this weekend?" Sally asked without waiting for Chloe to finish her sentence.

"Girl, you know the answer to that." Tamara stepped forward, pointing to her face. "Thanks to Jimmy, I got a swollen nose, two shiners to go with it, and a permanent restraining order. Chloe ended up with a big mess on her hands."

Chloe held up a hand. "The truth is I needed a little time to regroup.

We're extremely lucky Tamara wasn't hurt worse last week, but it made me reevaluate the toy store's mission. I know each of you has been dedicated to The Toy Chest, and I appreciate that."

"It's because of you," Laura said quietly, but everyone turned to look at her. It was unheard of for the reticent woman to voluntarily speak at one of their meetings. "You've given us back our confidence, and in some cases, a new start for our lives."

"It's true," Sally added. "Do you all remember Marsha, who left just after I came? She's a manager at Macy's now. In charge of the whole perfume counter."

There was a round of aahs from the women. Chloe felt tears prick the backs of her eyes. Yes, this was what she'd set out to do with the toy store, but in a different way. She'd wanted to change her own life, and she had. But not how she'd expected—her change had come from helping these women, from learning that she still had something to give.

"I appreciate—" she began then heard an insistent knocking on the front door and recognized Gloria Rees, her contact from the property management company, waving her hands to get Chloe's attention. Chloe grabbed the key from the counter and unlocked the door, opening it just enough to peek out. "Can you give me a few minutes?" she whispered. "I'm telling everyone now."

"Don't." Gloria flashed a bright smile. "Ben Haddox is renewing your lease. I've got the paperwork right here. He's also lowered the rent back to where it was when Stan owned the building. The store is safe, Chloe."

A chorus of cheers went up behind her, and she whirled around. Gloria pushed open the door to give her a hug and her employees lined up to follow suit.

"This can't be happening," she muttered, turning to Tamara, who'd come to stand at her side. "It's more than just the money. I promised Abby I'd make this right. Ben's brother went crazy when he found out the kids were helping me. Ben has to shut us down."

"No way, honey." Tamara smiled. "You went up against the Beast, and you took him down. This is the best news ever."

"I'll email the new lease agreement to you as soon as I get to the office. We'll have a contract locked in by this afternoon." The realtor gave her another small hug. "Enjoy your celebration, Chloe. You've earned it."

But she hadn't earned anything. Right now, she felt like she'd stolen the happiness of an innocent girl. Abby was so insecure about her place in the Haddox family. If Cory blamed her for helping Chloe to turn around sales, it could destroy the girl's fragile self-confidence. Chloe knew what could happen when you stopped believing in yourself. There was a good chance Abby would bury her talent and throw away her future just to prove to Zach, Cory, Ben, and Harry that family was more important than anything else.

Chloe couldn't let that happen.

She made her way back to the register where Karen stood, a wide smile on her suntanned face.

"Can you open for me today?"

"This is good news, right?" The older woman's soft eyes were concerned. "It's what you wanted?"

Chloe shook her head. "Yes. Maybe. I don't know at this point, but I need to make sure Abby and Zach are ok and figure out why Ben is renewing the lease."

"Sometimes we get the thing we wanted all along, only to realize it wasn't what we needed the most."

"I don't . . . this isn't . . ."

"You've done so much for all of us," Karen said gently. "It's ok to want something more for yourself now."

She hugged the older woman, grateful for someone to say the words out loud. "I've got to go." Without looking back, she grabbed her purse and headed for the door.

◆ ◆ ◆

She hesitated at the front door of the Haddox house a few minutes later, her hand poised to knock. Maybe she should have called first. Maybe Ben didn't want to see her. Of course he didn't, not after the things he'd said to her. Whatever his reasons for pulling the offer on the building, they probably had nothing to do with her. It was silly for her to think otherwise.

But she couldn't walk away. Not now that she was here, so close to looking into his stormy blue eyes again. She wanted . . . no, she needed to know that he hadn't compromised his promise to his brother for her. She had to know that Abby was ok. That's all this was.

Yeah, right, a voice that sounded a lot like Sam's said in her head.

The truth was she missed Ben with every breath she took. As much as it would hurt, she had to do this. Before she could knock, the door swung open.

"How long are you planning on standing there?" Harry asked. He took a drink of his iced tea, watching her over the rim with the same blue eyes as Ben's.

"Long enough to get over being a wimp," she admitted on a harsh breath.

That earned a snort. "You're quiet but not a wimp. I've never seen a woman handle my bull of a son the way you do."

"Did," Chloe muttered. "The way I did."

"You still have some stuff to learn." He motioned her into the house but didn't wait to see if she followed, just turned on his heel and stalked down the narrow hallway. "I got my hands full today, girlie. Could use some help."

"Is Ben here?" She waited a few beats but when Harry didn't turn back around, she followed him toward the kitchen. The counter was filled with boxes and bags of varying sizes, all of it junk food, from what Chloe could see. There were Pop-Tarts, powdered donuts, at least four different kinds of chips, sugary cereal, bags of licorice, and cookies.

It was a kid's grocery dream come true, but Zach sat at the kitchen table, his hands folded over his thin chest while Abby held out a plate to him. "You love frozen waffles with Cool Whip," she said, a pleading note to her voice. "You have to eat something, Zach. Anything."

Harry whipped around to Chloe. "Hell, no, Ben's not here." He pointed at Zach. "If he were I wouldn't need fifty pounds of that crap just to coax my grandson into taking one bite."

Abby looked up, her distressed gaze settling on Chloe. She dropped the whipped cream container on the table and came forward. Chloe braced herself for whatever Abby had in mind, whether it was a sucker punch or a shin kick, understanding the girl's anger and willing to be an outlet for it. Instead, Abby threw her arms around Chloe's waist and pressed her face into the crook of Chloe's neck, sobbing loudly. Zach didn't move, but his anxious gaze nearly broke her heart.

Harry cursed and lifted his hands to his ears, as if he couldn't stand to hear any more crying. Chloe shot him a dirty look then stroked her fingers along Abby's back as she gave Zach a hopeful smile. "I'm sorry. I'll make this right. I promise."

"Y-you can't." Abby's voice was hoarse but clear.

"I can. I'll close The Toy Chest, and I'll make sure Cory and Ben know you convinced me to do it."

Abby sniffed, pulling back to look at Chloe. "Why would you close the store?"

Chloe glanced from Abby to Harry then to Zach, who'd turned to watch the scene.

"Because that's what Cory wants, and Ben made him a promise. It represents something to this family, and I get that. You all are more important to me than anything else."

Fresh tears welled in Abby's eyes and she hugged Chloe again.

"Dad is fine with the shop," Zach said from the table, pushing away the plate that held a rather sorry-looking waffle.

"Eat that," Harry shouted, pointing a finger at Zach before switching his attention to Chloe. "Cory had no right to make Ben promise what he did. The kids and I went down there and straightened him out. He understands that your store isn't to blame for his problems and also how much you've helped Abby and Zach this summer. He sent a note back for Ben, releasing him from that ridiculous vendetta."

Chloe held on tighter to the girl in her arms. "Then why . . ."

"Ben's gone," Abby said on a sniff. "He's not coming back, Chloe. He left."

Disappointment settled in Chloe's stomach. "Gone where?"

"Vegas." Harry spit out the two syllables like they were acid on his tongue.

"Why?" The word slipped out on a hiss of breath.

"To open a fancy restaurant." Harry shook his head. "The big lug thinks that everything that's happened, from the online photo that led to the attack at your store to Cory flipping out, is his fault. He's scared to pieces that he can't control his temper and will hurt someone. He thinks the only place he's safe is in a kitchen where he can channel his anger."

"That's not why he cooks," Chloe whispered. "Food is love for him. It's why the show has been so hard. He needs to be cooking the kind of food he wants to for people he cares about. If he takes another contract to develop a menu that isn't his passion, it's going to kill him."

Harry let out a breath as if he was relieved she understood.

"He says we're better off without him," Zach said, biting down on his bottom lip.

"We're not," Abby said, sounding a little desperate. "Chloe—"

"I know." Chloe smoothed the hair back from the girl's face. "You need him. We all need him."

As she said the words, she realized how true they were. Ben was a larger-than-life presence, and while his temper was maddening, she understood now that it wasn't scary the way her ex-husband's anger had been. Ben was all bluster, hard and tough on the outside, but that rough shell was only a shield to hide his soft underbelly. He had a protective streak a mile long and had spent his life trying to take care of everyone in his life. She felt safe with him, not just physically, but emotionally, and even when he lashed out, she knew it was more about his own fear of failing his family than anything else.

She'd wanted a love that was easy and calm, but that wasn't what she needed. What she needed was Ben.

"I've got to stop him," she muttered, only realizing she'd said the words out loud when Harry, Abby, and Zach all started to move at once.

"I'll book the tickets on my laptop," Abby said. "Harry, you've still got the credit card Ben left?"

The older man pulled a piece of plastic out of his back pocket. "First class, Abs. Ben owes us for trying to stop him from making the biggest mistake of his life."

The girl flashed a cheeky grin. "First class all the way."

"I'm going to grab my iPad from my bedroom." Zach sprinted up the stairs.

Harry pointed at Chloe. "I'll drive to DIA. You have your driver's license on you?"

"In my purse. But we can't—"

"We can and we are," Harry interrupted. "He needs us right now as much as we need him." He narrowed his eyes. "Are you with us or not, girlie?"

Abby's fingers stilled on the laptop's keyboard as she glanced at Chloe.

Zach came charging back down the stairs. "Come on," he yelled, grabbing the waffle from the plate on the table and shoving it into his mouth. "We need to rescue Uncle Ben."

Chloe swallowed, squeezed her fingers into a fist, and pressed it to her chest to try to stem the tide of her heart racing. "Let's go," she whispered. "We're in this together."

♦ ♦ ♦

His head pounding from two days of meetings, tours, more meetings, and a dinner at one of James Wyatt's other Las Vegas hot spots, Ben rattled the ice in his water glass and took a long drink. "No."

Four men stared at him from around the large conference table inside Wyatt's plush offices.

"Breathe, Michael," he said to his publicist, who sat rigidly still beside him. "This isn't the end of the world."

Suddenly the stout, portly man at the end of the table jumped up, pounding his open palm on the polished mahogany. "It's the end of your world, you cocky prick." James Wyatt was as well known for his outbursts as he was for his world-class restaurants. He and Ben had that in common. "Is this some kind of a fucking joke? Some sadistic mind trick cooked up by the producers of that crock-of-shit show of yours?"

"It's no joke, James."

Another string of expletives erupted from the restaurant mogul's mouth, so colorful and inventive that Ben thought he should take notes.

"I'm sorry." The words felt rusty in Ben's mouth, but he found he meant them. His temper, always simmering just under the surface, was shockingly passive. For the first time in years, he felt peaceful. Well, not in years. He'd been at peace with Chloe wrapped in his arms. She'd changed not only his life, but also his heart. This time in Las Vegas had showed him that he couldn't go back again. He didn't want to go back again. He wanted to move forward, with his family and with the woman he loved.

He wanted to be a man who deserved her love, but first he had to get back to her.

"You string me along for weeks then refuse to sign? I'm going to open this restaurant without you and fucking have your balls as the nightly special."

Ben smiled. He couldn't help it. The thought that he knew what he wanted in life and was going to go after it made an unfamiliar bubble of joy . . . actual joy . . . inflate in his chest. "I hope you season them better than the scallops we were served last night."

Just as Wyatt launched himself across the table, the door burst open and Ben's father, Chloe, Abby, and Zach ran into the room.

He was so distracted at the sight of the four of them that he took his attention off Wyatt, who landed a swift punch to his jaw. Ben reeled back, his chair flipping over as Chloe and Abby screamed. By the time he lifted to his elbows, his father had hauled the short owner off him as Michael helped hold back the man.

"You'll never work in this town again," Wyatt spat out. "I'm going to fucking ruin you." He tried to shrug out of Harry's grasp, but Ben's dad was like a pit bull when he wanted to be.

One of the man's lackeys moved forward. "Sir?"

"Get your fucking hands off me," Wyatt hissed to Harry. "I'm done here."

Harry let him go, giving the man a hard push toward his assistant. Everyone in the meeting except Michael cleared the room.

Chloe was at Ben's side in an instant. "Are you ok?" she whispered, cradling his head between her hands. He rubbed a hand along his jaw. It stung, but he'd had worse hits.

"It wasn't as bad as being maced," he told her and earned a small smile. He should get up now since he really was fine, but he didn't want her to take her hands off him. This felt too good. He could smell her, the combination of flowers and citrus that was uniquely Chloe. He glanced at his niece and nephew, his dad, and then back to Chloe.

"What are you all doing here?"

"We came to rescue you," Zach said.

"You can't move to Las Vegas," Abby added. "We need you in Denver."

Zach pointed at Harry. "Grandpa bought a ton of junk food at the grocery."

111111111

Harry playfully smacked the kid on the back of the head. "Not supposed to rat me out, boy." His blue eyes met Ben's. "But, yeah, we want you to come home."

Home. That word echoed in his mind. Nothing had changed about the house where he'd grown up except . . . everything had changed. He'd changed.

"I said no to the restaurant." He turned to Chloe with a smile. "Maybe we should get off the floor?"

The blush he loved so much flared in her cheeks. "Right. Of course." She scrambled up, away from him, and he followed, straightening the chair as he stood.

"You're coming back to Denver?" Abby's voice was quiet, and the uncertainty in it melted away the last of his walls.

"Yes. We're a family, and we need to stick together."

"You'll do the cooking, right?" Zach asked, pointing at Harry and making a gagging noise.

"We'll share the cooking," Ben told the boy. "I'm going to teach you."

"What about traveling for the show?" Abby still didn't look convinced.

Ben glanced at Michael. "There's been a change to my contract. I'm not doing a full season of *A Beast in Your Kitchen*. There's going to be a new show where I bring chefs who need an attitude adjustment to Denver for boot camp. We've even hired an anger management counselor to help the hot-headed chefs find better ways to deal with their tempers."

Harry leveled a look at him. "All the hot-headed chefs?"

Ben glanced at Chloe then nodded. "Even me."

His agent let out a long-suffering sigh as he headed for the door. "I can't believe you convinced EatTV, but they love the idea."

Ben nodded. "Of course they did. I'm fucking brilliant."

"Language," Zach and Harry said at the same time.

"I can't give up all my vices at once, you people."

Michelle Major

"Tell them the best part," Michael said. "And I'll go smooth things over with Wyatt's people."

"I don't give a damn about—"

"It's my job," the agent said. "I'm part of the team, Ben."

Ben nodded then turned to Abby and Zach. "I'm also going to open my own restaurant in Denver. Something for families, real food done my way."

Finally a smile broke across Abby's face. "Then it's settled. It's all working out just how it was supposed to."

Out of the corner of his eye, Ben saw Chloe backing away. "Almost settled," he told his niece and turned to Chloe.

"You came for me," he said softly and held out his hand to her.

♦ ♦ ♦

Chloe eyed Ben's outstretched fingers, but didn't place hers in them just yet. If she touched him again, she was afraid she'd totally lose all control. This was what she'd come to Las Vegas for, to reunite him with his family. And now . . .

"I want you to have the building," she said softly. "If you're really going to open a restaurant, that's where you need to do it."

He shook his head and took a step toward her, the heat and scent of him crowding her senses. "The toy store is yours, Chloe. Cory understands that his fight isn't mine anymore."

"But . . ."

"The Toy Chest is yours if you want it," he repeated. "Just like I am." His voice was solemn in a way that made her heart clench. "Take the store or leave the store. I don't care as long as you stay with me. I'm bullheaded and loud, and I know I hurt you." He placed his fingers on either side of her face. "I'm sorry, Chloe. I'm sorry for being an idiot."

"We hurt each other," she answered. "I'm sorry for wanting you to change."

"I have changed." He crouched down so he could look directly in her eyes. "Loving you has changed me, sweetheart. And I do love you. So much."

"I love you, too." She sniffed and blinked, trying to stop the tears she knew were coming. Happy tears were so embarrassing. "But I love you just the way you are."

"God help her," Harry muttered, and Chloe giggled as Abby punched him in the arm.

"I want to spend the rest of my life with you," Ben whispered, ignoring his father. "You're my home, my one true place in this world. Let me take care of you, be gentle to you. Not because you can't take care of yourself, but because I love you. I want to be your safe harbor, Chloe."

"You are."

He kissed her then, sweet and full of promise. "Marry me," he said against her lips.

"Really?" Chloe flushed as hope and anticipation thrummed through her. She never expected to be in this place again with a man. But Ben was everything she never knew she wanted in her life. He wasn't perfect, but he was perfect for her.

"I hope by 'really,' you mean yes," he said with a laugh.

"I do." Chloe wrapped her arms around his neck and he lifted her, holding her tightly against him. "Yes, Ben. Every day, yes."

"You can get married right now."

They both turned to where Zach stood at the window of the conference room, pointing across the street to the garishly painted wedding chapel with a neon-pink steeple anchoring it.

"The sign says they're open until midnight so we've got plenty of time."

"Oh," Chloe said on a breath. "I don't think—"

Ben's grin widened. "It's perfect. Marry me today, Chloe. Now."

"No way." Abby's voice cut through her shock. But when she looked at the girl, Abby was smiling. "You need a dress. A white one."

Harry nudged the teen. "Still got Ben's credit card?"

Abby nodded. "There's a mall around the corner. I saw it when we drove up. We'll meet you at the wedding chapel in an hour."

"Awesome," Zach shouted.

Ben pulled her close again. "What do you think? If you need more time . . ."

Chloe didn't need more time. She'd spent hours and days and years planning and worrying. But this moment, full of uncertainty and spontaneity, felt more right than anything that had come before.

"I think I'll see you in an hour." She kissed him then grabbed Abby's hand and headed for the door.

It didn't take an hour. On the racks of the first shop they went in, Chloe found the perfect dress, a simple chiffon sheath with cap sleeves that was both elegant and understated. Turns out money might not buy happiness, but it could pay for an amazing wedding gown with just a swipe of a credit card.

The men were waiting and had managed to find matching deep-blue Oxford shirts. Harry walked her down the aisle while Zach and Abby served as best man and maid of honor.

It felt exactly right to stand with this family—her family—and officially join her life with Ben's. Already her heart belonged to him, and Chloe couldn't stop giggling during the ceremony, until the moment when the minister pronounced them husband and wife. The intensity and love in Ben's gaze as he looked at her nearly took her breath away.

He kissed her again, and it was perfect. This moment, this perfect kiss, was the start to the life she'd always dreamed of having, and so much more.

EPILOGUE

Chloe stood in the doorway of the café's ramshackle kitchen for a few minutes before Ben noticed her. She never tired of watching him work. His broad shoulders filled out the white chef's jacket he wore, and the muscles in his forearms bunched as he lifted a heavy pot off the stove. He dumped its contents into a sink strainer then finally looked up, a wide smile lighting his face. He smiled a lot these days, and she loved being part of the reason for it.

He crooked a finger in her direction. "Come here, wife."

"That sounds like a command," she said but took a step forward. All Ben had to do was look at her to make her melt.

"Please," he added and met her halfway. He swung her into his arms as they kissed, heat pulsing through her at the first touch of his mouth.

"Give it a rest," Abby hollered as she bustled through the kitchen door. "We're working here, people."

"Your friends act like they haven't eaten in months," Harry added, hefting an empty serving bowl as he followed Abby toward the prep counter.

After another quick kiss, Ben set Chloe to the ground. "The food is *that* good," he told his father, earning a hearty chuckle from Harry.

"Then stop screwing around and let's have more of it."

"If tonight is any indication," Chloe said, moving toward the trays of appetizers waiting to be served, "the restaurant is going to be a huge success."

"We've got a ways to go before Not Your Mama's is ready," Ben answered but couldn't quite hide his satisfied smile as he met her gaze.

Renovations were set to begin on the café next to The Toy Chest the following week. Tonight they were hosting an intimate engagement party for Kendall and Ty in the old space, a chance to try out a few of the recipes Ben had developed for his new restaurant, which he'd named Not Your Mama's as a nod to the recurring compliment Abby, Zach, and Harry gave to their favorite recipes.

After their whirlwind wedding two months ago, they'd returned to Denver to figure out how to merge their lives and what the future held for each of them. Ben had decided that his dream restaurant was one that merged classic, down-home dishes with fresh ingredients and an eclectic twist. Although the café was outdated, it was the perfect size and location. Ben wanted a place where families felt comfortable dining with their kids and to keep it small enough that he could get to know his patrons. Gone were the thundering rants that had become the hallmark of "Ben the Beast." Her new husband still had a tendency to yell, but he was learning to control his temper and not the other way around.

In fact, he was about to begin filming the first week of the new EatTV show, *Boot Camp with the Beast*. Ben was actually excited about the idea of hot-tempered chefs coming to Denver to work with him and gain access to both his culinary expertise and his growing skill at keeping calm under pressure.

For her part, Chloe had retained ownership of The Toy Chest but made Karen the manager of the business. Chloe had applied for her social work license and taken a position as the Community Outreach Coordinator for the Safehouse Shelter. She wanted to help more women gain the confidence to rebuild their lives away from the domestic violence that in many cases had dominated it for years.

They'd bought a rambling home in the Highlands neighborhood and moved Abby and Zach in with them. Chloe had gone with the three of them to visit Cory, and from what she could tell, he'd made peace with Ben's decision to abandon the plan for revenge against The Toy Chest.

"I'm getting money." Zach bounced into the kitchen from the dining room. "I took some lady's empty plate, threw it in the trash, and she handed me five bucks."

Abby rolled her eyes. "You're wearing a shirt that says 'Tipping . . . it's not just for cows.'"

"I don't even know what it means," Zach said with a grin. "Grandpa brought it home and told me to wear it."

"Stick with me, buddy." Harry winked at Zach then nudged Abby with his hip. "I had one for you, too."

"So embarrassing," Abby muttered.

When Harry's face fell, she gave him a small hug. "But I appreciate the thought, Harr—"

"What do you call me?" the old man asked with a growl.

"I appreciate it, *Grandpa*," she amended.

"That's better."

"No more sappy stuff," Ben shouted. "We've got people to feed."

"We just caught you and Chloe kissing," Abby shouted back. "What the hell?"

"Language," the four of them said in unison.

Ben laughed and came up behind Chloe, wrapping his arms around her. "You're about to see it again if you don't get out of my kitchen. Be off with you, faithful servants."

The rest of the Haddox clan groaned as they picked up dishes and bowls and disappeared into the dining room.

"We've got to get out there," Chloe said then moaned as Ben dipped his head to capture her earlobe between his teeth.

"Give me a few minutes," he whispered against her skin.

"Two?" she asked with a laugh.

"That comment will cost you." He whirled her around and claimed her mouth for a slow, languorous kiss that made her want to ignore their friends and family for the rest of the night. But after a few glorious moments he pulled back. "Thank you for making me happier than I knew I could be."

The love and devotion in his gaze made her insides melt all over again. "The happiness goes both ways, Chef Hottie."

"Your Chef Hottie," he told her. "I'm yours forever, Chloe."

"My everything," she agreed and kissed him again. There was no more hiding, no more fear. With Ben at her side, Chloe knew her life would be a perfectly imperfect, chaotic, joyful, satisfying adventure. And she planned to savor every moment of it.

THE END

ACKNOWLEDGMENTS

While writing a book is a solitary endeavor, it's way more fun with a fantastic support group. I want to thank the people who help make my job the best one in the world.

Kelli Martin, my amazing editor, who puts a smile on my face with every e-mail or phone conversation.

My agent, Nalini Akolekar. I thank my lucky stars each day to have you in my corner.

Melody Guy, developmental editor extraordinaire, whose insights on my stories make them infinitely better and who is an overall rock star.

The Montlake author relations team—I'm thrilled to have such a talented group of people on my team.

Lana Williams, my critique partner, who keeps me sane and motivated. Every. Single. Day.

All of my writing friends, especially Annie and Jennie—whether on Facebook or e-mail or over lunch, thanks for helping me refill the well.

My family, who love and support me and don't complain when I take my laptop to the beach.

My mom "co-parents"—carpools, playdates, sleepovers, and general life support. You do it all and I'm eternally grateful.

ABOUT THE AUTHOR

Michelle Major grew up in Ohio but dreamed of living in the mountains. Over twenty years ago, she pointed her car west and settled in Colorado. Now her house is filled with one great husband, two beautiful kids, several furry pets, and a couple of well-behaved reptiles. She's grateful to have found her passion writing stories with happy endings. Michelle loves hearing from readers, so find her on Facebook or Twitter or at www.michellemajor.com.